In Life everybody has a Few…

OPTIONS

BY

REGINALD GIST

REGGIE GIST

A T&P Publishing Book/Published by arrangement with author.

Printing History

First Printing: September 2014

Copyright 2014 by Reginald Gist

Cover Design and production: Mayhem Graphix

ISBN: 9780991358106

Printed in the United States

Dedication

I would like to dedicate this book to the love of my life, my beautiful wife, Tiffany Gist who held me down respectfully for several years while I was incarcerated. She gave me the motivation to successfully complete this body of work. Also I would like to dedicate this book to my wonderful sons Jalen & Jacoby Gist to whom my life is totally dedicated to making their lives better than mine. I love you all and thanks for the unconditional love and support which kept me strong throughout my time away….Love, Daddy.

Acknowledgements

I would like to take this time to acknowledge those that played a major role in my life. First and foremost, The Almighty Allah (GOD) for breathing life into my lungs and giving me the ability to experience all that I have. Also my mother Theresa Gist and my siblings Edwina, Cornell, Cortez and Rell for being a major support group throughout my life. The entire Gist family along with the Thomas's, Moore's, Evan's and Benton's. To all my friends and companions: Chuck B, Charles O, Live, Dris, Elc, Rock, Boski, Dean, Sho, Ed, Darcell, Hank and Herbie, Tone a.k.a Twin, Joey and all the soldier's in the game. I sold drugs with the best of them and buried the rest of them: Mat, Nat, David, Little David, Uncle Clif, Keyon, Lionel W, and those that I just can't mention. Last but not least I would like to acknowledge all my brothers in the struggle inside the belly of the beast who helped me to stay sane and focus during my stay and journey with M.D.O.C.: All my Bright'Mo Family, M. Evon, Brandon, Jabar a.k.a. Blood, Doc C from the wood, R-Dub, M. Price, and all the rest that I just couldn't name to the lack of space. Ya'll are never forgotten and will always have a place in this world…."KEEP YA HEAD UP"……"PEACE"…………..

OPTION

[**op**-sh*uh* n]

1. something that may be or is chosen; choice.

Prologue

In the early hours on July 30, 1974 approximately 3:25 a.m. the room was filled with cries from Ms. Giles, a soon to be single mother, who lied in a hospital bed surrounded by loved ones. Only fourteen years old, she shared a room with another young expectant mother. Sweat infiltrated her cotton flowered gown and hair cap that she wore as the doctor instructed her to push.

Her mother wiped the sweat from her brow and chanted, "Push, now breathe, push baby, now breathe."

The young girl followed her mother's direction as she peered over the crispy white sheets down into the face of the African American doctor between her legs, who gave her a look of encouragement.

After thirty minutes of intense pain and labor, the doctor motioned for the nurse to retrieve the cold metal tongs that lay amongst the other sterilized utensils. After a few more minutes she heard the doctor say, "The baby's head is almost out."

She braced herself as she felt her body naturally expelling the child from her womb. The newborn slowly emerged from the womb and took its first breath in a world that had already labeled him a statistic. As the rest of his small body slid out to perfection the doctor yelled over to the screaming patient that it was a beautiful baby boy.

Ms. Giles relaxed with ease knowing the hardest part of the labor was complete. The assistant rushed to the newborn and injected nose and mouth plugs to allow the baby to take its first breath and screams. Once smacked on the sticky bottom the baby complies as expected.

"May I cut the umbilical cord?" asked the new proud grandmother.

"Sure," said the assistant as Tosha Giles smiled with excitement and joy at the birth of her first baby boy and grandchild to Ms. Francis Giles.

"What is his name?" asked the proud Grandma.

"I'll call him Romelo James Giles after his father, even though he's not present to witness God's creation."

"That sounds wonderful," says Grandma.

The baby looked around in amazement at the people who loved him already. He weighed in at 6 pounds and 3 ounces then was taken to another room to be cleaned and the appropriate test were administered on the tiny body.

Tosha embraced her son and stared into his eyes and vowed, "I will love you until the Lord above calls you back to him. Even when you're wrong or right in this world, you'll always have the option to choose your destiny I swear, by the very breath I breathe in me. Cause I'll forever have your back. I love you, Romelo."

From that point on in her life she realized that no matter what she would be the best mother she could be for the both of them. And she would not allow her son and herself to become a statistic based on the worlds ideology…time would tell if her goals and dreams would manifest into success, and allow both of their lives to become one of prosperity and gracefulness…

CHAPTER 1
The Birth

After the birth of Romelo, he was finally brought home to be joined with this family. Being born in Louisville, KY in the 70's was a life altering experience. Crime was up, opportunity was down and everyone had Afro's and problems during those days. Racism and cop's ran hand in hand and growing up in a home with six or so siblings residing in them was a common thing to see.

In our household there were five not including myself. There was Frankie, Wanda, Cody, Jr, and my mother Tosha. My grandparents were hard working common citizens who expected the best from all of their children. With me being the first grandbaby I had all the reasons to be spoiled rotten. Trust me, after years of growing up I had my fair share of whooping's and punishment though.

Around the age of four I had the privilege of not only watching, but being a part of my mother's graduation ceremony. I even had the chance to walk across the stage with her while she received her High School diploma. Man, I was so proud and at only four years old I was heading in the right direction and following the right footsteps. I guess you could say I was a "Mama's Boy," huh?

Shortly after the graduation, my mom's figured that it was time to spread her wings and fly the birds nest. So we packed up the 72' Chevy, all gold with black trim along the side and moved to the big city of Detroit, the home of the Big 3. I can remember being amazed once I saw the big buildings and wide streets. My mom got settled and all the family we had here, all grabbed my cheeks and called me Lil Romelo or Rome for short.

We moved into a small house located on the west side near a large park with everything a child could want and more. I was very happy and content with the new change of environment. My mom had plenty of friends of all kinds. One lady named Barbara use to give me candy and money to put into my pocket. She was also the baby sitter and a friend to many families.

When it came to men, Mom would never let me get attached to any, especially since my Dad only came around a few times. I believe this was the reason why we moved from Grandma's home to the city, in search of bigger dreams and my father. Eventually after many years of neglect I came to realize that my mom would come to play both roles in my life.

But the streets became my father around the age of six. I was ready for my first year of school at Burt Elementary located in the heart of the neighborhood of Brightmoor, which was affectionately known as "Brightmo." My first few years of school were pretty normal like the average youngin' in this inner city. It consisted of teachers and girls who I didn't think about and a few older bullies. I never really got picked on cause my uncle, who was a few years older than me, always watched over me.

Once when I was entering the 3rd grade, my cousin Lucky moved in on the same block as me. He was only none or ten, but he was built like a thirteen year old. He had a light complexion, heavy set and funny looking glasses. His mom, my aunt, was a quiet person who worked at one of the Big 3 automotive companies. We used to walk to school together.

My grandparents had recently moved into the city from Kentucky a few years after my mom and me. My Uncle Cody was a brown skinned, built guy who was advanced in street activities. While walking home with Lucky we were approached by a few of the local bullies who were at least three times our size and at least a few years older than us.

OPTIONS

"Hey let me get that money, lil Bro," one boy suggested, while the other one who was younger balled up his fist.

Truthfully, I was scared out of my mind along with my cousin who eventually ran off faster than I could have expected. Being caught off guard by the two hyper young men I prepared for a beat down because I had no money to give. By the grace of God, this would be the one day that my Uncle Cody was allowed to walk to my house so that he could babysit for my mom. Once he saw the bullies surrounding me, he ran up to rescue his lil nephew, who was in a heated confrontation.

"Hey is there a problem, Fam?"

"Fasho, homeboy," the bully replied.

At the last second of the conversation without hesitation my uncle swung so fast and hard at the older dude. A straight right then a quick left hook to the face as blood dripped down the cheek of the bully. While engaged in a one on one battle the other younger bully tried to intervene in the scuffle by rushing hard and fast towards my uncle. I quickly dropped my book bag and ran to assist my family member. I tackled the boy and starting punching as fast and hard as an eight year old could swing. Impressed by my actions and lack of fear, the reaction caught everyone off guard as the safety school guard rushed to break up the battle.

After the incident we brushed the sand and gravel off our bodies as the other boys ran away from the crime scene as if they were fleeing from a murder case. The guard didn't give us any trouble, only a lecture on how to be aware of none school members and their after school tactics.

We continued our walk home as Cody acknowledged my heart and eagerness to aid in the situation, "Damn Lil Rome, I see you got a little bit of skills."

REGGIE GIST

"I grew up watching ya'll fight and wrestle every day," I said as we got closer to the house. Plus in the early years wrestling was a big event in our hood and on television. Pro fighters like Hulk Hogan, Iron Sheik, Jake the Snake, British Bulldogs, and you can't forget Rick Flair. Guys like this fought in the WWF in the early 80's, a new world of entertainment which would last for years to come.

Once we arrived at the house, my mom gave me instructions on the do's and don'ts of the house while she went away to explore whatever avenue she chose. Calmly I entered my room which at the time I had to myself. I placed my books down and thought to myself, "My first fist fight," and even though I didn't win, to me I still felt like I was victorious.

In the small but average sized living room, my Uncle Cody sat and talked on the phone with girls bragging about how he saved my life. As Prince's new hit, Pop Life, played on the large floor model stereo system that was made out of pure Oak wood.

On the same block there lived a few young females from my school and neighborhood. One in particular was Meka, and boy was she cute to me and popular in the hood. Over a few years of learning and mimicking my Uncle Cody, I became interested in females in elementary school and she was my first kiddie crush. We use to play with the rest of the kids on the block, but all I could think of was showing off to catch the attention of Meka.

We use to ride bikes, play tag and sometimes told jokes about each other's family and lifestyles. But eventually we would grow older to only become great friends as we both got caught up by what life had to offer.

After about nine years my Mom had a new boyfriend who would become my stepdad and the father of my sister Pooh. He was a cool guy with dark skin and short hair and sometimes he would teach me things about life that would stay with me forever. His idea of family morals was to eat, pray, lay as one and never be afraid of opportunities. He taught us about table manners and family values as their relationship turned into a short marriage.

Mom was always around during these times as she continued to work to help make sure that my sister and I had all that we needed to survive and more. It was kinda hard at first trying to compete with my little sister being that I was used to being the only child. We got along well as siblings and became a real force to deal with also.

A few months later I was ready to graduate from elementary school and so was my crush, Meka. While enjoying my last year of school I started to notice a small change in my mom and society. It was the mid 80's and this was era of Regan and the coming of crack cocaine and drug dealers. After noticing my mom's activities start to change and my stepdad's attitude start to change more to the, " It is what it is," stage, I began to observe my Uncle Cody becoming more like the cats I saw on TV, in videos and movies etc. See Cody was a hustler and as he became older he became wiser and notorious. I can remember watching him cook and package drugs until skinny men and women ran for blocks to purchase his product.

Along with my other Uncle Cliff, they formed a gang as a team but would only let me observe from the outside. I watched as my mom started to become a product of her environment and lose weight and become addicted to the drug. But I was still infatuated with the lifestyle and swag that my Uncle's possessed. They wore pagers on their side, Kangols with the fur around them. They drove different cars that were rented by the skinny people. The shoes were Nikes or Pumas and their pants were Guess and sometimes Lacoste Sportic. All the kids they hung around with sold drugs and breakdanced on card boards with boom boxes playing loud music.

REGGIE GIST

In '85 things were changing so fast and I was amazed by my surroundings even though I was only ten, I was ready to enter a new dimension. My mom and uncles would shield a lot of things from me. I guess they were protecting me from their world or myself. Eventually, I graduated from the 5th grade and was on my way to view the world as my egg, and it was waiting to be busted.

CHAPTER 2
1986 – MIDDLE SCHOOL AND LOVE

Well the year was 1986 and I'd finished my graduation ceremony last summer. I was officially on my way to middle school. As a student of Murphy Middle School located on Fenkell and Telegraph, I would be going through 6-8th grade and I loved it. No more little kids to deal with no more one room class all day and the girls were pretty from head to toe.

At this time my family or my moms and little sister were all that I had and adored. Even though my mom was addicted to drugs, she made it a habit to keep her abuse hidden from us. Now after my stepdad departed due to personal reasons I've never known, my mom had a new boyfriend. I knew he was special to her cause she would allow me to sit and talk with him.

Some days he would babysit my sister and me and we enjoyed hanging with her new friend Darius. Darius had a few other kids prior to meeting my Moms. His oldest sons name was Rick, but everyone called him Rook for other reasons. Rook and I became the best of friends until we became actual brothers from another mother.

Rook and his grandparents lived on the same block as we did growing up, so it was always easy for us to stay on the same team. Whatever I did, he did, whatever he got, I got. His father was always keeping us together. He taught us how to fish and play chess. We also went to the same school. Being that I was only one year older than he was, I was one grade higher. Moms treated him like a son from the start of the relationship to the end. We were one big happy family and soon to be "partners in crime."

Rook was about 5'3, 135 pounds and loved to wear his hair in all the latest styles like the Kid and Play high top fades or the Dewayne Wayne Mohawk. Me, myself I sported the Michael

Jackson curl and sometimes a plain old afro. Well, back in those days you either loved Michael Jackson or Prince. I was a true fan, Motown 25 was the shit to me!! The moves, the artist and the reunion, Yes!!! MJ's Billie Jean or Thriller blasted on every radio station. Guess jeans were still popular but Levi's, Calvin Klein and Nautica were the in thing to wear. In 1986 you had to have Kangaroo boots and a Starter coat, the coats with the football teams on the back and no hood.

I used to love going to my Granny's for the weekend because I could sneak and wear my Uncle Cody's clothes. They were always gone and they lived in the basement of Granny's house. I would play dress up and dope dealer at the same time, until my Uncle would return home unexpected! He said little but his actions were a little more dramatic. He would scream and preach about the money he made etc., and empty minded me would listen to every word and dwell on every story.

My grandparent's hood was a little wilder than mine, but Seven Mile and Greenfield would be the very hood that they killed or fought over to protect their turf. I had learned the basic characteristics of a hustler from my uncle and now it was time to teach my little brother Rook the slang and swag I had learned in the little time away from him and my hood. Boy, we were ready for school and anything else that came along.

Our first year was pretty uneventful as we caught the school bus or the "cheese" as the others called it, to Murphy Middle School. We would make the bus ride exciting by rapping and joking on the others on the cheese. Some called it capping, others called it playing the dozens. Once we got to school my grades were average, but my attitude was changing a lot. See at the time the placement of students was different, kids from every hood went to Murphy so a few gangs were formed as I tried to stay neutral.

In my home room class, I became good friends with a few guys, one in particular whose real name was Kiambu, but we called him Dean. He was about 6 feet tall, played basketball and Lived in a good hood called Rosedale Park. Dean and I got real close and he became my best friend all through middle school. My bro Rook liked him too and had no problem accepting him into our fold.

One day after home room we all were walking to our classes and we noticed a group of 6th graders in the hallway. It had to be six or seven nice looking females. I had on my new Lotto's and my black Levi's with the matching jacket. I had grown to 5'6 and my dark skin and deep dimples accented my outfit. I just knew I was the star of the bunch of guys I was with or at least the freshest! I was kinda afraid to make a move on one of the girls who was checking me out as we got closer. Once we got a few steps in front of them, I zoomed in on one girl who had on a tight, red, Guess shirt on with the pants to match. Her hair was jet black and hung down her back. Her smile was so bright it could have lit up the whole hallway easily. She was with four other girls who I assumed were her clique.

"Excuse me shorty, haven't we met before?" I asked her in my deepest voice with no mustache.

"I don't think so, but I've seen you in my math class," replied the young lady.

"My name is Rome, and yours?"

"Jennifer," she said flashing her brilliant teeth. Damn, a feeling that I had never felt before coursed through my body into my stomach. I could have passed out right there, but I remembered my homeboy Dean was standing on the side of me, wearing a silly smirk on his face. He had peeped me.

Since the bell was about to ring, most of the students scattered off to their classes while the others that were going to skip made their way to the most discreet exit. I had about one minute to try to get her number or at least give her mine.

"Let me give you my number," I said as I wrote it down on a piece of paper I pulled from my Nerf Notebook.

She took the number, smiled and said, "I'll think about calling you because my brother be tripping!" Her and her crew turned around and walked away.

Me and my boys walked away, but that would be a turning point in my life and hers.

Once school let out, we were at our lockers talking about what happened when my little bro walked up and engaged in the conversation that Dean and I were having. I felt really cocky over the encounter as I explained to Rook what happened and to my surprise he already knew the story. See, he and Jennifer had a class together and he had overheard her and her friends talking about a few guys at the school they were interested in. Once my name came up along with Dean's, he listened closer to the gossip.

We went to school a few weeks with no phone calls exchanged, but I did pass and see Jenn each day in my class. My days at home were filled with homework and hanging outside until the street lights came on. My crush Meka and I were still cool even though she went to a different school across town. We would talk and compare days every night and that is what made our bond so tight.

While we were sitting on my porch one night after basketball practice for the Pal League, "Road Runners" team, I heard my mom call my name to get the phone. I usually got calls from a few people, but this call was the one I had been waiting on. My mom had her hand over the phone and whispered, "Some girl named Jennifer."

I grabbed the phone so quick, but I got myself together before I said, "What up? Who is this?"

"Who you want it to be?" she asked in a soft voice.

"It took you long enough to call," I said half mad.

"I had to watch you for a minute and make sure you were cool," she said.

Our conversation went on for over an hour and we talked about everything. Even though I'd had plenty of calls from females, this one was special. As we discussed our past, schools, like and dislikes we became real cool friends.

Later on that week we walked and talked during lunch and home room class. I had a chance to meet her brother, Bam, who was in a higher grade than us, but went to the same school. We became cool too and he encouraged me to ask his sister to be my girlfriend. Bam was tall and light skinned and all the girls liked him. See in those days light skinned cats were the shit. Cats like Al B. Sure, Will Smith, Prince and you can't forget the group GUY, were all the girls crushes.

After a couple of months I took Bam's advice and Jenn and I became a kiddie couple. All throughout the school everyone knew we were going together so then we were like one of the school's cutest couples. I really enjoyed our time together and late night phone calls. My brother and mom liked her too after they met at one of our favorite hangouts, the skating ring. All the kids would either walk home after school, skip school, or hang out at Wheels or Northland skating ring.

Over a course of three or four months, we kinda got used to staying at her house during school hours in order to spend quality time together. Her brother and his girlfriend would stay at home also and chill out in the basement where his room was located. Jennifer and I never really spoke about the subject of sex, but we would always watch TV in the living room while she sat between my legs. I would slowly kiss her neck and rub between her thighs and massage her special spot through her tight pants. Boy! Was that a turn on for both of us. She was a virgin and so was I kind of. This was common at our age so the first time had to be special for the both of us.

After skipping school one morning we were at her house. Her brother Bam was busy in the basement with his girl, Tameka. Jennifer and I were upstairs watching TV when she asked me to come with her to her bedroom. I'd seen her room plenty of times before, but this time was different. I mean, these were the times of Slick Rick's first tape, Biz Markie and Bobby Brown's 'Tenderoni.' So it was no doubt that shit was on!

When we got to her room, 'Let's Chill," by Guy was on the small radio beside her queen sized bed. The room was pink with flowers along the trim of the wallpaper. The covers were pink and pulled back just enough so that we could slip between them. She guided me by grabbing my hand and walking me over to the bed. I must admit that I was nervous, especially being my original first time and the fact that Bam could come upstairs at any time. As we sat on the bed I looked into her eyes and ran my fingers through her long black hair. I could feel her body getting warm as I watched the goose bumps appear on her caramel colored skin. We started kissing each other slow then faster. I slipped my hand under her shirt to unfasten her bra from the back. She was very petite in size and so were her breast. They were the size of small Hostess cupcakes and tasted like them too. I slid her shirt off and then she stood up so I could take off her pajama bottoms and panties. Her body was smooth and she had the perfect gap between her legs.

Once I undressed to my boxers and socks, we laid underneath the fluffy covers and kissed for a second. I laid on top of her sucking her neck then her small chest trying to put a hickie on her caramel skin. My hands ran between her legs touching her wet spot and man was she ready. Her panties came off while I fingered her tight, young pussy with my middle finger as she moaned and grinded to her own rhythm. I didn't have any protection on and I was willing to take my chances. Looking down at my hard, nice sized penis I thought twice before she grabbed it and guided it to her soft, wet pussy. The first couple of strokes were off beat, but once we got past the tightness, our rhythm came together. In and out, up and down, nice long pumps, heavy breathing and suddenly she made her inner muscles clinch my hard on while I was in the motion of sliding into her then it happened. Out of my body poured my entire soul and energy as she wrapped her legs around me in the heat of passion.

We lied there while she told me that she had experienced her first orgasm. Afterwards we went straight to the shower to wash up as a pair. Shortly after Bam came up from the basement with no doubt that things had gone down. They talked in the kitchen and later they walked me to the bus stop to go home. Not only had I lost my virginity, but I had finally found out what this love thing was about. I thought about it the entire bus ride home.

Back at home, things were cool, but strange at the same time. I discussed the experience with my brother over a game of Mario Brothers on the Nintendo system. Detail by detail I told him what had taken place while he bombarded me with questions. I never asked him if he was a virgin or not. Later that evening, Jennifer and I talked on the phone and represented each other in school the next day.

My neighborhood was growing as the drug game expanded into the everyday life. My next door neighbor would turn into a high level kingpin who lived with his beautiful wife and their three year old daughter. He was an older guy with dark wavy hair. He had to be in his mid-thirties and drove a brand new black Corvette. I knew he was dealing to my mother, but they tried to keep it from me. I knew she still had a habit and she was pretty good at hiding it, but I wasn't stupid.

Me and the neighbor became cool on a different level. He always made sure I had money in my pocket by allowing me to do side jobs and chores around his house. When it snowed outside he allowed me to shovel his snow and he would pay me a few hundred dollars. In the summer, he would pay me to walk his pit bull, named "Biscayne." I would walk the dog until he became too big to handle. He bought me a red, twelve speed bike just to walk the dog at a faster pace.

One day around Halloween, I was sitting in a tree in front of my house when I saw several nice cars and men with large gold chains walking into my neighbor's house. They stayed for a few minutes then left. He daughter was with him because he was watching her while his wife ran errands. His wife trusted me with their baby so he called over to me and asked me to watch her cause she kept crying. I didn't mind, because I had a little sister of my own and was used to watching kids.

While we were playing in the living room, a few more men came over. I could see straight into the den where they were sitting and could see everything that was going on. The men stacked all their one dollar bills at the corner of the table and then they placed all their big bills inside a green duffle bag in the closet. I swear it had to be at least fifteen bags filled with cash in the closet.

Around this time Coleman Young, YBI, Best Friends, Maserati Rick and the Chamber Boys ran the streets of Detroit and the underworld. I truly believe that he was connected on a major level, but just kept a low profile. My theory would soon prove me correct. That same day I babysat for him he made all his partners place the dollar bills in the corner and once there were done, he told me, "Always stay firm and follow your desires and dreams to be the best." Then he gave me all the ones on the table.

After grabbing all the money and running home to share the profits with Rook, we counted $647 and from that point on I knew that fast money was the best money to get. It wasn't nothing new to Rook because he was use to me bringing money and gifts home from my neighbor. So going to school or skating it was always my treat.

Moms was also cool with the extra cash laying around and her relationship with Darius was still going good. They allowed Rook to move in with us so he could continue to go to school with me. My sister wouldn't be the youngest for long because later that year my Mom and Darius had a son and we welcomed Cornell with open arms.

As the months flew by a lot of things changed in my life. My relationship with Jennifer was solid and the time we spent together, the late night calls and sex adventures were all intact. Rook, Dean and I were still the best of friends. My moms and I were cool, but since I had become aware of what the underworld had to offer we started to get into it more often. I still looked up to my Uncle Cody and his friends, along with my neighbor who I visited frequently when I came back to my hood. Both hoods were a treasure and everyone wanted a piece of the gold and silver.

CHAPTER 3

Once my uncle's connected with the neighbor things went uphill for the collaboration of commerce. Over the summer life was pretty average for my family and friends. We continued to hang out at the roller rink and movie theaters. The Norwest and Mercury theaters were common grounds for all the local kids. I can remember watching *Krush Groove, Breaking, Purple Rain and Nightmare on Elm Street* in these theaters. A few fist fights would break out which was cool because guns weren't as common in violent crimes in the 80's.

Crews were formed and many younger kids took heed to the dope game for support. The beginning of 87' was the start of a new school year and new experiences. I was in the 7th grade along with Rook and Dean plus a few other people I had met over the summer. The first day of school was a blast. Kids wore their newest outfits that they had begged their parents for over the last few weeks.

In my class, Jennifer and her crew still were at the top of the food chain. I allowed a new member to join our squad of the elite. His name was Howard. He was a skinny little guy that wore glasses and acted like a real nerd. Even though he wasn't, we still got used to treating him like one.

A few of the classes had changed like instead of music, I had home economics. I was cool with it because Jenn had to share the same transition too. Rook on the other hand was starting to form his own identity and swag which only helped the crew to be more popular. We wore white Air Force Ones, Reeboks, and Adidas this year, especially, since D.M.C. came out with the hit song for the shoes.

A lot of the females that year wore short tennis skirts and flip flops along with the finger waves in their hair. How cute were they and their sexy attitudes? School was still pretty much the same except a few of the older dudes started selling drugs and became more popular. Me myself, was not dealing at this stage but I was getting accustom to that life style from my neighbor and being spoiled by my uncles.

Throughout the year it was pretty much the same routine and same group of people. At home things were a little rocky due to the fact that I wanted to venture off to my grandparent's home where shit was totally different. My grandparents loved me and allowed me to be myself in a respectful manner. I always came in on time and never gave any reason to expect anything bad of me. I liked the freedom and neighborhood because it was always something happening; females chasing after my uncles and their crews, fiends staggering up and down the block.

I also had a few friends that lived in that area. David was a younger version of me and also lived on the same block as my grandma. We got along real good and became the best of friends, whenever I was at my granny's house. All the younger girls loved "D". He was brown skinned, 5'6" and 150 pounds. He kept his hair in brush waves. We did everything together as we both learned and watched the older cats hustle into day break. Every other week I would visit the Seven mile area, but on a regular basis I continued to live with my mom, sister, and Rook on Fenkell. Rook and I were still bonding like brothers and I still was having encounters with my balling neighbor on many occasions.

Dean and Howard were still part of the school crew and we all continued to hang out at the movies and skating rings. Jennifer was starting to grow more and more on me as we went through the school year as a couple.

The school dances were still a major event. Two guys and a girl dancing in a 'sandwich' to a classic or new song like, Special Ed, Rob Bass, Eric B, and you can't forget New Edition was the hottest shit. We would drink punch and talk as the D.J. would yell "Switch," after every chorus. Kids from other schools would try to crash our dances as we did the same to theirs.

My crew had become connected to Jenn's crew of girls so each one of us had a girlfriend. Rook had Chalon, Chino had Cynthia and Howard had nobody so I thought. Our skip school adventures were still sexual as ever. Jennifer and I became more sexually active as the months rolled past. To be young was beautiful and in love, the sex was the bomb, with or without protection! So 87' went past kind of quick, a few new experiences with no major trouble.

My mom still was with Darius and our family Lives were a complete family with struggling parents trying to conceal their habits. Now 88' was a different story. This was the year shit got crazy. It was my last year of middle school and the beginning of a whole lot of shit.

Remember Big Daddy Kane, Kool Moe Dee, MC Hammer, Ghetto Boyz and DJ Quick? Or if you are from the "D", rappers like Kaos and Mystro, Awesome Dre, Rap Mafia, and Smiley. These were the stars in our hood and boy did we love they ass! School was about to start and I would be in the 8th grade and starting my new identity as a teenager with vision. My crew was still the same, but we all had new looks. I no longer had a curl, Rook no longer had a high top fade, but was more like the Kwame type of hair style. Howard and Dean were still my aces boons coons. Jennifer was getting older and wiser as the days went past.

Our homeroom class remained the same and a few of our classes still switched around because now instead of home economics I had wood shop with Dean, a class I personally hated. The dress code was wind breakers and Levi's, playing a significant role in our appearances. But Top Ten Adidas and Forums were a high statement in the fashion world.

Being our last year things went well except a few life altering changes. First at home my mom was getting on my case about my after school activities so our bond began to fade toward the worst. I spent a lot more time at my granny's house to stay sane, which was cool because David was always there to help me out.

In school things started looking strange and attitudes were forming due to the fact that we all would be splitting up to go to different high schools next year. Then for some reason my relationship with Jenn was changing and I felt like she was hiding something from me. During the course of the year my grades were stable, home was so-so and my eagerness to be more like my uncle became more and more within reach.

Close to the end of 8th grade my sex with Jenn was slowing up and Dean, Rook and Howard were all getting ready to go to new schools and so was I.

Over the last four months I noticed that our skip parties were slowing up. So after a few phone calls to Jenn I questioned her about our relationship and she said things were cool. But I had an inside ear that nobody really knew about named Chino. He was Cynthia's boyfriend and we became cool on the side. He told me that the parties were still going on at Jenn's house, but I wasn't invited. I started noticing on certain days, Jenn, Chino, Cynthia, Bam, Tamika and last but not least Howard were all absent.

Realization slowly set in. I remembered Chino and Dean telling me that Howard didn't live far from Jenn, actually within walking distance. So one day I felt kind of suspicious while catching the bus from school with my friend, Chris. Chris was a tall light skinned brother like Dean but instead of playing ball he played the streets and ran with a crew called "W.B.S" which stood for "Y Bull Shit." He was teaching me a new lifestyle in gangland and preaching to me about what he observed from the rear of the group. See he only dealt with me and he always hung with me over my grandma's crib with David. My mom was cool with him because his Mom would call every time we were together.

OPTIONS

This particular day it was raining outside and Chris told me to go check on my girl since it was a Friday and everyone was absent from school. I thought about Chino and our conversation and before you knew it I was ringing the bell to let the bus driver to know to stop at the next stop.

Once I got off the bus, Chris and I headed to Jenn's house which was about a twenty minute walk from the stop. We talked and talked until I got to her crib and knocked on the door. After no one answered, I rang the doorbell a few times. Still no answer so we decided to walk over to Howard's crib. I didn't know exactly where he stayed, but I had a good idea from the details that Dean had given me.

We walked about ten minutes around Outer Drive until we reached the Grayton Place Apartments. I looked at each mailbox until I saw his last name on the shiny plate. I rang the bell to Apt. 104, but there was no answer. Just as I was about to turn away, another tenant walked out the big door and Chris grabbed it before it closed. We laughed as we entered the building. We had no idea if he was even at home.

When we got to his door I listened at the door. We both heard voices coming from the small two bedroom apartment. I knocked several times and Chris said, "I see somebody looking at me."

The door slowly opened, "Hey, what's up?" Howard said blocking the entrance into his house.

"Shit, just trying to pop up on you since I was in the hood checking on Jenn," I responded.

"Yeah, she over here in the back," he said in an aggressive tone.

Chris's crazy ass saw I was about to snap so he pushed his way in while I followed him. Man, I saw her not in the living room or kitchen, but she was in his bedroom laying on his water bed. She was dressed, but as shocked as I was. My pride was hurt, especially in front of my boy who understood and had my back.

Somehow I kept my cool and found my voice, "What the fuck?" I said waiting on an answer.

She couldn't even answer me. I looked first at Chris who was ready for any drama, then at Howard who was looking back at me with a smug look on his face. I smiled back at him to hide my pain and walked out of the room. All I could think of as I made my way out of the tiny apartment was that my first love had just got banged by my so called homeboy.

"Life and Hoes, Hoes and Money. Choose either one of them and you're the dummy," Chris rapped, making me laugh. We headed to my Granny's for the weekend.

While I was over Granny's I didn't call Jenn, but my mom told me that she had called me a few times and so had Howard. I couldn't believe that so I told Dean and Rook what happened and kept it moving to the skating rink. I had a few dollars in my pocket from stealing a few of my uncle's rocks and selling it to a few neighborhood fiends I knew. It was crazy but it was a rush to me and fast money. At around 11:30 I would sit on my Granny's porch with Dean until 11:45 cause I would watch him walk home which was about twelve houses down. We both had curfew at midnight and we had better be in or we would get locked out.

So Sunday was considered a school night and we were about to call it a night until next weekend when I would come back to chill. But before I was about to go in, a neighborhood fiend named Ursula and Joey came walking by the porch that I sat on. They saw me and asked for my Uncle Cody who was gone out for the night to a club called, "Page One."

"Hey can you get us a twenty?" asked the lady fiend.

"What is that?" I asked.

"Come on Rome, hook a bitch up. We won't tell, plus Cody and CB ain't answering their pagers," she pleaded while waving the two ten dollar bills.

I already knew where they kept their guns and stash because they did everything in front of me to show off. They kept the drugs behind the dresser so my grandparents wouldn't find them. It was almost midnight and I only had $7 to my name until after school tomorrow. Then I would see my neighbor at my mom's house.

I told her to be quiet while I ran and grabbed two stones that looked like clear salt out of the stash bag of a hundred small salt rocks. I came upstairs after putting the stash back in its hiding place and went to the curb and gave it to her hoping it was the correct amount or size. I got the money and gave David $10 as he walked to his house and I walked to mine. The feeling I had could not be explained. My first sale and it was so easy, it gave me a full rush. Now I could see how my Uncle and neighbor felt doing their type of work.

I sat in the basement looking around for a minute until I thought about what to wear to school and the crazy shit that had happened Friday with Jenn. Once I fell asleep for a few hours it was about 3 a.m. and my uncle still wasn't home which meant that they missed their curfew at 2 a.m. and weren't coming home. Usually I would sneak and let them in, but some days my Granddad would double lock the door and they would be pissed.

At 3:05 I heard a tap on the basement window. I thought it was them so I raced to the door to let them in and to my surprise it was Ursula!

"Girl you tripping! Granny will kill you if she catches you here," I said in a whisper.

"Please Rome, the other ones you gave me was straight and I won't come back tonight, promise," she begged while scratching her neck.

I ran down the stairs to the stash spot and did the same routine. After I got the money I went to sleep happy. I woke up with $40 in my pocket and got ready for school. I called Chris and told him to meet me at the Coney Island for breakfast, on me. After the bus ride we talked about what happened and entered school with a full stomach.

I figured the word had gotten out about the Jenn incident so during home room I stayed to myself. I saw Jenn and Howard and they tried to speak, but since I had money, a new hobby and was fresh to death in my all black Damage outfit, I just kept it moving.

Me and my pride survived that day and the next few that followed, until I finally gave in and accepted a message from Jenn through her girl, Cynthia. We spoke and I explained that I wasn't tripping and that we could all be cool. But she had a different objective since she had seen me in Damage jeans one day and Used the next.

I learned early on that the word 'friends,' meant nothing like the description in the Webster Dictionary. The school year barreled by and right before we got out for summer break, I ended up getting into a scuffle with Howard about his dealings with Jenn. Cynthia and I exchanged numbers so we could talk more about Jenn and the "Duck." Truthfully, I wanted to fuck with her anyway because Chino had told me some wild stories about her and her freaky ways. I kept the gossip a secret and continued to have late night conversations with her and created a bond that I would use to my advantage.

My friendship with Howard had dwindled to nothing because he couldn't be trusted and my brother Rook was always talking sideways about him. Dean and Chris were still close by my side by the last few months, as Jenn and I had to reconcile our differences. My visits to Granny's house were still a regular while I usually floated back and forth from my Moms house.

Eventually, my neighbor the big baller would get raided by SWAT and the FBI for his illegal money schemes. So once he was bailed out of jail he moved away to a different hood by Fenkell/Greenfield. We still linked up, but it wasn't the same cause he was always stressed out or paranoid. The entire neighborhood would be upset after his move cause in the neighborhood there would be smaller dealers with more traffic than before.

Shortly after the change I went back to Seven Mile where I had a reputation for petty hustling. A few fiends knew of me because I would always be available after my uncle would leave for hours at a time. They never found out about the missing rocks because at that time my aunt and older Uncle L, were using so my uncles thought that they had found the stash and attributed the loss to them.

After watching them drink and shoot dice on the corner, a few fiends approached my uncle for some credit. Man, he went off into a rage, just to still say, NO! The way he treated them was crazy, but I guess you had to be that way in his line of work. When he saw me looking puzzled he stopped and told me, "Little Nef, the streets are what you make em'. Trust nobody and make your own rules."

I took heed to his statements and immediately made my proposition to him. "Dig, I watched you for years and I understand the game you play, so let me join the team," I whispered.

He burst out laughing so loud, I was so embarrassed. I almost wished I hadn't asked, but his reaction wouldn't stop me. After a while David came and joined the group on the corner and we kicked it about the money situation. School was about to be out and we need money for the summer. My uncle saw how determined I was so he eventually gave in.

A couple of days later he was going out partying and he felt like if he left he would be missing out on money. So he gave me a post. My post was on the front porch until 2 a.m. and to watch all the fiends he sent my way. He gave me $500 in rocks, fifty small rock salt stones to sell in his absence. My pay would be $30 off each $100. So at the end of the night I could stand to make $150 for the night. I did my job while Dee watched my back. I didn't worry about them though, all the fiends loved me.

This went on for the rest of the school year. Finally our graduation was here. It was to be held at a local church that was filled to the rim with flowers, teachers and parents. The inside was all white and our robes were royal blue the color of the school basketball team. Chris and I caught the bus to the ceremony because my mom would ride with Darius and Rook later.

I was dressed in blue slacks, a white button up and royal blue Stacy Adams. Chris and Dean were dressed to impress as well. Howard and Jennifer showed up separate with their parents. When my parents arrived we sat down next to Jenn and her Mom who knew me very well. We engaged in conversation briefly about our future as I explained to Jenn that she was my first love and first heartbreak. She cried and tried to make amends with a "promise to be loyal" speech. I listened then excused myself as the principal called my name to receive my award and certificate.

My family was so proud as I walked across the stage. I could hear them cheering for me as I accepted my awards. Later we huddled together in the reception eating cake and ice cream. "It's going to be a great summer," I thought to myself. The song, "I got it made," by Special Ed played like theme music in my mind....on repeat.

CHAPTER 4

Summer 88

It was a scorching day in 1988 and the sky was clear of clouds. Everybody my age was riding mopeds and had earrings in their ears. I did the same shit but it wasn't at my mother's expense, I bought my own. I bounced back and forth between my moms and my grandparent's house. Me, Rook and a few other kids were hanging at home, playing basketball on the rim we had mounted to a tree in our yard. When we finished we all hopped on our Sprees and my black and purple Elite 80 and rode through the small hoods on the west side.

Each day was filled with excitement and adventures that would give us a lifetime of memories. One day in July, we were riding in the same hood that Jenn and her girls used to hang out in. It had been a few weeks since we had graduated and since I had seen her so I was kinda looking forward to bumping into her. I guess getting over her was harder than I had imagined it would be. I knew she would stay on this block from the phone calls we had shared a few times a week. My brother Rook had started hooking up with her girl, Chalon so when we saw them I suggested we slow down and show off our toys.

We all pulled over to the side and started kicking it. Cynthia came over and took off my helmet and said, "Let's take a ride around the block." She hopped on back and wrapped her arms around my waist.

"I'll be back, right back, stay here," I told my crew as they all looked at me crazy as hell because they knew Cynthia was Jenn's girl.

We rode for a minute then I stopped at the store and we got a pop and chips and talked about Jenn, Howard and school while we munched.

"You know I got a crush on you, Rome. Why don't you come back later and pick me up after you and your boys are done riding?" she asked.

"That's cool. I'll call you around nine," I promised as we got back on the Elite and headed back around the corner. When we pulled up, everybody had partnered up and had exchanged numbers. Rook and Chalon were making plans to hook up later so I figured we could make it a double date.

Later on that evening Rook made arrangements for us to pick them up and we brought them back to the house. Our room was in the basement so it was easy to slip our company in. Moms and Darius were in their room and only came in the basement to wash clothes. I started having second thoughts when I thought about Jenn and Cynthia being friends but shit, Howard was supposed to be my friend and that didn't stop her.

Cynthia had on pink short shorts and a white tank top and white K-Swiss gym shoes on. I led her to my section of the basement. My walls were covered in posters and my bed which happened to be heart shaped was neatly made. I had a small radio on my dresser right under my Uncle Luke, "Nasty as she wanna be," poster.

Rooks section of the basement was similar, but he had a TV on his side. We went into the "living room" section and talked for a minute. Rook and I explained that my Moms could hear a mouse fart so they had to be quiet. We all decided to go to our own rooms so we could get better acquainted.

Cynthia played no games and after about twenty minutes of talking we were locked into a lip locking session so heated that we both were sweating and highly aroused. I slipped her shorts and panties off and she pulled her tank off exposing her young titties. I could barely contain myself as I took off my clothes and slid under the covers with her. She was 5'5, maybe 135 pounds with all the right tools to be our age. Her chocolate brown skin and short curly hair turned me on even more. The sex was better than I could have imagined and we laid in the bed for what seemed like hours afterwards talking.

We snuck them out and took them home and this became routine for the rest of the summer. The ride was real smooth and we agreed to keep our arrangement on the low. I didn't feel guilty at all, but it still didn't make it right what we were doing. Plus I was starting to like Cynthia a bit, but I still had feelings for Jenn. I just couldn't shake her.

One day towards the end of the summer I was talking to Jenn on the phone and she told me she would be going to Redford High School too. I was happy to hear we would be going to school together, but Cynthia was also going to "Red" so I knew this school year was going to be Live and I couldn't wait!

Rook was going to Southwestern and Dean was going to Mackenzie so my squad was breaking up, but at least it was for a good reason. I was still talking to Jenn and she started asking strange questions about who was fucking who and like the man that I am, I lied.

She lied and made me think that she already knew I was lying so I talked her into letting me come over. My mom and Darius were sleep earlier because they had come home from a dinner engagement and crashed. I pushed my moped down a few houses then started it when I was out of range. I made it to her house in record time and pulled my moped up on the side of the house. When I got to her house she let me in. Her mother was a nurse that worked nights so it was cool for me to be there. Usually Jenn and her brother would be home alone until seven in the morning. Jenn opened the door wearing a long white gown and slippers. Man, she looked good.

I walked into the house and we sat and talked for a minute and before I knew it we were kissing and she was leading me to her room. The mood was always right when it came to her.

I was so excited to be holding her that I was dripping before I could even get to her. She was so beautiful and her skin was so soft and sweet. We laid in her bed and I could smell perfume as we made out. The sex was the bomb, still tight and wet. Her movements had only gotten better since our last encounter.

When we finished, we talked about always being friends no matter what. That night we decided to give our teenage love a try, once again. I rode home around 12:30 to find Rook still awake on the phone with Chalon and Cynthia. He could tell from the smile on my face what had gone down. He wanted details as I blasted, Bobby Brown's "Tenderoni" on my little radio in my room. After I showered him with details we came up with a plan to avoid the drama at all cost.

The next few weeks things were cool with Jenn, Cynthia and I. I started getting restless sitting around the house with no money and big dreams. Having two girls, paying for food and gas was getting strenuous. That's when I decided it was time to hit Seven mile to get my chips together.

My mom's was cool with it cause she knew that I was a "Grandma's Boy," and a small time hustler. Her addiction was starting to slow down also, but it would take more than that for our relationship to get stronger. When I got to the Mile it was Live as usual. Cars, fancy trucks and plenty of fiends to go around. I jumped right into position with my boy David who had my back even though he was younger than me. My uncles trusted me and knew that they could Cody on me to be accurate and loyal.

Since the block we stayed on was considered a drug zone or spot we usually sat around and "Hustled off the hip" as we called it. Money was good for me especially because I had no expenses except girls and gas. My grandpa was a chef and he always made sure food was done and on the table. As I watched my uncles play with profits I found myself being different and saving a little bit for rainy days and plus I wanted a car.

OPTIONS

David was my little soldier and he looked up to me as did Rook and Chris. I would always buy shoes, food, even movie tickets for all of us. Not to show off, but to keep us close.

Over the summer I would grind and hustle back and forth between hoods. My relationship with Jenn was shaky. I guess I was pussy whipped and couldn't stomach the fact that she was fucking someone else on the sly, so she thought. I was still fucking Cynthia, but she had a boyfriend too. Our relationship was still a secret and that was cool with me. I finally told her about me and Jenn. She was upset at first, but she understood she wasn't the only one having her cake and eating it too. It was no problem on my end because I loved the attention and the random extra sex.

I would visit both girls who were still friends and school them in the same lifestyle. They both were excited to see that I was a hustler and stayed fresh. It was only a matter of time before I got caught up so I got all I could, while I could.

One day we were all parked at the swimming pool at River Rouge. We were sitting on our bikes when I group of females walked by wearing two piece swim suits. One was tall, had hazel eyes and a body like Buffy. When they passed I gave her a smile and asked her to come over to me. I wasn't wearing swim trunks cause like most of the dudes. I hadn't come to swim, just came to watch the girls do their thang.

I had on my gray Polo shorts with the shirt to match and my first Ram pager stuffed in my pocket. I looked like my Uncle's secret project, like he had put me together. As the female walked my way I got off my moped and approached her dripping with swag.

"Damn, sexy. I gotta get at you. What's your name?"

"Angie, but they call me Legs," she said smiling.

"Yeah I can see why," I said looking her up and down. "Can a brother get your number? So we can chat under better circumstances?"

She whispered her number in my ear and I slipped her a card that already had my beeper number pre-printed on it. We flirted for a minute then she moved on to the pool. We met a few more chicks, but I knew that Angie was going to call. She was too cute to play a nigga.

Throughout the summer we would go to parties. A few days after I met Angie we went to a party on Seven mile. Now this party was laid out! I mean, catered by Steve's Soul Food, a DJ and a vast selection of females. While sitting on a bench I saw my boy Chris and his other crew. He spoke to me and David and allowed us to join them.

The DJ played Salt and Pepa's, "Push It" and everyone rushed the dance floor and mimicked the dances from the popular video. I noticed one of Chris's boy's from W.B.S. talking to a group of chicks. To my surprise one of them was Angie, the girl from the swimming pool. She wore Nike gym shoes with stretch pants to match the color of her shoes. She had a tight cut off shirt that read, "The Wifey Type," across the bust. Her hair looked like she stepped off the pages of the latest "Hype Hair" magazine.

We made eye contact and she motioned for me to come over to the swings to talk for a minute. I had second thoughts because she hadn't really reached out to call me like I thought she would, but I left David and walked over allowing my herringbone chain with the gold Benz emblem to swing as I walked.

"What's up stranger?" she asked before I could say anything.

"Yeah, what's up with you stranger?" I asked as she gave me a hug. All my ill feeling slowly lifted.

I was disappointed to find out she was about to move to Atlanta with her grandparents. The party was so loud and kids were all over the place so I asked did she want to blow the party and take a ride on my moped. Much to my dismay when the DJ played NWA, Angie declined my offer and started dancing to the music.

Me and David hung around Chris and his crew for a few hours until several small fights broke out and it was time to go. No major drama but we departed after pulling a few more cats and kittens. We rode around until the wee hours of the morning searching for more girls.

Once we made it back to the hood where my uncles were smoking and drinking on the block. Cody was sitting on his new Lebaron as we parked and hiked our bikes in the driveway.

"Rome, come holla at me real quick," he said.

I walked over and he showed me his new 38. Snub nose revolver that he had hidden in his stash spot in his car. "See niggas always gotta be prepared for the unexpected."

I looked at David as we both thought about our safety on the block but dismissed the idea. For the next hour we kicked it about our days and the big boys talked about fucking this hoe or that one etc. I personally liked to hear about their different experiences so I could learn from them. These boys were crazy into the life and what it had to offer and I had to follow their lead.

At around midnight while we were chilling in the driveway, my pager went off. I didn't recognize the number or the code behind it so I asked Cody could I use his cell phone to call the number back. I grabbed the phone out the bag and it lit the car interior as I dialed the number.

"Hello," some young female answered in a low voice.

"Anybody hit a pager? This young Rome."

"Yeah, what's up baby? This Legs from round the way."

"Bout time you popped at a nigga. What's up wit' ya?"

"At my cousin's chilling and you crossed my mind," Angie purred into the phone.

"Well I ain't on shit just on the block watching these cats gets blowed cause I don't do that either," I answered.

After a few minutes my uncle started complaining about his bill being high so I cut out conversation short in the driveway.

"Rome, let me holla at you real quick," he said.

I walked over and he showed me his new 38. Snub nose revolver that he had hidden in his stash spot in his car. "See niggas always gotta be prepared for the unexpected."

I looked at David as we both thought about our safety on the block but dismissed the idea. For the next hour we kicked it about our days and the big boys talked about fucking this hoe or that one etc. I personally liked to hear about their different experiences so I could learn from them. These boys were crazy into the life and what it had to offer and I had to follow their lead.

At around midnight while we were chilling in the driveway, my pager went off. I didn't recognize the number or the code behind it so I asked Cody could I use his cell phone to call the number back. I grabbed the phone out the bag and it lit the care interior as I dialed the number.

"Hello," some young female answered in a low voice.

"Anybody hit a pager? This young Rome."

"Yeah, what's up baby? This Legs from round the way."

"Bout time you called a nigga. What's up wit' ya?"

"At my cousin's chilling and you crossed my mind," Angie purred into the phone.

"Well I ain't on shit just on the block watching these cats gets blowed cause I don't do that either," I answered.

After a few minutes my uncle started complaining about his bill being high so I started to end the conversation. She didn't seem happy about it so I asked her could I hit her up on the house phone.

"Why don't you just bring me and my cousin a drink so we can just relax because my peoples are gone and we trying to chill," she said in her sexy voice.

"Shit, what ya'll drinking and what's the address? Im'ma bring my homeboy with me, he cool as hell," I said convincingly.

"Cool. Gin and Orange juice and she live on Seven mile and Archdale. It's the green house on the corner."

A few minutes later I asked my uncle to go cop the drinks for me while David copped a $20 bag of weed in case shit needed a lift. Once we had everything we needed we stashed the weed and drinks and hopped on the moped and made our way to our destination.

David really wasn't feeling the blind date at night tip, but he went along with the plan and agreed to take one for the team if need be. We got to Angie's cousin's house in about fifteen minutes and pulled up on the walkway to secure our bikes. Trina, Angie's cousin, was standing in the doorway looking like a tall version of Toni Braxton, short hair, curves and all. David's face lit up.

The midsize house was pretty nice. Angie was sitting on the leather wrap around sofa looking gorgeous as ever. She had on a long shirt and some shorts.

"What's up?" I said handing her the brown paper bag.

"Nothing, waiting on you," she said as she rose from the sofa and took the bag. She went into the tiny kitchen and made us all some drinks.

Trina and David were already joking and laughing like they'd known each other forever. They went into the next room to smoke the weed that David had bought. That gave me and Angie some time alone.

"Why it take you so long to hit me up?" I asked as I watched her sip from her drink.

"I know you used to girls sweating your ass. I ain't that type of girl. Plus I'm about to move so ain't no sense in starting something I can't finish, you know what I'm saying?" she asked as she moved a little closer to me. I could tell the gin and juice was working on her because she started rubbing the back of my head while we talked.

I was enjoying the affection as we got closer and she slipped me some kisses. I was rubbing all over her body when the thought of Jenn and Cynthia crossed my mind. It came and went to so fast I almost didn't see it! I had about an hour to get Angie naked and that was all on my mind.

I was up in her shirt in a matter of seconds massaging her nice sized breast seeing she conveniently had taken her bra off before we got there. I played with her nipples and they became hard as metal screws every time I flicked my finger over them. The moans that came from her throat let me know I could go further. I put my hand down inside her tight shorts and felt how wet she was. I pulled the shorts off and she laid back on the couch with her shirt pulled up exposing her beautiful body.

We smiled as we heard Keith Sweat turned up to abnormal levels indicating that Trina and David had their own thing going on. This was literally music to my ears as I pulled down my pants and boxers and laid on top of her small, smooth body. I guided my dick to her tight pussy and we both moaned as

I entered her. We slow grinded for about ten minutes while I took my time and made sure she came all over me, then I felt my time coming. It was time to release my inner soul as I pulled out and aimed at her flat stomach. My juices sprayed all over her body with a few drips hitting her neck.

She smiled and said, "You nasty Rome."

My body was still tingling from the moment as I got up and went to take a quick bird bath in the bathroom. I peeked in on David and Trina and she was going to town on his dick. I watched as she expertly went up and down, jacking his dick with her mouth and hand until he exploded into her mouth. He looked up and gave me the thumbs up as I pointed to my new Movado watch. "Time to go, Fam," I motioned.

A few minutes later we were out the door, hopping back on our bikes headed back to the block. When we got there the block was clear except for a few fiends staggering along the dirty curbs in search for misplaced money or a package. We talked about the girls for a minute then parted with our special handshake used by the 'Seven Mile Dogs' everywhere.

The rest of the summer was more of the same. I now had three girls in rotation. At any given time I would receive pages from either of the girls. I was milking this situation until the well ran dry. Angie was leaving in a week and I wanted to get all the sex I could. Even though I felt bad I had to chop it all up to teenage love maybe she'll keep in touch or maybe she wouldn't who knows. The choice would be hers, ya dig?

The main focus was getting my life together and getting ready for school along with the rest of the squad. I can't wait to become a freshman and experience the life of the mature crowd. Moms was still on my case and Rook was preparing for the same changes as I was. We talked a lot on the phone and all through the summer I still visited my old hoods to show off and pursue my old crush Meeka who was heading to a special school for overachieving children called Cass Tech. A lot of schools were being rebuilt and since my mother stayed near Redford that was the school for me. So now that things are cooling down, I was ready to get heated up at the start of my new semester.

CHAPTER 5

Yeah, this was it! My first day of high school and I was ready. The tall building that set across the street from the eighth precinct on Grand River was my new home.

There were so many people and so many classrooms it seemed surreal to me. Being that it was my first day it was really weird being by myself and not people from our previous school. But people I had never really dealt with. However after traveling through the large crazy hallways that were designed pretty awkward trying to locate my first hour I bumped into Jennifer and Cynthia walking together trying to locate their locker. We talked for minute then they moved on both looking fly as hell. I don't know what was worse, them walking together or me wanting the both of them.

Once they found their locker they realized it was down the hall from mine. I stopped them and we made plans to grab a bite to eat after school. The traffic in the hallway was crazy. There were restless teenagers searching for their classes and their friends while showing off their newest fashions.

I entered my first hour class and noticed that each hour I would be presented with new classmates. This was exciting to me. More people meant more girls. Around third hour I bumped into an old friend of Chris's. Since Chris was going to another school this was cool. At least I would have a few friends that I knew. Being a freshman in high school wasn't the easiest thing.

"What up doe?" he said when he saw me.

"Shit, what it do?" I replied.

"Ain't you my dog Chris's peeps?" asked the big dude.

"Yeah, that's my people. I've seen you a few times, but we never were introduced. My name is Rome," I said extending my hand for a play.

He complied and said, "They call me Big Phil."

After our first conversation we became cool and started to hang out during and after school. Over the next few weeks we met with the rest of his crew at school and at that point I began to smoke a little weed drink the famous mad dog 20/20. We would skip class and some days Chris would come to our school to pick us up or roam the halls to pick up girls. This is when I noticed that I had become a member of the gang called W.B.S. We did everything together during and after school hours. It was crazy because I lived off Five mile a.k.a. Fenkell and they all lived off Six mile road. So there was a small conflict of area claiming through the school/hood, but I dealt with it because these were my 'mans.'

Whenever I wasn't hanging out with Big Phil, Chris or my dog Chin, I would chill and hang out with Rook, Dean and my neighborhood crew. Moms was still on and off drugs and my sister and brother were in good health and starting school and etc. Jenn and Cynthia were a hot commodity to any guy that wanted them. Some days Jenn and I would hook up and play the boyfriend/girlfriend role, but I could feel myself growing away from the drama. In fact, I think she felt the same way too.

I continued to sell small amounts of drugs through my grandparent's house where I loved to hang out with David and others. One day I was over Jenn's and Bam, her brother was over there with his girl. We chilled and talked and as usual engaged in sex for a few minutes. Once we were done she got a call from Cynthia and that's when hell broke loose.

"I can't believe this shit, girl! I just found out I'm pregnant!" Cynthia yelled into the phone.

"Damn! Oh! No! Your dude done knocked you up?" Jenn screamed into the phone covering her mouth and shaking her head at me.

I was shocked to hear that Cynthia was pregnant but before I could let that sink in. She hit us both with the okeydokey.

"Girl, it might not even be his though. It could be Sam, Black Mike or Rome's. I don't know which one of these niggas is the baby daddy," Cynthia said knowing full well what she was doing.

"I'm gon call you back," was all she said to Cynthia but she had all kinds of shit to say to me. "Damn, Rome! My friend? For real? I mean, I know I slept with Howard, but I thought we was past that. You really gon play me like this?" she yelled in my face as tears ran down hers.

I was confused because, one, Jenn had slept with my friend and it wasn't a big deal. We got past that. But mainly because I couldn't believe I might have finally got caught up.

"Jenn, I haven't slept with Cynthia in three or four weeks so I can't be the daddy," I said trying to smooth it over, but of course that didn't help. After a few "I love you's" and "You're the only one I care about's" she forgave me for the moment.

Rook called me when I left Jenn's house and I gave him the run down. I told him I couldn't be the unlucky gentleman. He couldn't help but laugh, "Man, bring some rolling papers."

A few weeks later, Cynthia's boy toy found out who I was and questioned out friendship in the hallway.

"What's up with you Rome?" he asked looking like Iron Mike Tyson.

"Yeah, what it do?" I said standing guard with RIP next to me.

"Cynthia told me the deal and I'm not feeling you fucking my BM," the cocky dude spoke.

"Fuck you and Cynthia dude," RIP said before I could say anything. Yeah, he had my back, I can't lie so "Q" the self-proclaimed Baby Daddy was outnumbered. He walked away with cruel intentions on his mind.

That same week a rival gang called S&S which originated from the projects on the West side started picking victims throughout the school to fuel their reputation. Well, this one day we were all in the hallway, I was holding Jenn while Cynthia stood by her when they came down our way looking for trouble. And to all of our surprise guess who was with them? Q, yes Q or little Tyson as I called him. They saw his pregnant girl alongside of me and Jenn and he went crazy.

He grabbed her and started yelling while I smiled at all eight of them looking stupid. RIP and Chin, who we called that because of his double chin and his height, approached the scene and declared that this was W.B.S. hallway and they had to leave. They looked at fifteen to twenty young men with fear in their eyes and grabbed Cynthia and marched away knowing that they would be back since they knew our whereabouts.

Later that day I was at our bus stop next door to the school off Six mile with the crew killing time as usual.

"Rome, Hey Rome!" I heard Jenn yelling as she ran up on me. "Can you walk me home since Cynthia left with Q?"

"That's cool," I said as I gave the crew some love and started our journey to take her home.

Twenty minutes into the walk and almost at her house I saw five S&S dudes trying to catch up to us. Now I could run and leave Jenn cause she'd be safe but then respect would run thin or I could stand to take a beat down and pray that I survive and maybe get a little sympathy sex. So I swallowed my pride and told Jenn to cross over to the other side of the street and walk home because they probably had a gun on them. She did as I told her. As soon as she did I turned and broke out towards the school as fast as I could.

They gave chase and one stayed to watch Jenn. So since they couldn't catch me they went back to their original plan. Who cared as long as I made it safe at home so I could regain my courage to react the next day?

The next day of school, I spoke to Jenn due to the lack of the phone call to ensure my safe journey home. I soon found out why I didn't get that phone call.

"One of those guys was Q's brother, and he tried to talk to me. So we exchanged phone numbers," she said as if it were nothing.

Cynthia had told her about him before so he wanted to get at her and she wanted him too, obviously. I figured they wanted to get back at me for fucking Cynthia. So she was falling for the drama I let her find herself. At lunch time the entire S&S crew set with Q, Jenn, and Cynthia. It was cool, I was with about nine dudes even though they still outnumbered us.

No confrontation took place, so we left out of the lunch room to go to our lockers. They followed us and once I told the boys what happened the day before they all got heated. So we stopped in our tracks in front of the main office and confronted the current situation.

"Dig, what ya'll niggas trying to do?" asked RIP.

"Whatever," a tall boy answered from their group. I noticed he had a twin, standing near him.

Before he could blink Chin ran up and kicked the guy into the trophy case and all hell broke loose. The entire hall was filled with punches being thrown and security tossing people around like a riot was taking place. Some got caught, many got away through the side doors the school used as exit routes. The entire school saw that both crews stood their ground and the rematch was sure to take place.

From that point on we had a few altercations with each other, sometimes directly in front of the school or in front of the police station. They even built a police mini sub-station inside the school to control the violence.

Not long after, me and Jenn kinda ended our relationship after one last booty call. She started letting Q's brother play in it, so to me that was too thick for my blood to handle. It was dangerous to get caught slipping in the hallway so no distractions, was cool. I learned quickly that to love, sometimes is to let go.

The rest of the school year was up and down as were my grades. My attendance started taking a turn for the worse. But I was a child who thought like a man and so my actions were soon to bring manly consequences.

CHAPTER 6

"89-90"

The summer of "89" was wild as ever and it passed by slowly. All that I can say is that it was fun with a few more experiences than usual. I was still hanging with the crew and switched from hood to hood under the umbrella of my Uncle Cody. Jennifer was pretty much a distant memory and my mom's addiction was getting worse. She would use until she decided to self-rehabilitate. That worried me, but she kept me at bay.

The drug game was still kinda new to me and I became more advanced over time. The absence of Jenn showed me a lot about feelings and kiddie relationships. I was primed for the next slew of girls, no feelings involved.

During the times I would stay with my Granny, I became more involved with Chris and David along with the rest of W.B.S. set who dwelled on violence and destruction.

One day we were at McDonald's on Six Mile and Greenfield. Chris, Chin, RIP and a few others set in a few booths talking and picking with a few of the female employees. A few guys from a rival group came in and started trouble by bumping Chin in the line which was a sure sign of disrespect. This was our turf and we weren't having none of that.

RIP with his 260 pound frame sprang into action and sucker punched one of the guys and seconds later the McDonald's became a front row seat to a royal rumble event. Punches were thrown from every direction as the four on four brawl ran the room. As I took a quick breather and managed to gather my senses from all the mayhem, I noticed everyone fighting except a short guy with long hair that was just about to pull out a blade from his pants pocket. Within seconds he rushed into the crowd and swung aggressively connecting with Chris's face. Before I could take him down I heard him screaming as he fell down over Chin's tired body. He and the rest of the crew hurried to the exit while we all tended to Chris as he lay on the floor holding his eye. Blood streamed through his fingers as we told the manager to call 911.

Unfortunately, he lost the eye. I couldn't believe it. I felt so bad because I couldn't help him in time. It all happened so fast, I don't think anyone could have. But I damn sure was going to be there for him as he recovered. Me and the rest of the crew vowed to roam the streets looking to exact our revenge as soon as possible.

Once my mom and grandparents heard about what happened they became adamant that I change the group of friends I was hanging around. But of course that didn't stop anything. I just got smarter and sneakier. After a few weeks I ended up back over my mom's to avoid any further altercations, so they thought.

As soon as I got back to the old hood things would be shaken up as usual only because I'd had so many experiences that I wanted to share with them. Chris and I were still friends until he moved with his dad out of town. That was the last that I heard of Chris a.k.a. Left Eye.

In my hood things were moving fast. The local hood stars like Chaos and Mystro were on the rise with their new CD. My neighbor was their best friend and also one of my former employers so I had the privilege of hanging with the "in" crowd. Me and my boy Dean would go to the video shoots and gigs with the crew. I can remember their first video called, "Mystro on the Flex," with the crew. We all wore our Top Tens and Starter coats. We had to be the happiest crew in the world.

That summer I received my drivers permit so I was able to drive with a licensed adult present. Dean had his too, so sometimes we would ride his parent's car around with his brother, Snook. Sometimes he would let us sneak and drive to basketball practice. We both played for Jake Boy's PAL League called the "Road Runners." We practiced at Webber middle school and it was an exciting experience. I learned a lot about the game in these early years.

To earn money when I wasn't playing on the team I would take trips to other cities with the crew. Javan was the "boss," in charge. We would travel to places like Flint, Grand Rapids and Albion, but the one I loved the most was Muskegon. On these trips we would blend in and conquer the drug trade making major profit. Sometimes we would double or triple our profits in their housing projects. For example, an ounce of crack went for $900 in Detroit, at this time you could cut maybe $3000 from it, and sell it in these cities in one night. If needed, an ounce of crack would cost a local $2200. So you can see how it was worth the trip.

Most of my money came from driving to and from these cities because I utilized my talents from my past and started slanging with the others. I had a smooth tongue and could make the devil fall for water, shit I could've sold him a few gallons too. The crack heads loved me, and so did the team I was on. They all called me, "a great earner."

With the money I earned, I bought clothes, food and shared my profits with my family when we got back. The trips were usually over the weekends so my mom wouldn't really miss me. It wasn't until my weekends became weeks that my mom started giving me hell. It was worth it. I had all the latest shoes like, Jordan's, Gucci's, Ewing's and etc. Plus all the best of the best clothes like Levis, Guess, Calvin Klein's and Cross Colors. I even was the first to have the Eight Ball jackets and card leather coats.

Boy, life was on the move for me and the crew. While spending many nights in Muskegon hustling off Moffat Street in the Heights and ZZ's party store on Hoyt Street, my females at home drifted a little because I was never there. But when we were home Dean, Rook and I would have a blast spending and enjoying what life had to offer.

The summer was going really smooth until I felt the need to venture into my own endeavors as a Boss. One night after watching Javan re-up with an old man named Dave, who was known around the hood as Uncle Dave. I saw that he only paid $750 for an ounce of powder (cocaine) and Unc would loan or front him another for the same ticket and since my mom and Uncle Dave were good friends due to her habit and his, I elected to use my inside connect to get a front.

We talked to Unc and explained that I was familiar with the hustle in "Skeet Town," and knew the route plus the locals. He agreed, so I gathered a couple of friends from the hood named Q and Tone and convinced my older Uncle to drive us there for a hundred. We would catch the Greyhound back to the city once we were finished since it only cost us $25 per person.

"It should take us two days tops," I told the two brothers that were only a few years older than me. I figured they would make $300 each in two days minus the $100 for travel. I paid for travel, food and shelter which would be some local female's crib that I met that month. Javan and his crew were still making the same trip we knew that there would be ill feelings for what they called "back dooring" the hustle. I learned the ropes from them and hoped that they would accept my power move.

I had my uncle cook up an ounce of powder for me and I sat at the table and cut the crack up into nice pieces. $3000 in all $20 rocks or "slabs" as they called them in the "Skeet." A nice profit would be made in a few days and the trip would be repeated until we saw fit to quit.

The night before we left, Javan was outside in his sweet, light blue pick-up truck with the dark blue cover on the bed. We talked and explained my situation out of gaining his respect. He understood, but deep inside I could tell that he felt like the move was a form of infringement on his business. I learned quickly that in the so called game everyone wants to win and win alone.

There was no guide book on how to be successful or the ruler of the underworld. A handbook that consisted of your experience or lack thereof, or maybe watching and learning from others situations. Even with gaining this brief knowledge as a young man I still needed and wanted to move forward with good intentions and confidence. Putting my wants in front of my needs would be another lesson I would soon learn about.

I was really excited about stepping out on my own, doing my own thing. Prior to leaving for "Skeet Town," me and the crew were going over our strategy and plan since this was their first time going up there. After telling Rook good-bye and calling a few females to do the same, we were off. The drive took about 3 ½ hours as we smoked weed and listened to the latest tapes. Our pagers and my cell phone in a bag were our only means of communication during the trip. Smoking weed really wasn't my thing since my asthma was bound to flare up, but occasionally I would take a small puff to blend in or to catch a quick head rush.

While driving into Muskegon through the back way to avoid police we became unlucky real quick. A young white officer was observing the traffic that entered and left out the lucrative city. We were spotted riding in our low key "84" two door Datsun. Four, black males at 7:30 am with a car full of dope and no specific destination spelled trouble. As the cop got behind us I grabbed the bag of rocks and slowly rolled down the window. He was following so closely behind that I had to really careful. Our initial plan was to ride down to the strip on Hoovey Street to flip a few hundred for a room for the night, but with the copper trailing behind us that plan was dismissed. We rode around making useless turns, but he stayed with us.

"Why don't we go down on Sherman?" one of the guys asked. Now let me explain what the strip looked like. There were at least six to eight drug dealers on all four corners of the three block radius, trying to sell rocks. A few of them were from Detroit and a few were from the "Skeet" acting as lookouts; and secondary hustlers. Whenever a car pulled up to the corner to purchase dope, everyone would run up to it as fast as they could and stick their hands in the window to show off their rocks to persuade the fiend to buy it. So at times you would have a number of people at one car until the deal was done.

It was the late 80's, early 90's and crack was new to everyone, especially the people in "Skeet." It was scary due to the fact that a lot of users were so young. I mean like sixteen to seventeen years old using and abusing the drug. A few saw it as a hustle by buying $100 worth of rocks from us and getting a deal for example six or seven rocks for $100 would allow them to make a profit, but still allowed us to move our product faster. It was cruel, but there was no weight or wholesale dealers at this time. This was the best deal any local could receive and they loved it. So all that was said to say, going to this location would be as stupid as searching for rice in the snow.

After making six or seven turns going nowhere, the officer reacted by turning on his sirens and lights to motion for us to pull over. Prior to this maybe a few minutes before, I had slung the sack out the window thinking that I would remember where I threw it. Once we pulled over, the officer approached our car demanding our identification and registration. After giving him this basic information he asked a few questions like, "Where were we going? Because we looked lost."

"My grandmother lives on Moffat, Officer," I said praying that he believed me. He took my ID then came back to the car and much to our surprise, he let us go. Only one thing, I needed to remember where I had thrown the $3000 sack. We drove around for another hour and I still couldn't find it.

This was the worst because now I had no money, no drugs and I still owed Uncle Dave and all this happened in five hours. So much for my new position as "Boss." We drove over to

Javan's to hide out in the Heights. What I didn't know is that Javan had given the order that I wasn't able to come into his house and his boys made sure I knew it. Fortunately for me, my lil dog Ray was there and since Javan wasn't in Skeet until tomorrow, he let me in.

Without any money, I couldn't call Uncle Dave. So we rested for a few hours then hit the road back home and tried to come up with a plan to make up the money. However since my skinny ass uncle, who had driven us there was paid up front, he had decided to go out and get high with the locals. So when his money ran out, so did he!

"Now what?" said the brothers as we sat on the porch the next morning. Shit was so fucked up for us we had to find a way to get back home and plus I had to bounce because Javan was on his way home and I couldn't get caught in his trap house.

So hours turned into days being stranded with only $45 to our name and getting on the bus without each other wasn't going to happen. We stayed a few nights at one of my chick's house. Her mom was cool enough to let us stay, especially since her mom liked one of the brothers. But we still had no money and dick can only pay for so much.

On our 9th day there, a friend of the family came to check on the girls and found out that we were staying there. I explained to him our situation and he was willing to help out. He told us to go buy a few packs of powder "Stand Back" which is a pain relief medicine along with a few tubes of OraGel toothache liquid. When we came back he took the items and made it into little pieces of rocks. Then after freezing them he dripped a few drops of OraGel on them to give them that numbing effect that crack has in case anyone wanted to test the product. In the end it looked like we had a few hundred dollars' worth of "gank" or fake crack.

Shortly after we hit the strip with the intentions of selling the gank quickly and getting right on the bus headed home. Unfortunately, this plan didn't pan out because before we could sell enough we got called out by a few unsatisfied customers. Word traveled fast in this little ass town. Maybe because we weren't the first to try this scheme.

Shit out of luck and nowhere to turn, we had to come up with another plan to get some quick cash plus our time at the girl's house was wearing thin. "No drugs, no hugs," was my motto at this time so we all were upset and irritated due to the long and restless nights. Dave had found out what happened when my uncle got back to the city. I found out when I called my mom to let her know I was safe. I was really fucked now.

The next morning one of the brothers came up with the suggestion that we strong arm someone and take their money and head straight to the bus station.

"That sounds good, but who?" I asked.

No answer. I figured they thought I was scared to pull off a robbery, so I let the silence ease into the small area we were in at the diner, where everyone ate with no worries. We all were having serious mood swings because this situation was so fucked up.

We went across the street to the Super 8 motel where all the locals hung out on the weekends to mingle. By it being early on a Sunday most guest had already checked out, but a few still wandered around the area eating and visiting the small shops that connected to the motel. While approaching the parking lot with my boys they noticed an older white lady going to her car and asked her for the time. As she reached inside her car, one of the brothers delivered a serious blow to the lady's face and the other brother snatched her purse off her shoulder.

With the lady slumped into her car, we broke out running towards the motel and found a bathroom to hide in. We checked the purse for money then I said, "Why didn't ya'll tell me the plan??"

"Man, I knew that you would freeze up, Rome," the oldest brother said.

Our streak of bad luck continued when we realized that there was only $17 and a gang of coupons inside the purse and to make matters worse, I heard walkie talkies outside of the bathroom. Before I could say anything the door flew open and a few officers burst in with guns drawn, ready to use them if necessary.

"Get on the fucking floor!" they all screamed and we cautiously complied.

Stretched out on the floor, they cuffed us all and separated us. They took us out to the cars and took our ID's. I was still a minor according to the law. At fifteen I was taken to the youth home while the two brothers who were over seventeen were taken to jail.

My stay in the home was brief, two and a half weeks to be exact. My court date came and I was happy to see my mom there but she wasn't happy. We all stood as the court officer announced the judge. My lawyer spoke as the charges were being read, they ranged from armed robbery to assault with intent. To my surprise they released me into my mom's custody until I had to come back to court.

Needless to say the ride home was pretty cold. My mom and grandparents chewed me out all the way home. Hey, you live and you learn and I still had a lot of learning to do.

CHAPTER 7

Sophomore Year High School "89-90"

This school year would be wilder than ever and by me being on my A-game I was fully ready. After recovering from my court case and the steady summer, I was able to hustle enough under my uncle Cody's wing to repay Uncle Dave and prepare myself financially for the upcoming school year. The first few weeks were calm as the old crew found their way around the crowded hallways and classes.

RIP, Chin and myself and a few others held our spot down next door to the school. After beefing with rival hoods during the summer it would be a matter of time before it caught up to us. And after Chris's situation my defense stayed on high cause anytime the shit could hit the fan.

Meanwhile at home my mom's still allowed me to come home so she could keep an eye on me. Especially after the Skeet Town incident. Though she still had a light addiction, our relationship was still off and on along with our attitudes colliding. Even though it was never physical it still left me exhausted.

As I tried to do my best to do well in school, but the street life had me by the neck and I could only breathe easy when I was in them. As I got deeper in the streets my grades began to slack. Occasionally I would see Jenn's pretty ass in the hallways, but we never spoke. To me it was the betrayal that had me bitter plus I had a bigger vision for my life then she could handle.

A few of my newer friends like Steve were always around to lead me in many directions. Steve was cool. He was a medium height, kinda built and loved to show off his rap skills. Then the popular groups were Ghetto Boyz and some local rappers like A.W.O.L., Detroit's Most Wanted and my boys,

Chaos and Mystro who again were close friends with my dude Javan.

Steve had his own group called "Self Paid," and many days I would hang with him and Aaron a.k.a Gangsta Slay. Steve's name was, "Out Cold." And we would rhyme and mimic the Ghetto Boyz. He stayed with his mom and three younger brothers who all accepted me into their lives and we became like family.

The crew was cool with my new friends as many of the other guys had either been incarcerated or killed off by rival gangs. The movie 'Scarface' was just released in the theaters and it had everybody wanting to be drug dealers on a major level. It was crazy because my Uncle and his crew followed the paths of the characters in the movie.

I would bounce from hood to hood and deal in small amounts of drugs, but my hustle was during school hours. I would sell joints during breaks or after school as kids drank Mad Dog 20/20 and escaped their problems by getting lifted. I didn't really smoke, but occasionally would to prove that I was a man and cool.

On the weekends I would hang out with Steve and polish my rap skills and other days I would kick it with Chris and David and continued to push a small pack of rock cocaine to my uncle's clientele. To me, life was moving fast and I still had a few female friends that would enter and exit my world. The only person who really understood me was my brother Rook, so at night I would call or go by to see him and talk the latest talk and he would give me some good advice. I have to admit that he kept me sane a lot of the time along with my little brother and sister. I figured if I made it then they all would be alright.

Between hanging and school my time was short trust me, but I learned to make the best out of every minute. Back at school we would skip classes and shoot dice in the hallways until girls came around. Then it would be off to Chin's house to enjoy a quick skip party that would end at 4:00 p.m. before his parents came home. A lot of times Chris would come through and hang out with us.

One day I came to school late and noticed nobody was there. So I rode my Elite straight to Chin's crib to see what's going down. As I pulled up I could hear MC Breed's new song, 'Frontin' blasting while a few teenagers mingled through the medium sized house. A few new faces watched as I entered the door with my Top Ten's and W.B.S. t-shirt. Nobody looked familiar so I dipped to the basement where Chin and the crew were entertaining a group of girls.

"What up doe, Rome?" they all spoke as we gave daps to each other.

"Same old soup, just reheated," I replied as I glanced through the cloud of smoke in the basement. Just then Jennifer came down the stairs with another girl and waved at me from a distance.

"Damn, she getting around," I thought to myself as I motioned for her to come over. I was hoping I could get a little "for old time's sake" sex.

Once we hugged, we sat on the love seat and talked for a few minutes. We spoke on school and tried to stay away from the past, but we both could tell that we loved and missed each other a whole lot. It was noon and she usually got home from school at 3:00 and time was moving extra fast. I tried to make my move by taking her upstairs away from her girl into the bathroom so we could talk on the one on one. In the bathroom she already knew what I wanted so we both took no time going at each other.

First a kiss as we embraced by the small sink, then off with my shirt as she unbuckled my pants slowly. Since she had on biker pants and a long shirt I easily pulled hers down to allow one leg to come out of them. With my help she softly sat on the edge of the sink with her legs open as we still kissed fast.

"Damn," she looked so sexy and her pussy was shaved bald, plus it was so wet from the foreplay that I needed no help from my hands to enter her. This was followed by long hard thrusting pumps. I repeatedly went in and out of her, allowing the tip of my penis to only reach the outer lips of her pussy then all back in at once. Making cumming sounds she bit her lips and grabbed me closer as she came all over me and the now slippery sink.

Shortly after that I exploded as I pulled out to let the cum squirt on her pussy. I looked up and she had the same look I had in my eyes. "I'll always love you," I said as we wiped off with random rags.

"Me too, Rome," she replied putting her clothes back on. We snuck back out to the party which was going on like they never knew we'd left. There was little to no conversation between us, so before I knew it she was gone and I rejoined the fellas. They knew what was up with me and Jenn, we hadn't fully gotten over each other.

As I was leaving, I couldn't help but to wonder why was she there? I dapped the crew and left the party. I had plenty of time to think on the ride home. I was all in my feelings and I didn't like it. I made it home and crashed.

Rook was still playing sports and going to Southwestern and we could get together at home and politic certain things. Once I told him I saw Jenn he laughed and spoke his piece. He was always on my side, but trust me he would speak his mind when he had to. If I was happy he was happy and vice-versa, that's it.

Every now and then David would come through and we would kick it about my hustling skills and the court case was still pending in "Skeet Town," that would now be transferred to Detroit through court motions.

The rest of the hood was the same, Meeka was growing up but couldn't give me a chance because of her new boyfriend that I knew, were in the same class. Power, she knew she had it and that made my crush even stronger because I wanted it back, and her. Anyhow, it was 1990 and I still tried to do the right thing and stay focus or balanced as I would call it by being active at school. The rest of the school year was kinda slow, but every now and then a little action would pop off.

I never saw or called Jenn since the skip party and Cynthia had started dating my cousin through a mutual friend, but I kept my mouth closed cause he thought he had a winner. Huh?!

Every other week, I still rode my moped to Granny's to hang out and hustle cause I loved that hood. My hood had become a moneymaker as well so I had the best of both worlds each day. As I finally passed to another grade, barely, the summer got underway. The Senior Picnic was held at Belle Isle Park in downtown Detroit. The picnic was always live as cars, bikes and sexy girls roamed the strip in search of their next jump off.

This year was the best because W.B.S. had the best mopeds and cars. We drank, smoked and enjoyed the view as loud music pumped through our speakers. This year there was no gang drama, but every hood represented with pride and stood firm by any means necessary to protect their set. As the day passed and the darkness grew near everyone climbed in their rides and headed for the "Jefferson Strip," to enjoy the route home.

I couldn't wait to get a page from one of the girls that I had met to get the summer, popping off the best way I knew how. "In due time, the world would be mine," I thought to myself as I turned the throttle to its max to race home to rest for the last few days of school.

"Two down, two more to go," I said under my protective helmet. "Welcome summer time!"

CHAPTER 8
Summer 1990

Loud music playing, ice cream trucks circling the blocks, girls laced in cute sandals and booty shorts, the smell of new Jordan's and Patrick Ewings permeating from the feet of the fellas. Yea, these all were the official signs of the summer and I was enjoying every single minute of it.

After the senior picnic, my pager had more action than usual due to all the new females I met at Belle Isle, so I was already off to a good start. Rook was silly as usual as he told us about his latest sexual experiences. He had hit a few girls already, like Lakesha, a chick from the block. She was pretty cool and her family had money. They had a large camper that they kept in their yard that we use to chill in. The other chick was Jameka who also lived on our block. She was cool too, but since she knew of Rook's secret play dates, she kept to herself most of the time.

My uncle was still the man and my idol to a certain extent. One day I was laying in my living room when my mom got a call from Granny. I could hear her crying and cursing. I knew something was wrong from the look on my mom's face. At first I thought I had done something wrong until she said, "Come on Rome, hurry up and get ready!"

"What's wrong?" I asked as I tied up my colorful Ewings.

As we rushed out of the house she explained to me frantically that my Uncle Cody had gotten into an altercation at the club a few nights ago and was beaten with a bat and left for dead. He had been unconscious until today and was able to tell the doctors who he was because he had no ID on him when he was brought in.

"Damn, the man who I had come to think of as invincible was in trouble and fighting for his life," I thought to myself.

REGGIE GIST

Once we got to the hospital and found our way to his room, I was told to stay outside while Mom went in and talked to Granny and my other Uncle CB about the situation. After an half an hour I was told he wanted to see me by myself, so I complied. Believe me when I say they worked him over pretty bad cause once I entered the room, I walked past him to the other patient who shared the room with him. He was totally unrecognizable. His face was swollen to the size of four human heads all in one.

I held back tears as I approached the bed to talk to him. "What the fuck happened?"

He spoke in a low, humble voice as he told me the story, "Rome, man, I was at the Dancery dancing with this dude's girl and didn't know it because she didn't acknowledge the dude. So he tried to cut in and I wouldn't let him." He cleared his throat and continued, "I looked around the club to see where my boys were, but I didn't see them and before I knew it I got sucker punched from behind."

I could barely hold my anger and tears in as I listened to the story. I was so hurt, but I let him continue.

"It was about five of them and I was hanging for a minute, but it's only so much you can do with ten fists coming from every direction. Then security broke the fight up and threw them out first, then me a few minutes later, which gave them enough time to get weapons and shit to beat the fuck out of me with. Then I woke up here, with tubes and IV's every damn where."

"Damn, all this over a bitch? Why your boy's didn't help?" I had to control myself because I was yelling. The medicine he was given was kicking in because he was nodding off and didn't answer my question. I figured I would leave and allow him to rest, but before I turned to go he said, "Yo, I can remember one dude. He looks like a cat that hangs out in your hood. He be hanging with Javan."

He described the dude and I took mental notes then told him to get some rest. We left the hospital just as the rest of his crew poured in to post up as extra security for their injured comrade.

Soon as we got home Rook was waiting on me to confirm the details. It hurt me to see my uncle in the hospital and all I could think of was revenge at any cost. But by me being a lil' fella my position was to stay in line and wait for future orders. It took me a few days before he was released. He was still in bad shape. His head was the size of two pit bulls due to the swelling. I could tell he had nothing but bad intentions. Somebody was going to die.

It only took a few weeks to connect the dots and find the guy who started the altercation. In the underworld everybody knows somebody, somehow and street codes come into play if you are ranked. So, I begged to ride in one of the many cars that would be used to ambush the target.

"Give me a gun," I said even though I was scared to death.

"Ok, here," Uncle CB said handing me a chrome 9mm with the heavy clip.

I felt a sudden rush of adrenaline like I'd never felt before holding that piece of metal in my hand. As we got closer to the location which was literally a minute from my moms, I listened to the plan that was orchestrated by my uncle. The first car would drive past to see who was outside the house then report to the other car. That was done.

"Hey, there are seven to eight people outside and he has on the blue jacket with the Detroit cap on," said Cody into the phone to CB.

"Ok, let's roll!" CB screamed. We rode down the street and slowed down as we got near the house. We opened fire as soon as we spotted the guy who Cody had fingered. People were running in every direction, but the guy in the blue jacket was firing back at us with a .357 in each hand. Bullets hit the metal of the cars we were driving and my heart almost stopped. I continued to squeeze the trigger at any one running or standing still. The target jumped up laughing and ran towards the back yard. As we drove off I saw several people lying on the ground bleeding. I checked myself and luckily I had survived my first drive-by.

Because all the drama had gone down in my hood, my uncles ordered me to lay low. Even though I hadn't been seen, it was known I was related to Cody so I could very well be a target now.

Only Javan knew both sides of the story. They had used him for bait and since he didn't want any drama, when approached he cooperated and gave us the guy's location. So we weren't worried about him snitching…again.

I hung out at Granny's for a while. Things were business as usual. The fiends were still visiting the block along with women and the crew. David and I still hung out and hustled through the hood even though both of our parents despised the idea. The weather was ninety degrees plus every day and I was loving it.

A few of the other cousins were staying with Granny, my cousin Ray and his sisters and my aunt who was younger than me named Tee. She was Cody's and my mom's youngest sibling. We would all share the house and time of our grandparent's giving them everlasting joy or headaches.

As my uncle recouped from his wounds, I picked up the slack and held down the block under his watchful eye. I saved money and treated all the grandchildren like brothers and sisters and tried to train my Lil' cuz Ray to be a good soldier. That's another story.

It was Saturday night and while I was doing my shift with "D," we were talking about Chris and how we missed him, Jenn and the crew. All of us had been out of touch since school was out and Chino found out that Cynthia and I had played a bit. "D" was cracking up when I told him that I had tricked Cynthia, her two sisters and her mom into thinking I was a twin so I could fuck all of them. It really worked for a minute until my mom got involved due to a small situation pertaining me and my "twin."

While we were talking one of my favorite fiends drove down the street in her new Escort with the hatchback. Escorts were one of the popular cars like the Probe, Honda Accord and Sidekick trucks. While she was trying to convince me to give her a couple of stones on credit, she made me an offer I wouldn't and couldn't refuse. She offered me her car for $1500 and it was an "86" model. I gave her a few rocks and told her to get the title and then we could talk to my Granny about the deal.

A few days later she brought back the car, title and her mom to seal the deal. Cody was glad to see that I was maturing in the streets as he was healing. Tensions had cooled down since the shootout, but we were still on high alert in case they drove down our block the same way.

Once Granny approved the deal after I told her I had saved my money and gotten a loan from my uncle. I was geeked to have my first car a few months after I got my license. The car was a beige two door with a tape deck and speakers. "D" and I loved the car because now we could cruise down Seven Mile or go to the Isle when we weren't at River Rouge flirting with the ladies.

We would sit inside the car in front of the house and sell drugs out of the car until curfew. I was working from sun up to sun down and "D" was like my shadow. The best part was when we would ride through the hood and see Rook and the crew. The look on their faces was priceless when they saw me achieve another goal. Mom was cool with the car too, but she was still keeping her eye on me because I was still her lil' man. She didn't want me to grow up too fast.

I drove the wheels off that Escort and treated it like a Benz. On certain days I would teach "D" how to drive and allow him to chauffer me around while we cruised the hood. My boy Byron stayed next door with his little brother and mom. He was cool because we grew up together, but he was a little wilder than I was. He did things like steal cars and guns and stayed in juvey for his actions. His mom and Granny were good friends and looked out for each other.

One day I was riding down Sussex and noticed Byron sitting on a porch with a few girls. So we stopped even though I wasn't driving to kick with for a few minutes. He was chilling with his girlfriend and another girl who was her cousin. She was about 5'3, 120 lbs, brown skinned with short hair that curled at her neck. I had to have her and she was looking like she was feeling me too.

I stepped out the car with my green Miami Hurricane short outfit with some Gucci shoes and my Ram pager. On my neck hung my herringbone chain and on my finger was a gold pinky ring with my initials in it.

"B-Dog, what's up?" I asked trying to sound cool.

"Shit, chilling with lil' Ma and her family," responded Byron gesturing to the two girls on the porch.

"Hey shorty, my name is Rome."

She waved her hand and said, "My name is Kamari, nice to meet you."

We kicked it for a few minutes then we exchanged numbers because my pager was going off, alerting me to get back to the hood.

OPTIONS

Later on that night Byron asked me to play wing man for him. Cool, as I expected as we drove to grab some Coney Island for the girls then to the crib which wasn't far from our house. We talked and chilled until Byron and his girl left us alone so they could do the nasty.

Kamari and I sat on the porch and got better acquainted with each other. We talked for hours until curfew. We decided to hook up later because she had to go home the next day. She lived on Fenkell and Schaefer which wasn't far, but explained that her parents were strict on her when it came to boys. So I kept that in mind and didn't call until she dialed me up. Plus I kept the power by leading the chase.

The rest of the summer was steady. Every few days Kamari and I would talk a few hours and built a bond that would last a while. She was a sweet girl and was preparing for school at Cass Tech to be a dance major. I was still going back to Redford with the crew, except this year I would be driving.

My W.B.S. crew stayed loyal and "D" stayed the same. Steve and Aaron sharpened my rap skills as a member of the Self Paid Clique. The block still bumped with opportunities to get money as I frequently visited my moms. I only saw Kamari a few times after we originally met and each time it felt special. Truthfully this was growing into another Jennifer situation, but I hoped it would turn out different cause I was falling in love…again. Damn.

CHAPTER 9

School Year "91"

The winter time was always extra cold and fun. The early part of the school year flew past and Christmas came and went before I knew it. My friendship with the crew remained the same as we stormed the hallways of Redford looking for women and trouble.

I hardly ever saw Jenn or Cynthia, even though they still went to Redford. Sometime I would miss them and slowly creep past their classes to sneak a glance at them.

Steve and the W.B.S. set would do as they always did and held me down, while Rook and Dean picked up the slack at home. Life was moving fast and so was my reputation. I managed to sell drugs in school and accumulated a few more groupies in the process.

Beef with the rival schools still existed, but stayed cool due to the light demo that was set last year in the hallways. Kamari and I were starting to build a stronger bond by phone calls and quick visits to her sister's house. My car was in good condition so I continued to drive to school and cruise with "D" at times.

The hustle was getting greater cause I was mobile and could meet the needs of more customers. At the same time Cody had fully recovered and he became even bigger than before because he was a survivor and a role model to us all. Granny was working selling insurance and my mom had found her way and was being a better parent to me. Since I had wheels a lot of time was spent with her while she tried to kick her addiction. I enjoyed getting closer to her because at this point in my life her sincere advice took the place of my dead beat Dad's. Since he wasn't around my journey through life would be filled with more obstacles and unanswered questions that only the streets could answer.

Back at school things were calm until a rival gang called S&S from the Smith home projects tried to get their reputation up by jumping our boy, Fatman, after school one day. Once it got back to us what happened, revenge was necessary and we had to stand firm and retaliate. One day, after spring break, the weather was nice and warm and we wore our W.B.S. hats and shirts out loud. We were getting ready to leave school and head to our chill spot when Fatman saw a few of the guys that had jumped him.

Almost simultaneously they noticed us as they motioned for the rest of their clique to enter the war zone which was located at the center of the school. At least twelve on twelve or more guys squared up and battled for ten to fifteen minutes. Punches flew and people ran for cover only to be trampled on by a spectator. Police stormed the scene quickly as the fight sprawled out into the middle of Grand River, stopping cars in traffic as they tried to avoid hitting any students.

Many got arrested and many were injured from the battle but only the strong survived and thank GOD I was one of them! A few days later the police did an investigation and it was determined that we were the instigators. Because of the amount of damage that was done on the school property we were all expelled from the Detroit Public School District.

When I got home and delivered the news to my mom she went crazy on me. That tirade was followed by the wrath of my grandparents. The words they spoke sunk into my brain and injured my pride. They threatened to take my car and I prayed they wouldn't go through with their threat. They all were adamant about me graduating and walking across that stage.

As I was sulking, another thought crossed my mind, the chances of me getting any pussy from Jenn or Cynthia was severely thin. No more school, meant no more Jenn or Cynthia.

So I spent my time off getting closer to Kamari. She was so pretty and fun to be around and she held me at bay by not allowing me to fuck her yet. This was unusual to me and I was determined to succeed in this adventure real soon.

After school was out for the summer, I promised my family that I would study to get my G.E.D. and a job to reduce my drug selling and I had every intention on completing all the task above.

I was chilling at Granny's helping her recover from a terrible accident that she and my aunt had gotten into a few months earlier. The car was totaled and they were lucky to be alive. As a matter of fact everyone thought they were dead at the scene, but GOD had a different plan. So since I was the oldest grandchild I stayed around to lend a hand where I could. My granddad loved her as much as anyone else and he made sure like always that he stayed by her side, three hundred percent. The rest of the family played their part as well as we all nursed her back to health.

After I finished my "watch" for the evening, I sat on the porch trying to get a few sales and the house phone rang, then my pager beeped showing Kamari's number. I had been feeling a little down and this made me feel a little better. We talked for an hour and I wanted to see her for a few minutes to get some kisses. She agreed as she told me that she was at her sister's for the night and it was ok to come over.

I jumped into my car and headed down Greenfield to Fenkell then turned left until I came to Coyle. I parked my Escort and ran upstairs to her apartment to see my baby. She opened the door wearing some cute shorts and a cut off top as she let me in. Her sister and her baby daddy liked me because I was a young hustler that held my own. They would sleep in the back and allow us to chill in the living room. This night they were sleeping hard by 12:30 am and we were sitting and kissing on the couch for a few minutes. She asked me to kick off my shoes and lay with her on the pallet she'd made on the floor out of sight of her sister's room.

We lied down and slowly kissed each other for what seemed like days. I was kinda nervous because unlike Jenn, she wasn't a virgin, but not a slut either. I swallowed my fear and proceeded to massage her chest and suck her neck to get aroused a little more. She smelled so good so I slipped my hand into her shorts trying to find that special spot as she did the same to me. Once I got to it, her breathing picked up and so did mine. One finger played with her pretty little clit while the other one entered into her tight wet pussy while she grinded aggressively. She slid out of her panties and I pulled my shorts down to my knees with my eye on her sister's door. I lied on top of her and guided my hard dick to her pussy replacing my fingers.

The first pump was so damn hard to get in so I had to pull out to let her juices pour down to lubricate my dick. After a few tries our rhythm became one as we kissed passionately while staring into each other's eyes. She breathed deeply and let out a low moan indicating she was about to cum. Then in one motion we both came together and the moment was so special.

I was really feeling Kamari and after that night we became a couple. A young couple who was willing to learn all about love, under the watchful eye of her sister and parents.

Back in the hood, "D" and I were talking about my days with Kamari and he told me that he liked her for me and the bond we had. That felt good to hear and after she met my mom and the family they all felt the same way too.

Shortly, after a few weeks of hanging and slanging in the hood, "D" and I were driving down Sussex making our play rounds, when we noticed Byron and a couple of our friends gathered around Kamari's cousins house that he dated. So as we pulled over everyone was looking though the window's like something was going on. As I approached I could see that she had another dude in the house. We later found out it was her ex-boyfriend. He was beating her ass! They wouldn't open the door to let us in because he was jealous that Byron was fucking her.

Watching him beat her through the window threw Byron into a fit of rage. He tried to kick the door down to no avail. The guy knew we were out there and he wasn't leaving until we were gone.

We all left and walked down to the corner to throw him off. We jumped into my car to go to Granny's to get my .32 special which was a chrome, long nose with the detachable revolver. I had bought it for $100 from Byron and now he wanted to use it for free. Cool, I gave it to him and drove to the liquor store to post up and call Kamari to tell her what was going on.

While at the pay phone we noticed the guy trying to slip away, but once he saw us he tried to head back to the house. We gave chase. I kept the gun with me as I drove down to the house only to see Byron, "D" and two other guys beating the guy up. I watched but didn't interfere. I was sitting on my car when the guy tried to get up and run but "D" kicked him in the face a few times. He bled and broke away running towards Seven Mile.

Tracy, Kamari's cousin surprisingly came running out the house yelling at Byron for fighting him. She said he was a member of the Schoolcraft clique. I had heard of the crew and had a few run-ins with some of the members so I knew that shit wasn't over quite yet.

Once the drama died down, a few days later things were back to normal. Each night we followed the same routine until 1:30 am which was close to curfew time. One night I was driving down the street and in my rear view mirror I saw a car following me real close. I told "D" to give me the gun and placed it on my lap as I drove and made a four corner turn. During the turn the person in the other car grimed us as he drove past slowly.

"Damn," I said to myself knowing that it was an enemy. Shortly after, we parked across the street from Granny's house to post up. A couple of homies came and told us that a man in a gray car had been riding around asking, "Who is Rome and where does he stay?"

I figured this was the same guy that had followed us earlier. That dude that they had jumped had went to the elders and told them what happened and they wanted revenge. It was no secret that Schoolcraft niggas hated Seven Mile niggas badly. It all originated from a concert at Harpos featuring a few famous rappers that spilled out into the streets. So for the next couple of days "D" and I stayed on guard and post making money each day.

I put Uncle Cody up on all that had gone down and tried to use his "Boss" pass to kill the drama. "You can't make money and beef," he would always say. We tried to live by those principles as best we could.

Since things were still hot on the streets, I spent a lot of time with Kamari and only came on the block when I was needed. After dropping her off one night with David, we drove to our spot in front of Granny's. As we set observing our surroundings, listening to Paula Abdul's, Rush, on the radio, a white old school Caddy or Lincoln pulled up in front of us and parked a few houses down. The night was hot and the skies were clear while Byron's mother sat on their porch catching a breeze.

My mom and siblings were over looking after Granny who was still stricken by her injuries from the car accident. The block was pretty quiet because everyone was at the AMC theatre to see Ice Cube's new movie Boyz in the Hood. They had left David and me in control to run the block while they crewed up and represented. Everyone wore their Ewings, shorts with the Jersey's to match with thick gold chains and pagers.

OPTIONS

We sat in the car under the streetlight as a neighborhood fiend walked up to the driver's side door where I sat and asked for a little credit cause she was fresh out of jail. "D" rested in the passenger seat buzzed off the coolers we had drunk with the .32 across his lap. Suddenly, out the front window I could see a tall dark skinned male get out of the Caddy parked in front of us. He had something in his hand as he walked towards Byron's mother on the porch. She looked like she seen a ghost as she had a blank look on her face. Then the guy crossed the grass headed for my Granny's home and got as close as the storm door. I figured he was looking for my uncle being that several dudes would come through and kick it with him and the crew. So I spoke in a loud voice, "Yo, my man? What up doe?"

He turned and looked back at me with another blank look then started down the driveway towards my car. It never crossed my mind that maybe the guy who got jumped told his crew what kind of car I had or that the girl Tracy told him that I was getting a little money.

I was in the middle of giving the fiend a twenty rock on credit so I had a pill bottle full of crack on my lap and her blocking my view when the guy walked up to the window. Right before he approached the car I asked D, "Yo, you got the gun ready?"

"Yeah, we straight," he said.

The stranger came close to the driver's side door and spoke, "What's up? Who are ya'll?"

"Shit, who you looking for?" I answered quickly. I was kinda thrown off because he didn't look familiar and his eyes kept wandering and casing the vehicle. I glanced over to see that D didn't have the gun in his hand and the stranger noticed at the same time.

Seconds later, I turned back to the stranger at my window as he raised a chrome and black revolver in the same motion hitting me in the top side of my head. This allowed the fiend to break out on foot across several yards yelling for attention. I could see the fear and shock on Byron's mother's face as she still hadn't moved from her spot. I was thinking maybe she thought this was a joke because we always played and fought amongst each other. Once the gunman had the ups he didn't shoot just yet, he spoke in an aggressive tone, "Nigga give me the money!" He looked over at D who was still lying back buzzed, "Don't move or I'll blow your fucking head off, lil' nigga!"

I never took my eyes off him at this point, but I did as ordered. First the ring, then the money on my lap with the pill bottle that contained small pieces of crack. With one hand he tried to grab everything as money and crack fell on the ground. I continued to talk to the man hoping to keep him calm as blood drizzled down my face. I prayed for someone to come save us from this frightening man.

I slowly touched "D's" leg and told him in a soft voice, not to move as I continued to eye the suspect close. Then shit started moving fast. I heard the gunman speak very loudly, "Nigga, I said don't move!"

The passenger door flew open and then I felt the wind as a bullet flew past my neck. Damn! What happened? Did the nigga shoot D or did D just shoot the nigga? Moments after the shot the gunman moved backwards, gun still drawn and aimed at my head ready to shoot. At this point the car felt lighter as he spoke backing up, "Nigga, I should kill yo ass."

"Keep your eyes on him," I kept thinking. "Be ready to duck." I was hoping D had ran to get help cause I could no longer feel his legs when I reached to grab the gun off his lap.

The shit moved fast again as the gunman walked to his car in front. I leaned over down into the passenger seat in case he decided to shoot through the front windshield. Only then did I notice D's shoes and saw him lying along the side of the car with his face towards the trunk.

Shit! He wasn't moving, only breathing hard and calling my name softly under his breath. Instantly, I reached under him and located the gun then hopped out the car and ran behind the tree and fired six shots from my .32 trying to hit the stranger as he pulled off.

By the time the shooting was over things got hectic and chaos broke out everywhere. Now everybody was coming outside to help or see what was going on. My mom ran out to me with Granddad who now had the smoking gun in his hand. People bombarded me with questions as my Auntie ran and got D's mother, as he lied helplessly on the curb bleeding out from the head.

The police and EMS were called and the EMS arrived first, but couldn't help him until the police arrived. Precious minutes were wasted as they waited on the police. I sat on the curb in shock, crying because I couldn't help my friend who was clinging to life. I went over to D's mother and sisters and we prayed over D as I rubbed his back. His mother began to speak in tongues and I knew right then it was over. I could actually see or envision his spirit, ghost and soul as the angels came to take him home. He moved his head to the left and that was it…

The police arrived and the investigation started. The call went out that David was pronounced dead on arrival and I blacked out. When I woke up, I was down at 1300 Beaubien being questioned by the lead homicide detective. I didn't know anything so I really couldn't tell them anything. My car was seized and taken in as evidence, while news reporters stayed glued to Granny's house waiting on any more drama.

Back in the hood, David's family prepared for his funeral and subsequently blamed me for the whole incident. Even after I explained everything about the fight and being followed, folks in the hood still shut me out. My uncle's business suffered, as he lost some of his clientele. Kamari was my only outlet, so she tried to comfort me in spite of her parent's orders.

My family was also a key support group during this time. But since everyone feared another death or violent situation I decided to hide out over at Stevie's house in Redford Township. His mother was like my mom and allowed me to stay as long as I didn't sell drugs or bring them near her house. She usually was gone because she was a Sergeant in the army and had done a tour in Desert Storm.

My stay there was calm and therapeutic for me. I had a terrible case of survivor's guilt. All kinds of thoughts went through my head like, "Why did I live? Why did D have to die? Should I go to the funeral? Does everyone wish it was me instead?" These thoughts entered my mind day and night. Meanwhile, I stayed to myself and replayed the scene and events trying to find something new that could help.

I paid my respects at the viewing, but I didn't go to the funeral. I sat alongside my best friend and talked and cried wishing he could wake up and my nightmare would be over. Things would never be the same again in my life or my hood.

After the funeral I returned to Granny's to help her recover, but she was so strict on me that I wandered back to my hood on Fenkell to hang with Rook. He was always there for me to vent to, as I tried to piece my life back together without my best friend.

Later in the year, my family got a call saying that charges were being brought up against me for the Muskegon case, and I had to report to court a few weeks later. I was so nervous, as the date approached us and prepared for the worst. So the night before, I sat at Granny's talking on the phone to Kamari who gave me her blessings. Even though we hadn't had sex since our last encounter our bond was steadily growing to a higher level.

OPTIONS

The next morning, Granddad and I got dressed and went to court. I was surprised that it was the trial already. The old lady showed up and identified me as one of the perpetrators and gave step by step details of the incident. A couple of minutes later the judge found me guilty and sentenced me as a ward of the state until eighteen years of age. My luck couldn't get any worse.

With no time for goodbyes I was taken into custody by the court officers and sent to juvey. Thank God I was seventeen and only could be held a year tops. In all my stay at juvey was so quick I transferred to the Burton Center to wait to go to my placement which was Camp Nokomis, a ninety day camp for troubled teens.

My family still had my back and so did Kamari who wrote and sent pictures each week. I learned a lot from being away from the streets and missed a lot too. I missed my mom, little brothers and sister, Rook, my uncles and grandparents and definitely Kamari. The one person that always remained on my mind and in my prayers was my boy David. If I could bring him back or replay that dreadful day, I would take his spot, trust me. But since I can't, doing this time was allowing me to become more mature and before I knew it I would be back home making my own path. But until I made it back I had to get prepared for this ninety day camp and learn all that I could learn.

CHAPTER 10

"92" Done it Again

After completing the 90 day course at Camp Nokomnis it was time for me to return home. The camp was fill of new experiences as we took trips around the U.P. setting up tents and going cross country skiing. I was taught new ways to think and many new viewpoints on life. My family still supported me as well as Kamari whom remained my girlfriend.

Now that I was on my way back home a lot of shit entered my mind as my heart tried to mend from the loss of my best friend. Life would be different now and people's reactions toward me would change because of my past. What would I do to better my life once freed from the rules of the system?

Once released on probation to star common wealth I moved back in with my mom and siblings on Fenkell. My first day home, they threw me a welcome home party in the basement. This was a great way to come home and enjoy my freedom. The house was full of my friends and Kamari had also come to support her man. Kids from the hood like Meka, Rook, Dean, Tookie and several of my new friends from the camp danced to the latest Tupac tape and Jodeci songs while they drank juices and ate snacks.

Everyone was so excited to see me. Uncle Cody came through and gave me a few hundred dollars to show his support. As the music blasted throughout the house, Kamari and I snuck off upstairs for some alone time. We sat off in the corner of the living room and shared a few kisses and chatted about our future. She looked so good and the smell of her perfume had me so aroused that she had to pull me off of her in order for me to chill. As bad as I wanted to fuck her, this was not the time or the place.

Eventually the party died down and we sat on the porch waiting for Kamari's parents to pick her up. My mom had introduced me to our new neighbor's son, Sam and he was waiting with us. When her parent's pulled up, I promised to call her later and Sam and I started kicking it.

Sam was a short, dark skinned brother who was built like a steam truck. He was a few years older than me, but he was cool. He, Rook and I started coming up with some money making schemes for the squad.

I hadn't seen Javan yet or any of my WBS leaders and Stevie had vowed to come through at a later date. So several days came and went by with no word from anyone. I had my GED so I decided to look for a job to hold me over and keep my family and P.O. satisfied with me.

After a few months at home I landed a job at Little Caesars on Grand River near Outer Dr. I worked hard and made manager within ninety days. I had a good work ethic and was always available to do overtime. I usually walked to work and then Sam or Rook would meet me at night and we would walk home eating pizza slices and kicking it.

I also took a computer course at a college to gain a certificate in computer office finance. While at work one day, I found a way to scam the system and make extra money in the process. All I had to do was work the register and take the money for the pizza's we sold and pocket the money. Then I'd destroy the original receipt that showed a pizza was ordered. Once I mastered it, I could easily make 300-400 dollars a day. I saved the extra money I made and my checks to buy weed or crack to sell, plus I was also saving for a car.

In a matter of weeks, I had saved over seven thousand and was ready to start looking for my dream car. I was over Granny's one day and a guy told me he sold cars. We went to his backyard and he showed me all the cars he had available. All of them were in good condition and older models. I fell in love with the 78' two door, two toned grey Malibu with the red seats! The asking price was 1800 that would still leave me with 5000 in the stash. I rushed home grabbed the money and came back with the money for the car and title.

I went straight to Murray's and copped a gold crown for the back window and a bottle of Armor-All for the tires. When I drove down the block with my six by nine's and Spice One tape blasting "Welcome to the Ghetto," I knew I was the shit. The whole block was looking as I ran in the house to call Kamari and plan a drive by so she could see the car.

Rook, Sam and my mom all jumped in to check out the ride and give advice on what to do next. After I got the plates and insurance it was on and popping! We went everywhere and met everybody! Even through all of this I still worked, sold drugs and robbed the company. Life was great!

Kamari and I were still kicking it strong and her parent's didn't really care for me, but her sister was cool so we had to spend most of our time over there. The sex was still the greatest and protection was not a factor because we loved each other enough to deal with whatever came.

The next few weeks I was hanging all over the city. We were at Rouge Park, Sparky's Arcade on Fenkell and Telegraph mostly. One day Sam and I were hanging out in the parking lot of the arcade when two pretty young things trailed each other into the game room. The slim, tall chick had on skin tight, biker shorts with a gap so wide you could see the people in front of her through her legs. Her friend had on a Nike short set with lots of plastic jewelry and accessories.

"Cute," I thought to myself. I approached her like, "Hey, sexy, what it do?"

"Which one of us are you talking to?" the slim goodie replied.

"You, since you spoke up," I said smiling. "My name is Rome and this is my boy Sam.

"My name is Ne-Ne and this is my girl Shyia," she replied over all the noise in the arcade.

We played games for a minute then grabbed a quick bite to eat. After a few hours their mother came and picked them up. We exchanged numbers and headed back to my car to patrol different hoods for other little cuties.

Things back at home had become better for me and my mom. We were communicating better and that made things much easier. The family was moving forward as mom started growing out of her addiction and started regaining our family structure again. I loved being around her even though she became more strict, but I knew it was all out of love because she only wanted the best for all of us.

A few days after meeting Ne-Ne, I got a page from her asking me and Sam to come through and kick it. I agreed and we headed to her crib on Schaefer and Plymouth, where she lived with her sexy ass mom. Over at her place we sat on the porch and talked about our life, our past and our future. We got along good and I was feeling her and it was vice versa, but I still had to keep alert because Kamari knew everybody. I felt kind of bad cheating or playing on Kamari, but hell, I won't tell on myself. It was funny because just as I was thinking about her my pager went off with her number on it with 69 after it. That meant sex and plenty of it, so I quickly ended our playdate and raced to drop Sam off.

Once we got to my house I called Kamari and assured her I was on my way to her sister's new house on Six mile and Meyers. So I erased the number out of my pager and was on my way to heaven. I pulled up with my car stereo bumping with a few joints rolled up for Dan and her sis. As soon as I walked in Kamari was ready to go into the kid's room to play.

It was around 11p.m. and everyone was sleep so we were ready to get it started. We started kissing roughly and then we fell onto the bed where I gave her hickeys on her neck then we undressed each other. She smelled like a fresh roses as I slowly laid her down to taste her sweet nectar. I watched her facial expressions as she motioned for me to stop and lay down so she could return the favor in the 69 position. We enjoyed each other briefly before we decided to move on. She lied down on her back and threw her legs on my shoulders so I could enter at a 75 degree angle. Nice, long strokes until I was inches from having my whole dick inside her, then I would snap the last piece in forcefully, allowing my balls to hit the bottom half of her pussy and drive her into ecstasy. Damn! Fucking her was the bomb and I enjoyed every minute of it. We both fell asleep happy.

The next morning we woke up and showered, then ate breakfast from the Coney Island on the corner. When we got back to the house Danny asked me did I have any weed and of course I gave him what he wanted. He mentioned to me that he had a deal on guns. I was on probation and didn't want any, but I still needed one because my hustle was moving and growing fast. He went into the basement and came back with three containers. The one I liked was a 9mm Jennings with a chrome tip and clip.

"Give me three hundred," he said with a slight smirk on his chubby face.

"Yeah right," I thought to myself as I began to talk him down and by the end of our conversation he was sold at 225 cash.

I took the gun to my car and placed it under the passenger seat. Kamari wasn't aware of the transaction because she would have gone crazy if she knew I was doing something crazy. I kicked it over there for a few more hours then headed back to the hood.

As soon as I pulled up at my moms, Sam came out to smoke a square and kick it. "Damn, nigga. Kamari had yo' ass on lock," he joked.

"Man, I gotta keep her happy," I grinned.

"What's up for the day? Ne-Ne and her girl trying to hook up. You down, nigga?"

"Yeah, I gotta work a few hours, then it's on," I said.

Later at work it was stressful as hell because the customers were always in a hurry or acting extra hungry. Since I was the manager, I gave away free pizzas to the girls I thought were cute. Being the only manager on shift had its perks and weed and my money scheme were just a few.

After a few hours on the clock it was time to head out. I went home and showered and threw on my Calvin Klein outfit and Nike Air Alpha shoes before Sam came over.

It was hot as an oven when we made our way over Ne-Ne's. We pulled up playing Keith Sweat and were welcomed in by the girls. We chilled in the living room watching Tupac in Juice for a minute before Ne-Ne grabbed my hand and lead me to her room. As we walked through the house I noticed how nice and expensive the house was. There were brand new big screen TV's, VCR's and jewelry laid out on her mom's tall Oak wood dresser. I took a quick glance around to make sure there was no one else there and then my focus was back on her.

She had on some tight legging and a long t-shirt that read, 'Too Hot to Handle,' and yes, she was. Her room was decorated in pink and grey with a queen sized bed with a matching comforter. She got right to business by laying me down on the bed and tracing her tongue all over my body until she reached my dick. Then she slowly took me into her mouth while I played with her little wet pussy. A few minutes into the head job she stopped because she couldn't take the pleasure of getting her pussy fingered and jumped on my dick and allowed me to watch her ride me. Being slim was no problem because she rode me for thirty minutes straight. I came at least two times pushing her off of me before I came. She would lick off my dick and jump right back on it until she got hers. It was an hour into our visit and a lot had transpired already. I went to check on Sam and he and the cousin were engaged in their own foreplay. I gave him the signal that it was time to wrap it up because her mother got home around three or four and that wouldn't be a good thing for her to come in and see us all laid up. We hugged and kissed for a few minutes then bounced.

The next morning I woke up to pages from Kamari, my job and a few other numbers. It was a Thursday and I headed to work for a few hours. But things were a little strange at the job. The Head Manager was there doing the close out books for the week, a job I usually did and came across a few missing tickets. He questioned me and from that point on all eyes were on me. Eventually my hours were reduced along with my ability to back hustle the company.

Since money had dried up at work, my street hustle had to pick up. Uncle Cody was doing his thing and I had adopted my cousin into the circle for help on my end. All my friends were drifting into other areas in their lives so a lot of the time we barely saw each other or only spoke briefly.

Kiambu was playing basketball for Mackenzie. Rook played baseball for Southwestern, Stevie was taking his rap career to another level and my WBS crew was fading into extinction from jail and death. Things went up and down on a daily basis.

A few weeks after making out with Ne-Ne things got rough. I got fired from my job and Kamari had gotten tired of me being missing in action. Being a player and hustler was taking a toll on my thinking pattern and had me off my square.

REGGIE GIST

One night Sam, Ray and I were sitting on the hood of my Malibu thinking of ways to get some extra dollars without using the gun that I had purchased from Danny. Then the thought crossed my mind about the jewelry and expensive things I saw at Ne-Ne's crib a few weeks before. So we collaborated on a simple plan to stage a B & E while I was over visiting her. The plan was to have Sam and Ray knock on the door as if they were friends of hers then I would tell her to open the door to see who they were. Once the door was open they would push in, fight me and take my possessions, then grab some TV's, jewelry and whatever else of value. Then we could take the stuff a block over to Sam's sister's house and hide it until later. Then we could sell the goods and split the profit.

The robbery would look like it was an ex-boyfriend of hers and both of us were victims. Yeah, that sounded good, but like all plans, they could fail. We all agreed on keeping it basic but since it was hard to trust the two of them, I kept my gun a secret. The night of the crime I called Ne-Ne and asked to come over and chill, she agreed. I did like her, but being blinded by my wants and needs left little room for a conscience.

The trap was set and I entered as planned. An hour into the visit the knock came on the door and I asked her to see who it was. When she opened the door, Sam kicked it open with force causing her to fall backwards. Ray grabbed me and we fought while Sam who wore a ski mask rambled through the house.

Ray took my rings, watch and my chain while I kept my gun concealed in my back pocket. To my surprise Ne-Ne had run out of the house during the scuffle and was being chased down by Sam. Ray went to work taking all the valuables like we had planned. I saw him leave out, but I wasn't sure where Sam had taken Ne-Ne. I took out my gun and placed a bullet in the chamber and searched from room to room. I went upstairs and thought I heard heavy breathing coming from a closet. I walked up to it and tried to open it, but to my surprise Sam came bursting out the door!

I flew into the wall barely missing a glass table that sat in the middle of the floor. As soon as I got up I rushed back to the closet and saw Ne-Ne with her pants down crying softly. I cocked the hammer on my gun and ran down the stairs after Sam. He had raped her and that was not part of the plan. I was hell bent on revenge as I raced down the street after him. When I caught sight of him I let of six shots all six missing him by inches. A few guys were on the block and ran in to call the police. I went back and checked on Ne-Ne but she heard the shots and hid in another spot. I immediately left to go to the meeting spot to kill him.

Of course, no one was there when I got there so I went back to her house again only to find that the police were coming down the street. Now it was time to put my acting skills into play. While talking to the police I learned that Ne-Ne was only fifteen years old and since I was seventeen she couldn't give her legal consent to have sex. I told them I was her boyfriend and yes we had had sex a few times, and her mother allowed me to be over there.

Into a pair of handcuffs I went, then to the patrol car for Criminal Sexual Conduct in the 3rd degree. While the police were making their report in the car, the two dudes who called the police had no idea, like Ne-Ne, that it was a scheme. They assumed that the guys had robbed us. The cops went door to door asking questions. They came to one house where one black male sat on the porch alone. One of the witnesses noticed his shoes and said that he was around when the shooting took place. It was my Cousin Ray's stupid ass. The cop's asked him did he live at the house and he had to say, no. They brought him over to the car and asked him his full name, that's when they noticed that we both shared the same last name. They began to search his pockets and found all the jewelry that I had reported stolen, then burst out laughing at us.

I figured that Sam had left Ray alone with nowhere to hide so he came back looking for me. Sam had gotten away and Ray and I were taking the fall for it all. They took us down to 1300 Beaubien.

I ended up pleading no contest and Ray begged for mercy as he told the whole story. Busted and being charged as an adult for my crimes while Ray got sent to juvey. I was in the county jail for weeks until my bail was set and my family bonded me out. Kamari was heated and vowed to leave me alone as I searched for Sam for my revenge. After a few weeks of searching with no results my uncle's sent for me to come to Seven Mile for a few days.

Life was hard waiting on my trial and my family was so disappointed in me, as was my probation officer and many others. Thank God in December I went to court and was found not guilty after Ne-Ne admitted that she had lied about her age. The truth came out about Sam as well, and he was still on the run. I was sentenced to two years for the gun they never saw or found and two to fifteen years for conspiracy to attempt a B & E. Ray had gotten two years in juvey for his part, but there were no more camps for me. It was time for the big house…

CHAPTER 11

"93-96 Life in Prison"

After a few weeks in the county jail, I was hauled off to Riverside until my prison placement was ready. All I could think about was spending four years of my life without my family, not being able to see my siblings grow or my mom fully recovered from her addiction. The feeling of being alone was overwhelming the entire stay in Riverside.

The terrible smell of pee and funk searched the hallways until they found rooms that were occupied with two roommates. Being in quarantine, movement was rare and visits were unheard of at this point. Over the weeks I would work and read until my turn came to leave which came shortly after. I was sent to the infamous MTU. MTU was very raw and looked like a college campus. I learned a lot from being there as time moved very slowly for me.

I lost contact with a lot of people, Kamari, Ne-Ne, Stevie, Dean all disappeared as soon as I was sentenced. I guess it was really, out of sight, out of mind, for them. I witnessed so much inside during my stint. Fights, stabbings, rapes, gang violence. You name it I saw it and learned from it. About a year into my bid, guess who I saw in the chow line at dinner? Yes, you guessed it, Sam. He was serving time on an alias for another crime. When he saw me, he almost passed out.

We couldn't speak due to the fact that we shared separate yard times, plus as soon as he realized that I didn't blow up on the spot on him, he requested to be transferred to a different prison. So I never had the opportunity to confront him about his actions.

So as time went on, I too was switched from several prisons like MR, Hiawatha up north, and URF. My stay in these joints showed me a lot as I hung out with the best of thieves, murderers, rapists, etc. It was towards the end that my calling came to explore my inner conscience and seek the highest power by studying the words of the Hon. Elijah Muhammad and the Nation of Islam. I researched and read every book that I could get my hands on like; The Message to the Black Man, Comer by Night, The Fall of America and the most important one the Holy Quran.

Reading these books gave me a deeper input on life and my purpose in it. I would call home and share my newfound faith with my mom, who was fully recovered from her addiction. Then I would write Granny and my Uncle Cody with powerful messages and questions to enlighten them of self. Eventually, I became a member of the Nation of Islam and then the minister. Throughout my time I contributed to resurrecting as many souls as Allah allowed.

The teachings were self-motivational and accurate, to help me to stay sane throughout my stay. After a few years in and out of several prisons I landed at Muskegon's level I. It's crazy because I had been a civilian once in the slow town.

In 1995 I was looking at feeling better than ever before. I gained a few pounds, worked out and controlled the Nation of Islam's actions. We became a force and encountered many obstacles and individuals. My family still remained the support group as everyone was older and wiser. My Uncle Cody still ran the streets and everyone eagerly awaited my arrival.

Early in 1996 I was eligible for parole but was fearful of getting it due to my previous actions before I became self-conscious. All I knew was that Allah was the best of planners and no man controlled his plans. My mom came to the interview and as a team we both supported each other and the outcome was a blessing. They gave me my parole which meant that I got my life back and a second chance to make a difference. I went back to my unit and prayed along with the brothers and celebrated the wonderful blessings of Allah.

OPTIONS

I had about four months to remain there then I would be released into society with limited restrictions. I had to report three times a month to an agent and maintain a job along with having a 10 p.m. curfew. I continued to teach until my release date July 3, 1996 a few weeks before my birthday. The night before I left I contributed all of my unwanted things to the brothers and stayed up all night filled with adrenaline and anxiety.

The next morning I was jarred out of my sleep by the frail white guard, "Mr. Gist, it's time to go."

I said my goodbyes to everyone and exited the unit leaving behind the dreadful past of incarceration. Only a few hours then I'd be home. I rode the Greyhound bus to Detroit were my mom and siblings waited at the station. I wore a new pair of Timberlands and a new short set by a college team that my mom had bought a few weeks prior to me leaving.

Once I arrived at the bus stop in Southfield which happened to be the wrong bus stop because I should have gotten off in downtown Detroit, I was alone. It felt so scary being free, the readjustment factor set in quickly. I started walking down Lahser then suddenly I heard a horn and screams. My family had found me! "Yes!" they did care that I had made it safely. Now it was time to go home…

CHAPTER 12

Welcome Home Rome

Finally we pulled up to the new house on Six mile and Lindsay to be greeted by a few family members, but since I got off at the wrong stop, everyone was waiting for me down town. Eventually, we all gathered and enjoyed my home coming event. This day I got to know my little sister who was now older and her new boyfriend. His name was Reggie, a tall 6'3, 200 pound young nigga. After talking and hearing about how he filled the void of me being gone by helping my mom, brothers and little sister, I gained all respect for him. He was only seventeen or eighteen and was more of a man than I was. We became real close and he helped me with my adjustment to the hood along with a few others.

The hood was filled with all types of people that did everything. My first day home was filled with excitement as Cody, Granny and my cousins came through to kick it. That night I was shown my room in the basement which was cool, because anything was better than prison. My mom had hooked me up with a co-worker who had seen my picture and had started to write and send pictures when I was locked up. Her name was Dykema. She was an attractive, petite, little chocolate chick. She and another girl that my sister had hooked me up with named Denise, had become my pen pals.

Denise was a child hood friend and cute as a doll. She was a light skinned chick with long black hair. I was feeling her for sure. It was my first night home and I needed the comforts of a woman. I called Dykema at work and told her to fall through since my mom knew her and felt comfortable with her in our home.

She got there around 12:30 and came to the back patio entrance where the family room was located. Everyone was sleep upstairs in the tri-level home. I let her in amazed by her smile since we'd only seen each other once on a prison visit and the rest through pictures. She was excited to play her part so we ate and talked for a few minutes, then I walked around to check to see if everyone else was asleep. She was already in tune to what I wanted so we wasted no time getting it started.

We took off our clothes and lied on the couch slowly. There was no kissing as she kindly went down to give me oral sex as I rubbed her head and spaced out. "Damn, this shit feels so good," I thought as she bobbed her head up and down on my big black dick. In and out of her mouth, fast then slow with fluid motion. It had been three years and eight months since I had this feeling that I'd yearned for.

After a few minutes I came all over her face and neck then turned her around to enter her from the back. At this point in my life eating pussy really wasn't my thing, so I didn't try. She understood as I grinded hard and fast, in and out of her juicy pussy. We came to together and fell asleep shortly after.

When I awoke the next morning, she was gone. The next couple of weeks we would come to a stalemate. The sex was ok, but I became disinterested quickly. I think everything was over rated when I was inside. She saw that my appetite was growing and slowly faded out of the picture.

My mom picked up on what had happened when she came into the family room and saw the Burger King wrappers. She knew Dykema worked at BK and put two and two together. She just shook her head.

Later that day, my sister took me around the new hood and introduced me to a few people that had been awaiting my arrival. All she ever did was talk about her big brother and the entire hood was interested in meeting me. I was a little bigger than before. I stood at 5"8 and weighed in at about 150. All cuts as they called it in the weight world. Attractive to many, plus fresh out the joint looking for any kind of action. I met my next door neighbor Eric and two brothers, Hank and Herbie that were cool as hell. Hank was the oldest and was cool like me.

A few hours into the day my sister took me to see my brother Rook who was cutting hair only a half a block away at the barbershop. It had been a while since we had spoken or wrote, so my coming home was a shocker to him. I entered the shop and every one noticed me because I somehow stood out. He was cutting hair and not paying attention. The manager asked me did I want a cut and I replied, "No, I just want to see Rook."

He heard his name and turned around, "Oh! Shit! That's my brother!"

We hugged and he gave me dap as he looked me over. "Damn, nigga. You done got a little bigger!"

"Yeah the joint will do that to you," I laughed as I noticed a few of his clients tensing up. "Dig, come by the crib later so we can catch up," I said quietly.

When I walked back around the block, Eric and the new crew were all hanging out on his porch like usual, talking shit. Eric was young but wise. His mom had moved to another state, but left the four bedroom crib to him and his brother. So of course, their home was the local hangout. All they did was steal cars, hustle weed and fuck hoes. I loved it even though I was on parole and couldn't afford any trouble.

I was given a level of respect because of my history and connection to the streets. My Uncle Cody and Reese stayed in the game, so I had access. I knew that if I rushed into the game, it would be the wrong move. So I took a different approach by finding a temp service to hold me over and keep my parole agent off my back. I landed a job with MetLife on Telegraph and Ten Mile as a mail room clerk. The pay was $9 per hour and the place was flooded with beautiful women.

I would work five days a week and get paid every week. My mom was so happy because I could provide for my family a little bit too. One day I came home from work and my sister had gotten into a big scuffle with a few hood girls. It was funny until about fifteen dudes showed up to help or watch. I had only been home for a few weeks and my connection with my old crew and friends had not been made. I hadn't talked to Dean or none of my WBS homies, so back up was a .38 special I had left with Rook.

As the crowd gathered for a fight I calmly displayed my piece and let them know that wasn't shit going down. To my surprise ten more dudes pulled up along with a few chicks. My sister had called a few of my female cousins to assist her, then all hell broke loose.

I was standing next to Eric and a guy I called Tee. Tee told me to chill and showed me his gun, then explained that he was a leader of a gang called Y.S.L He said that he respected my position and knew my sister who was deep into a head to head fist fight. He only came around because he got a call that I was around and had a gun.

Once everyone calmed down as we broke up the fight, he and I had a quick talk. He dug my attitude and invited me to his hang out on Puritan/Greenfield. Since Herbie, Hank, Eric and the entire hood was Y.S.L, I felt safe around them even though I wasn't a member. I didn't go this night, instead I told him I would fall through after work.

My Uncle Reese had sold me a few ounces of weed for $175 that I had bagged up into $10 bags at 1.5 grams a piece to gain a small profit. The workplace and hood loved it and since I was close and available they loved to shop with me. After my third check I bought me a cell phone, the hand held kind that was just becoming popular. It was a prepaid cell phone and I was the first to have one in the hood or family. I knew I was the shit as I hustled, worked and became a hot commodity to everyone.

OPTIONS

Over the course of the summer I met so many people, especially women. I must have fucked at least every female within a 20 block ratio. It was crazy. I hit all of Eric's female friends and all of my little sister's girls who were legal. She hung with an older crowd anyway so I felt better about kicking it with them. I fucked Denise, Crystal, Jeli and her sister, Lynn, my Aunt Tina's girls, Kim, Lisa and the list went on.

I had a few chicks at work that adored me and me and Hank kept a gang of women running in and out of his mom's basement. That month Tupac was killed and it was crazy because we rode around banging his music in my little Tempo I had bought a few days before. We switched from Pac to "Elevator Music," until we found a chill spot at Tee's house.

Tee was a lot like me and appreciated the fact that I had hustle skills and stayed neutral in the gang life. He labeled me his twin and that's the name that we used from that day forward for each other. Everyone else called him Mr. Tensy. His house was big and was the control center of the gang's territory. I enjoyed being around them and became an honorary member with high rank after a short time.

I kept my low profile throughout my first summer home. With work, hustling and being a player I stayed pretty busy. Mom and my siblings were all happy to have me around as we enjoyed family time together doing everything. Eventually, Rook and I lined up and caught up on old and new things. He had a little boy at the time and was a proud father and barber. We would sit and talk for hours about what our new plans for the future would be. We talked about opening our own shop and studio for our music label.

His baby mom was a trip and he wasn't fucking with her physically anymore because of their differences. He had another woman named Vivica or "Vicky" for short. I was proud of my little bro and looked up to him for being so responsible and in control of his life.

As the weeks went by, a lot of shit moved in and out of my life. Cody came through every now and then, but he wasn't the same hustler he used to be. He still made money, but not like the old Cody. Granny was still Granny as I would fall through the Seven Mile hood to chill and check on her and Granddaddy. My side kicks Eric and Hank were always down for a ride in the Tempo as we went from place to place just to show our faces. The family loved them just as much as they loved me. I was Eric's oldest son's Godfather and was present at the christening. My life was ok and I felt relieved not to be in prison anymore. Staying out meant staying focused on all levels.

Kim and Denise became my two main chicks but I had a nice stable to sneak and play with when I felt the need. They gave me something to do as the fall and winter months came. Other than that, I worked, hustled and stacked so by the summer, I would be ready. Now it was time to hibernate….

CHAPTER 13

"97" Moving Forward

Winter 1997 was slow but steady. During that time period my mom crashed the Tempo on a late night drive, doing God knows what. I woke up for work to find broken glass all around my car. I was pissed but had no choice but to tape up the passenger side door with plastic and keep it moving. She tried to explain what took place but I paid it no mind and just started saving for another one.

After a month of saving I purchased a 1988 Cherry red Thunderbird coupe. One of my co-workers took me on Livernois to their dealership and I paid $2500 for the car and drove it off the lot. Of course I headed straight on Seven Mile to show Cody and my Granny my newest accomplishment. While over there I ran into my boy Aaron who lived on Seven Mile and Sussex. He specialized in stealing cars and rims and hooking up sounds. I had about $700 left in my savings so I asked him to show me the goods.

He sold me a pair of nineteen inch, one hundred spoke Dayton's with the fat tires and put them on the car. Then he put in a CD player, all for $500. Damn, I was geeked up! Once he was finished you couldn't tell me nothing as I drove down Seven Mile to Southfield headed home.

The fam loved the new look and so did Eric and Hank. The 88' turbo coupe looked very nice with the cherry red seats and gold trim to match the rims. I took my mom and sister for a test drive while Eric followed in his stolen 96' drop top Mustang.

Later that night, we decided to hit Rouge Park and coast the city looking for girls. What a terrible idea. Driving down Lindsay trailing Eric to our first stop we came across a side street that didn't have any stop signs. Eric cruised through and I followed him and a car came through in front of me. I almost missed it, but I clipped the rear end of the car and spun out of control.

Everyone froze and Hank and I got out of the car looking dazed. Eric turned around as the car that I hit stopped to make peace. I was heated as I ran around the car to see the damage. He didn't have on any lights or I would have seen him coming so I was ready to kill him. People came out on the block after hearing the crash and me arguing and called the police. The entire front clip of my car was ruined. We decided it was best to just take the car and leave.

My car was parked for a few days, but was still drivable. My mother's boyfriend took me to some place to buy a front clip bra and a few headlight bulbs to fix the car a little. After we were done it didn't look so bad so I could drive it. It was fucked up that I crashed my new car the same day that I had bought it. But the Tempo was a bad look, and I still managed to pull it off.

We started hanging out at clubs like the River Rock, Warehouse and our favorite Maxi's on 96 and Telegraph. Maxi's was a college crowd club that stayed packed with all types of kids and young adults. The Dancing Bears, who were a group of young guys who male danced, kept all the ladies on the dance floor. One of the members was a close friend of mine from Granny's hood named Chucky. They also always had a guest DJ or special appearance on the weekends.

Hank and I were regulars and knew everyone of importance in the club. One night in April, we drove his mother's new Neon to the club to catch a few females and take them to the IHOP on Grand River and Outer Drive. That was the spot that everyone went to for breakfast after the club.

We went in that Saturday, dressed to impress. Hank wore a Versace shirt and denim jeans while I rocked my Fila jogging suit, the snatch off warm up one. I sported the newest Grant

Hill's with the Fila hat and socks to match. We wore Movado and Wittnauer watches with gold rings to match.

We entered the packed club while the music blasted, Rapping Forte, and located a spot to chill in the VIP section. A few fellas came to speak as we ordered Moet and orange juice to catch a buzz and look good since I couldn't smoke. I never smoked weed or cigarettes while I was still on parole.

Out the corner of my eye I saw Hank was talking to a group of girls and they were pointing my way. So I started walking towards the crowd to assist my boy. When I got closer I noticed a light skinned girl with a body suit on that showed off all her curves and her pussy print with some strange looking space boots. It was a different look but it looked good on her. She had long hair with green contacts and a bright smile.

Hank was busy with her sister so I slid up and introduced myself. Her name was Rochelle and she was interested in everything about me. We kicked it for a minute there then I invited her over to our space in VIP so we could have a few drinks. She reminded me of Aliyah or T-boz from TLC, she had that star quality look. I noticed I was getting a lot of looks from the fellas and I figured it was because she was bad as hell and everybody wanted her.

She fit in really well as we sat back and kicked it, listening to the music and talking. Then Montell Jordan's, What's on Tonight, came on and she asked me to dance and I gladly accepted. We got our slow grind on. It wasn't long before I noticed people staring at us dance. I really put on a show then.

A little while later I convinced her to go to IHOP with us to eat and chill. She declined at first but then I told her I would pay for her friends too. We left the club in Hank's Neon and followed them to her house to drop off a friend and her Caprice Classic. Then we all piled into the small car and stopped at my crib so I could grab my car.

When we got out to get into my car, she asked me, "Is this your car?" Like she didn't think I had one.

"Yeah, it's mine. Gone and ahead and jump in, I'll be right back," I said running into the house. I checked on my family and grabbed one of the fifty teddy bears that my mom had brought home so I could pass them out to the ladies at work for Valentine's Day.

Rochelle was surprised when she saw me return with a box filled with bears. I jumped in the ride and Hank followed to IHOP where we chilled and I started feeling something different for her. From that night on, I knew this chick was special.

We talked a few days after and she told me she had a son named Ike who was five, and we planned to get together one day after work. She worked at A & W in Dearborn, so that was a plan.

Back in the hood, shit had gotten crazy. A rival beef had stirred up between Y.S.L and some of the newer members of WBS since this was some of their territory too. On a Wednesday night we were chilling on Eric's porch shooting dice and talking. Out of nowhere a long Cadillac rode down the street and there was one guy looking at us like we were crazy. We thought nothing of it as I clutched my .38 in my warm up jacket.

See I never had questioned Eric and the rest of the guy's past when I met them because I had just come home and everything moved so fast, it just never happened. One of the members of Y.S.L had done some crazy shit to a few guys on the other side of Six Mile and they wanted revenge. Everyone knew about our hang out spots and Eric's house was one of the main two.

So as this car rode past I became more alert and ran and sat on the hood of my car which was parked in the driveway of my house. Suddenly the car came back driving slow and did the same thing. So I yelled to the five guys shooting dice, "Heads up!"

They looked up and noticed the car and came off the porch to confront the driver. That was the wrong thing to do. The driver drove to the corner which was about seven houses down, put the car in Park, got out the car with two chrome guns and started walking towards us shooting! He started letting the rounds go so fast that everyone took off. Even me with the gun! We ran for cover, jumping gates, diving inside doors and kneeling behind cars for safety.

At least twenty shots were let off before I could get one off. The hood sounded like Iraq as the shooter fled back to his car and sped off. We all recovered and checked to see if anyone was shot or hurt. Everyone was cool but I noticed a bullet hole in my fender right where I was standing before the attack.

"Close call," I thought to myself as I went inside the house to gather myself and analyze what had just taken place. To my surprise I was met at the door by my Mom and two brothers looking hysterical. They had heard the gun shots and thought I was either shot or the shooter. Mom went into a fit of rage as the block filled with police and neighbors asking questions and checking for damage. As expected no one saw or heard anything so everyone returned to their own private lives.

I knew it wasn't over and I knew either they would seek revenge or we would. It was a never ending cycle dealing with this type of beef. Later that night after everyone disappeared I sat back and called Rochelle and we spoke for a minute. We covered a lot of ground before she had to get some rest for work. I called Kim, Denise and Lynn to chat before I had to sleep for work.

Soon as I finished my late night call, my mom came in the basement to talk to me. "Rome, I really think you are moving too fast. You've barely been home long and this type of stuff is happening already. I'm scared for you son, and I'm scared for myself and the family. You gotta stop," she said looking desperately into my eyes.

"Ma, it wasn't my fault. I don't know where that came from, but don't worry about me or this family. I will figure it all out. Trust me," I promised her.

As the days flew by, I and Rochelle got closer. I hadn't been to her apartment yet out of respect for her son, so I was surprised when she invited me over one night. This particular night he was over at his Dad's. Her apartment was a tiny one bedroom, but was set up really nice. I scanned the rooms and was happy to see there were no male items lying around, but there were also no pots, pans or dishes in the kitchen. I glanced in the fridge and there was no food either.

"Damn, are you human? Do you eat?" I joked when I closed the fridge.

She laughed, "I eat out all the time because I'm always at work." She was the head manager and her son was always in good company. She had at least four sisters and her mom and her fiancé, CB, who I met later.

This particular night would be special because she allowed me into her home where I chilled on the couch watching T.V. as she slipped into something a little more comfortable. Thank God she was clean and smelled wonderful. Maybe it was because of her age and experience.

Rochelle was five years older than me at the time and I was almost twenty three years old. She loved her teeth and pussy just as much as she loved herself. We sat on the couch watching T.V. until she leaned over and gave me a long wet kiss, letting me know what time it is. I was cool with it so I kissed her back the best way I could, considering that I wasn't too keen on kissing. She stood to her feet and pulled down her pajamas. Her pussy looked good enough to eat. She took my hand and lead me to the pallet she had made for us on the floor to protect the couch.

My eyes slowly observed her smooth caramel skin through the glare of the moon that entered the kitchen window. She was beautiful and her pussy was shaved and juicy. She looked like she wanted me to eat her out but that was a no-no in my book and a small turn off to her.

"Damn, this pussy is great," I told myself while deep stroking her. I had dealt with a lot of women but she had some good pussy and after five minutes of being inside of her…Splash! I pulled out and shot all over her stomach, but she still wasn't finished. We wiped off then she gave it to me doggie style allowing me to enjoy her as she moaned and pumped back on me hard. Once again I came all over her back then we wiped off and fell asleep until morning.

Rochelle had become my favorite for the time and we grew into a couple as I realized she had a lot to offer me on many levels. I appreciated her for many reasons. She made me look good, too.

Back at home things were still cool, but tense in the hood. I continued to work, slang and hang. Hank was always around because he was dating Rochelle's sister Tricia still. Eric was still being Eric, Rook came through each day because he worked a block away and Twin was allowing me to become a team player. He introduced me to his big bro 'B' and allowed me to deal with him on a 1-on-1 basis. He would front me work and allow me to do me.

At this time my name and game was becoming a household name. I was getting two pounds for $1,800 and selling an ounce for $150. My clientele grew so quick because I was mobile. All the women in my life were still adding up as my hustle life increased. Being that I still hadn't really eaten any pussy, I was doing okay. Yet, I did grab a couple of porn tapes for pointers. I really wanted to impress Rochelle due to the fact that she enjoyed it. We had several dates and a few more sex adventures over the past few weeks. I enjoyed everything about her as she introduced me to her family. They loved me once I grew on them knowing that I would be around for a long time. Before you knew it me and her step-dad, 'CB' became very close friends. A month or two into our relationship I asked to move in with her and she quickly said yes! So I packed my things from my mom's and moved in with her.

Mom had met her only a few times and didn't trust her because of her beauty and age. She actually was against me moving and expressed it often, but I knew I had to get away from the hood the best way I could. A few homies had gotten killed and I feared I would be next. So the timing of transition couldn't have been better.

Living with a female was strange at first. It did come with its pros and cons. A few were: Live-in pussy, comfort, and being the head of state. On the flip side was the arguing, getting tired of each other, no freedom, and having to answer to someone every moment of the damn day. I dealt with it and matured as time went on.

I still blew through the hood to hang out and catch up on the latest. Only a few cats knew where I lived, including Rook. Rochelle and I got along good as I cooked, worked, planned events and hustled extra hard to provide all that she needed. Plus I was actually being loyal until a few of her ex-boyfriends started calling and popping up.

CB and I hung out every day as I eventually came in contact with Steve, Dean, and a few more friends who smoked weed. I was expanding my clientele to earn more. As the game progressed I met up with a cat named Tashaun who was from Brightmoor like myself. He was a year or so younger than me but carried himself like a real 'G'. Through an acquaintance we became cool and started doing business together because he also sold pounds and had a few extra connects.

This dude was an animal; kind of like the new era '50 Cent'. He sported the finest jewels and drove a new Grand Cherokee with crazy sounds and Dayton wires. We became a force to be reckoned with as time went on. Together we learned a lot and formed a tight bond as I watched him be a father to his only son and mentor to many. Tashaun and I did everything together and a lot of times he would front me pounds like 'B' even though I still had pounds from 'B'.

Things had changed between Twin and B due to the ongoing beefs in the hood so I tried to keep my distance. Plus 'B' was out the game and going legit and getting married soon. This allowed me to spend a huge amount of time with Tashaun, CB, Rook and Hank. Rochelle really didn't care for Tashaun because she thought he was wild and kept me out too late with women. She respected everyone, but still kept her eye on all of us. I found out later, just why.

While living with Rochelle I learned a lot about how to please a woman. She never knew why I didn't like to eat pussy or even never even tried it on her. So I left it alone and continued to do my research and finally was ready to show off.

Late one Saturday night after a romantic night on the town, we came home as usual and prepared for bed. She always slept in her panties and a t-shirt and if her hair was tied down then I knew it was time to get it on. She was beautiful, I'll admit. As she strolled into our room with a slight buzz from the drinks we shared over dinner. Once she laid down getting ready for a regular sex session, I changed it up on her. I commanded her to take her t-shirt and panties off and to relax while I did all the work. The look on her face was priceless.

I started to kiss on her neck allowing my tongue to slither over her collar bone to her breast. I spent a few minutes sucking and kissing her nice sized breast by forcing them into my mouth one at a time. My hands would cup them as my fingers gently pinched her nipples. The moans that I heard signaled that I was doing everything right. The sweet sounds were exciting me as well, so I traveled down her stomach stopping at her navel, then proceeding to her sweet land of ecstasy. My tongue extended like a snake froze in time as I glided down her shaved pussy which was already dripping wet. I watched all the pornos that I'd watched to prepare me for this moment and went to work.

I licked around her thighs then started to lick from the bottom of her pussy hole all the way up to the clit where I paid special attention by doing a figure eight with my tongue until her facial expression showed I had found the right spot. It tasted so good to me so I explored every inch of it with my tongue. I licked the outer lips and the inner lips then sucked the clit hard and fast moving my tongue like a lizard. She began to tremble and moved her fingers past my tongue into her pussy which was now hot and wet from my actions.

"Faster! Faster!" she whispered in the sexiest voice I'd ever heard. My dick was pressing against the bed ready to explode. All I heard was wetness as she fingered herself rapidly. Once my mouth covered her swollen clit and pussy she surprised me by closing my head in between her thighs tightly while she came all in my mouth. That moment I realized the effect that eating pussy had on women. It's just as special as getting an amazing head job from a woman.

This was one of her talents and a must have for me from any woman I ever encountered in my lifetime. That night we slept better than ever before. I laid there thinking to myself as she slept, "The moves worked. Now what else could I do to become the ultimate lover?"

As time went on things became more intense in our relationship and in the streets as I tried my best to balance and separate the two. While hanging with CB I had become closer to her family, and while hanging with Tashaun, I became closer to the streets. I had a lot of female clients and tried to stay loyal by not mixing business with pleasure. I remained true to the one I loved as hard as it was.

I met a beautiful brown skinned woman named "Sharice" who had a boyfriend that was a local MC. Alaya who I pulled up on at a bus stop while riding with Tashaun on Schoolcraft and Evergreen. She was young, but had a nice smile and a fat ass, high yellow with normal size breast. I also met Jay and Will who were residents at Grayton Park apartments which were directly across from where I was staying. They both smoked weed and not only became good customers but became good friends. All of us got along and became one big family with me at the head of the table.

Life was moving fast. Work, play, hustling and being the head of the household was pretty stressful. Being in the game on this level was scary. More money, more problems, more women, more temptation, more clientele, more risk, things were cool, just a handful. Then to top it all off me and Rochelle's little sister had gotten cool. She had come through a few times to cop weed from me. Rochelle trusted us so she never made a fuss. She had slipped out of Hank's grasp, but they were still cool too. We would hang out and every now and then I could get info out of her. It was amazing how people acted when they were high.

One day she fell through the apartment with one of her home girls. Now let me explain something about this chick. She was medium height, about 115 pounds, smooth chocolate skin, perfect white teeth, a radiant smile with cat like eyes that made her look sexy and sneaky. To top it off this girl had the nerve to be bowlegged with a gap that made her pussy look fat and good as hell. Being that Tricia had brought her through to cop a few bags I kept my composure and introduced myself. Tricia quickly interceded by mentioning that I was Rochelle's man.

She smiled shyly, "I'm Tee-Tee, Tricia's friend from the hood.

Our eyes connected as we did the exchange and she took the few bags. I still remained cool though making sure not to show any signs of interest to Tricia. They left but the thought of this little slim bitch stayed on my mind for days. She soon became one of my clients along with a few other females that Tricia introduced me to. Rochelle wasn't that fond of me having female customers, but shit, girls smoked weed too. Their money was helping to pay the bills so she accepted it.

Now, I was ready for Christmas and the New Year. My first Christmas at my own house and it was going to be wonderful as the entire family enjoyed it together. Granny, my mom and the rest of my family were all doing good. My new life was on track…or at least that's how it seemed. Let's start a New Year!

CHAPTER 14
98' Moving Backwards

It's a new year and winter was coming to an end. I'd had a wonderful New Year's celebration with my family and friends. Things were going pretty smooth still as I continued to work at MetLife and hustle a little harder to prepare for the summer.

Rochelle and I were getting along and the sex was still erotic and experimental. Moms, Granny and Cody were all coming through to check on me on a regular basis. CB and Tricia were still playing a major role in my life along with Tashaun, Rook, Jay and Will. My parole term was almost at an end and I couldn't wait to be free from restrictions and urine drops.

A lot of my spare time was spent playing video games on the PlayStation and Dreamcast with the fellas. Our hangouts were at Jay and Will's place in Grayton Park apartments which is kinda funny because these were the same apartments that Howard the Duck used to live in back in the day. Over here I could relax plus give Rochelle a little freedom once she was off work but still remain close if she needed me.

I would break down ounces of weed into quarters and grams and leave it with Jay and Will to serve to all they knew plus a few people that I would send through while at work or at home. See Rochelle was getting a little jealous of the females that purchased from me. So I avoided conflict by redirecting the traffic and still being available to serve. So Tricia, Tee-Tee, Sharice and the others would go through them to get their stuff. After a few attempts the females would request that I be around so that they could chill and smoke at the apartment. Eventually I gave in and became a regular at the hang out while still allowing Jay and Will to profit.

It was truly fun as I hosted various smoke out's to the clientele. Rochelle had gotten kinda used to my routine and became a little looser than I expected and accepted. A few of her ex-boyfriend's would call or drop by unaware that I lived there and this became a problem. She started feeling a little trapped by my presence and needed an outlet. So she started sneaking around while I was at work or she would let the men visit her at work.

Fortunately our next door neighbors were three young dudes who had love for her because of their history and love for me because of my product. They would inform me of her actions while I was at work. I could never catch her in the act, but she started getting sloppy. She started hanging out at the same club every Tuesday called Slammers. Then she would go to the River Rock on Saturday, so I would be hanging out with Tashaun and often we would pop up at the club to see who she was hanging with. Most times she wasn't by herself.

This started to get embarrassing to me. This one dude named Clarence used to be in love with her and I think she loved him too. He would call, show up or visit her job even though he was well aware of me and our relationship. This made me and Rochelle fall out and I moved out to a good friend's house named Crystal. She was still in school in Grand Rapids and I would house sit for her a few months until she graduated. The ironic part was she lived three blocks over from my mom's.

Even though Rochelle and I were on again and off again we would still fuck and fight mentally. We both were drifting off with the opposite sex and Tee-Tee was still coming around with Tricia but we had yet to hook up solo.

On Rochelle's birthday she gave a party at Reggie's club on Chicago and I showed up and so did Clarence and his twin brother. Things immediately got heated and he got thrown out of the club where he waited in the parking lot for Rochelle and me.

Thank God Will and Cody were with me as I sported my Coogi jumpsuit and Hushpuppies to match. She played both sides as the beef erupted in the parking lot. Since I drove a different car, they never saw me leave so I waited and followed them to her house then drove to his house. I studied the route and a few hours later got the crew together and did three drive-by shootings at this house to send a message. First, don't try to threaten me or try to play with my bitch! The show down was stupid and later came back to haunt me.

The next day I spoke with Rochelle and tried to get things back on track only to find out that he had spent the night over her house. I drove by to holler at Jay and noticed his truck parked at Rochelle's and went crazy. I shot the truck up and her apartment, then went out to Tricia's out in Inkster to hide out.

After the tension died down Rochelle and I talked and I moved back in. After being gone for two months a lot had changed and I figured that Clarence's Mom told him to leave her alone out of fear for his life. Yes, my actions were stupid but necessary. I didn't cheat on her or lead anyone on after this. A week after moving in I found out she had fucked Clarence several times without a condom and she found out she was pregnant. By whom, we weren't sure. So we got her an abortion to solve that problem. That's when I realized that she was weak and let another man in. I became a little more confident with myself and started expanding my stable and poker face.

This was the year that the "Hot Boys, started showing up everywhere with their music and videos. Tashaun and I hung out more as my feelings toward Rochelle had changed and were barely there. I explored more options as my street cred rose to a high. Tashaun's sister Kay Kay and I became cool. There was her, Sharice, Alaya and a ton of others who I had never fucked. Now I had to have them all. I was the perfect example of a Good boy gone bad.

First Sharice, then Alaya, then Kim a few others all while living with Rochelle. I needed revenge but hurting her wasn't enough. So I kept all my women secret. Did it feel good cheating? Well, I'll say it felt better than being cheated on.

Over the next few months Rochelle would sneak off but I was so focused on work and making money to live above average that I didn't care. Ultimately, I would have the last laugh. In September, I lost my job at MetLife because I was only a temp and they were downsizing us all. So I found a midnight job at Ford Trucking in Romulus which was close to Tricia's housing project in Inkster.

She was still cool as hell even though she was Rochelle's youngest sister. Right was right and wrong was wrong to her. She never took sides and always remained neutral. My working midnights caused a major problem because Rochelle would sneak dudes in while I was gone. I found this out from my neighbors. They would call me at work to tell on her and she never even knew.

This shit was getting boring so I started saving my money for a rainy day. Shit was moving fast in my life and I had no sense of direction. Rochelle and I were falling out of love. My mom was in need of my help when she transferred out to Southgate. My brother Rook went on the Maury show to find out the son that he had taken care of was not his. Tashaun had gone to jail for six months for some bullshit over his baby mom's and CB was getting ready for the wedding to Rochelle's mom.

One day on my way home from work I got pulled over and gladly handed over my license assuming this was a routine traffic stop. It was far from routine, I found out there was a warrant for my arrest in Wayne County for destruction of property! Clarence and his mom filed a police report saying that I had committed a crime against them. I called Rochelle and explained the problem and to my surprise, she had my back on this one. The bad thing was this was a parole violation.

When I got to the County jail, Clarence's gay ass showed up crying and I was waived over to Frank Murphy. With no bond because I was on parole, my family and job were all in an uproar. I spent three weeks in the County and Rochelle came to visit weekly and sent money. I had left her my Thunderbird and small grey pick up I had bought from a friend.

I was transferred to Western Wayne for parole violation while the charges were pending for forty-five days. I had Rochelle contact Clarence, Twin and my Uncle Cody to resolve the issue of Clarence coming to court to testify. It went well and he never showed up to court and I was released on parole until the outcome of the case was decided. I was super happy as Rochelle picked me up and took me home and fucked me for several days.

Things were looking up as I found a new job and got things back on track with the streets. Tashaun was home also so shit started working out. After a few weeks home, CB and I were out hanging at a job function he took me to at a bar. Being out with him didn't make me feel bad and I thought it would be cool with Rochelle because it wasn't like it was with Tashaun, Tee or Will. When I came home around 2:30 am she had locked the screen door so I couldn't get in and then once I did get her to open the door, she threw a fit. This is where I learned yet another lesson, "Never move in with a female, let her move in with you."

Since my mind was made up I started looking for another place to live because I know she wasn't 100% happy anymore and wanted to spread her wings. So did I, in a way. I talked to the manager at the apartments who knew me well since I paid the rent anyway and asked him for an open apartment for myself. After a while the apartment downstairs from Rochelle came available and I rushed to rent it. I put down $1650 which paid my deposit and two months of rent. I never told Rochelle about it, only CB, who kept it a secret.

Late one night we were lying in bed and I left my wallet inside my night stand on my side of the bed. While I was sleeping she went through my wallet and found the receipt to the new apartment and went crazy. I stayed calm and lied to her. I said, "It's not final yet. But if you continue to trip on me and lock me out and shit, then I'm moving!"

I know it was crazy to move literally a few feet from her, but since I had a record, I couldn't pass a background check and it was all I could get with such short notice.

Of course she started acting better, but I was already full throttle with a full tank of gas. We had our good days and definitely a few bad ones. I figured it was the best thing for me to move if we wanted to maintain a half way decent relationship. But since I was literally seconds away, things were bound to get ugly.

Once I claimed my own, all types of pussy, money and opportunities came knocking. Even Tee-Tee starting standing out and falling through without Tricia, to cop a few bags and to flirt. She was cool and sexy in her own little way and I liked the fact that she knew I had a girl and we could still be friends. Everyone else I dealt with never knew until it was too late....

CHAPTER 15
99-Back on Track

My new place was all that I wanted it to be. And I'll admit the freedom was a little different. I had to be careful of my actions because Rochelle was still my main chick and lived upstairs from me. We didn't have keys to each other's apartments, but we usually spent the night in one place or the other. People knew we were having problems because of the move, but they weren't sure what the problem was. Maybe they thought that my place was a stash spot or a play pad. However Rochelle kept a close watch on whoever visited my house from sun up to sun down.

I had visitors every day. My place became the chill spot for all my boys and occasionally a few chicks too. I would break down an ounce and we all would smoke and chill. Tee-Tee, Sharice and Trice, a female that my sister had recently hooked me up with would fall through every now and then. Trice was a cute small framed chick with a long ponytail. She worked with my sister at a drycleaners out in Southgate.

My business was growing as I landed a new job through a temp service. No more night shifts for me. I was now working at Simon and Schuster's Accounts Payable firm, in Livonia. The job was great and had plenty of perks like, my own office, phone, flexible hours and the location was ten minutes from home. I was able to leave on lunch breaks and make a few sales or restock Jay and Will with more product. Besides, at the new job there were a few co-workers that became loyal customers.

I was surrounded by women of all sizes, shapes, races and religions. Being that I was one out of ten men who was actually available or attractive, my attention was unlimited. They offered and made so many advances by flirting or spoiling me with food and gifts. The flip side of this wonderful job was that

Rochelle hated the fact that I was surrounded by women all day. She was working at J C Penny's as a manager on the day shift and a lot of days she would come home late from working overtime so I had plenty of extra time to play in the streets.

A few months on my job and my secret savings account in my closet started growing. Tashaun was still throwing me a few pounds and I was buying a few on top of those. B and Twin were still around but fading because of B's life style changes. Hank had started working so he rarely came through. Then he ended up moving to Atlanta with his mom, because of some trouble in the city.

My uncle watched as me and Tashaun grew as hustlers. I met all types of street niggas who were heavy in the game and loved me because of my ability to control, manage and produce large amounts of money. They all trusted me and started allowing me to handle more work. I enjoyed the benefits and shared the wealth with my circle and Rochelle. I would take her out to the best places, buy her the best clothes and jewelry and give her money whenever she wanted. Yes, she was spoiled but she deserved it because she put up with a lot. I think she wanted me to be the man she met before she allowed me to change into my alter ego. I was a bad boy now and my goals were set to an all new high.

Once I got a taste of the street life and money I was hooked. I had no limits because the money was coming in so fast. Tashaun always had the hook up on the latest shit like clothes and electronics. While in the movement I bought me a '79' Pontiac Bonneville. It was a brown two door and had the gearshift in the console. I loved it as I transferred the rims from the Thunderbird on to it. Then I took it to get the windows tinted and sounds from Jam Sounds on Seven Mile and Telegraph. My car was nice and over a few weeks I added three TVs and a PlayStation to it to make it stand out a little bit.

OPTIONS

Everyone loved it as my reputation continued to grow bigger and bigger. A few weeks later I bought an '88' Blazer and painted it red and altered that with the tinted windows, sounds and TVs. Now with two cars my street cred was rising even higher. I was finally feeling complete.

I started hanging out at the River Rock and Floods with Tashaun and the crew. We would still catch Rochelle on her flirt shit, but I just downplayed it until we got home, then I blew the fuck up. Back at work things were flowing like water. I had met a few new women to add to my stable like this white girl named, Stacy. She was kinda cute and spoiled me like crazy. She would take me shopping and let me use her car even though she knew I had a girl at home. For real, she bought me my first gold chain with a key for the charm and got me a Wittnauer watch and a ring to match. She would buy me clothes every pay period and even got me a Quacom cell phone on her contract and paid the bill.

Our only problem was we had to keep our relationship a secret at work because it would cause a major problem. All the women had a crush on me and threw themselves at me all day. Like this big booty woman named, Rhonda P, she was older and really thick but loved me like crazy. We became fuck partners and close friends at home and at work, but that didn't stop other women from flirting with me.

I had a young chick named Val who was a virgin and a Jehovah Witness who gave me that V card and loved the fuck out of me. It was hard trying to juggle all these women at work, but I was smooth and somehow pulled it off.

Back at home, a chick named Jazzy who had a twin named Teesa, had moved into the apartment complex. I had gone to school with her at Murphy and now she had a son and a man who used to abuse her. Once she moved in and saw me, her man went crazy and they would fight over all types of shit. She knew about Rochelle, but didn't give a fuck which I found out later.

One day I was outside my apartment on my way in from the parking lot in back. At the inside mailbox Kessa was getting something out of her box. It was 11:30 at night and you could tell she was trying to sneak and grab her mail quick being that her apartment was only a few feet away. I had caught her wearing a short night gown with her robe half way open. Damn!! Her body was perfect. She was 5'7 about 140 pounds, caramel complexion with a flat stomach. She caught me looking and heard me say, "Damn Kessa."

"What?" she said with a flirty smile on her face.

We talked briefly and I gave her my number to call once she got inside because her man was at work. That night we talked for hours until Rochelle came in and we hung up with promises to keep in touch.

A few days later she called me when she knew Rochelle was at work and asked could she come down for a few minutes. Maybe she wanted to talk, or to smoke a blunt but I damn sure wanted to know what was up.

I was chilling when she showed up with a tank and some shorts on. She came down in her robe and ten minutes later we were fucking like crazy. She rode me so good and looked pretty as hell doing it. It was so damn good that we lost track of time. I had to admit we were cutting it real close, but this pussy was worth the risk. She knew she could fuck and the look on her face said as much. That night after we finished we vowed to keep it on the low because of her man and my girl.

Over time, we would sneak and fuck and avoid being caught, but Rochelle always suspected that we were doing something because our hello's and goodbyes were way too familiar. I felt bad doing a lot of the shit I did, but it wasn't my fault. I had a lot of women that needed me to make an impact in their life and I respected and accepted my role.

OPTIONS

This would also be the year that I got Tee to let me into her life. She had become a little distant from Tricia and so I jumped when the opportunity presented itself. Only because Tricia's family always thought that we had a secret love or something and we didn't. She had a boyfriend that she was staying with in Inkster so we kinda fell apart but still stayed in touch.

Tee-Tee was working at a drug store in Redford and would call me to meet her at her job to serve her friends a few bags. Tricia was working there part time, but got fired for some reason or another. This is how Tee and I stayed in touch. After work one day she called me and asked was it safe for her to fall through because Will and Jay weren't at home.

"It's cool. Fall through and I'll have you gone before Rochelle comes home."

She and Rochelle had fallen out over a pair of missing contacts. One night after the club Rochelle accused her of stealing her contacts and they hadn't been cool since. Whatever, I didn't care either way.

When she showed up I sized her up at the door. She was really cute with her bowlegged self. I just knew she had to have some good pussy. While she smoked I made up my mind, it was now or never. I started kissing her neck and body as I kneeled in front her. She didn't resist so I assumed it was cool or she was just high. I moved her shorts to the side and then her panties, as she had on a pair of baggy shorts. I eased them over just enough to get access to the pussy.

Her pussy stayed consistent with her little petite frame. It was so small and pretty. Her pussy was so wet and smelled so sweet. I placed my head between her legs and explored her pussy with my tongue. She lifted her legs up on the couch as I ate her pussy until she came all over my face. As bad as I wanted to fuck her little sexy ass I knew my time was running short and

Rochelle would be pulling up soon. I knew I left an impression with my pussy eating skills, so I decided to concede and send her home without a fucking, but if she came back to finish I knew I had won.

She washed up real quick and we checked the parking lot for Rochelle then she left to go home. I prayed she wouldn't tell Tricia or Rochelle. I had learned a lot about the cheating from Rochelle and I pretty much had it perfected. A man would be fine as long as he didn't pillow talk, and a woman would be fine if she knew her position and played by the rules.

While I was doing more than a little multi-tasking, everything was in control but it was exhausting. Too many women required too much time, energy and self-control. Between Tee, Jazzy, Rhonda, Val, Tricia, Sharice, Alaya and Rochelle my schedule was locked. Then I had work and my street life, along with hanging with Tashaun and CB.

Jay and Will stayed close like best friends and Rook was in the process of moving into his Dad's old house on Lyndon and Livernois. For some reason one night Rochelle started asking me all these crazy questions about my spare time and new gifts. She accused me of cheating, can you believe that?? I avoided the fire by dashing a little water on it, hoping that it wouldn't rekindle.

On Wednesday, me, CB and a few other guys would rent the gym on Hamtramck to play basketball, workout or relax. It was the same routine in and out every week, but this Wednesday seemed a little strange to me. We would all meet at my apartment then travel to the gym in CB's truck so we could all catch a buzz before the game. We would usually get back home around 11:30 then chill out for a few smoking blunts or playing the PlayStation.

I had started smoking a little weed after I got off parole to ease my stressed mind. When we pulled up to the crib we did just that, fired up as Jay and CB played the game. I jumped in the shower then made a few calls to my female friends before work the next the day. Whenever Rochelle wasn't around I called everyone up to say goodnight, it made them feel special.

While I was making my calls I noticed Rochelle's car wasn't in the lot. This wasn't a club night so I became a little concerned when she wasn't answering my phone calls.

"Cool, she must be out fucking," I thought to myself. I mixed it up with Jay and CB about a few hoes I was dealing with lately. Even though CB was Rochelle's stepfather, he never got involved in our personal life, because he was my friend. After a few blunts everyone left and still no word from Rochelle. I got ready for bed and called Stacy and told her to bring me lunch to work tomorrow.

"Of course I will, baby. I love you," she cooed into the phone.

"I love you too," I answered hanging up the phone.

I fell off to sleep after a few minutes, but was awakened when I thought I heard something rustling in my closet. Before I could react because I was still half asleep, Rochelle came running out of the closet at full speed with a big ass knife in her hand, headed right towards me.

I rolled out of the bed and out of her reach just in time. She was crying uncontrollably because she had been in there for hours and had heard everything. What I didn't know is the night before when she came over and fucked me to sleep she had unlocked my kitchen window since she no longer had a key to my place. She snuck in while I was gone and had been listening to everything!

We wrestled around with the knife between the two of us. She wasn't satisfied until she had drawn blood. Luckily it was only a finger that was cut. She was huffing and puffing as I stood on one side of the table trying to convince her not to listen to her lying ears.

"You told that bitch that you love her Rome! You love her??" she screamed at me. After hours of trying to explain she finally put the knife down and left my apartment, but not before she said, "Oh, and I'll be at your job tomorrow, Bitch!"

I let her leave and lied down in my bed. After all the shit she had done, including getting pregnant by Clarence, I didn't think it was shit she really could say. I mean two wrongs don't make it right, but at least I did my shit in the dark.

Fortunately for me, the next day she didn't come to my job. She'd only heard the name Stacy and didn't know what anyone looked like. The other girls I had talked to in the living room so she hadn't heard those conversations. Thank God.

It took a few days before I got her to talk to me. She wanted me to get another job, but she knew that wasn't happening. My money was steadily stacking and she knew it was true because she wanted for nothing so she knew I had the money and the power and she had the heart and the pussy.

Things went back to normal as best they could until one day when my phone bill came in the mail. I made Stacy get it sent to my house since she was going through the numbers and tracing my calls. Well, of course Rochelle got a hold of it and did the same research that Stacy had done. She got the exact dates, times and numbers of everyone that I called. Then she got cocky and called every person and tried to exploit our relationship. A few of the women didn't feed into it and a few were shocked, but even still more eager to play the game.

I didn't find out that she had called people until Rook called me and told me she had called him too. Then when I went to work a few females approached me with the situation. I kindly explained that my girl and I were on rocky terms because of her own mistakes. Most of them told me that they hadn't told her anything and kept it moving. I learned quickly that a lot of women don't care if you got woman, especially if they already have a man. It's less of a headache for them because they don't have to deal with you every day and vice versa. Besides, everyone had someone to serve whatever purpose in their lives.

My last lesson was every woman wants a man that is taken. It makes them feel better to steal or out do another bitch by stealing out of their garden. Men are the same way except that it's a bit more complicated. We try to kill any insect that invades our garden. Mainly because if she steps out we feel that were lacking on some level. Whether its money, sex or time, she looked somewhere else for the missing link and that is a blow most men can't sustain.

It's something about white women that makes them want to talk or tell when confronted by a black woman. Once Rochelle manipulated Stacy's dumb ass with her "It's cool, I just want to know the truth," shit, Stacy told her everything. She told her about the shopping sprees, me driving her car, all the other women at my job that I fucked with, on down to the sex we'd had, that I secretly hated but had to give to her as a down payment for all the benefits she gave me.

Rochelle was heated and used it all against me as she stepped out and did her own thing. I knew our relationship was strange and most people thought we should let go and stop hurting each other. It was just too hard to let go for some reason that I couldn't explain.

The days and months flew by and not much had changed except Tashaun had a new Expedition and had tricked it out. I still was kicking it with a few broads. Every so often I played with Jazzy and a few women at the job. I even fucked Val who was a virgin at the time at the Ford and Wyoming Drive-In. Ironically, Rochelle was acting better and staying around a little more. However, Tee-Tee was making a small impact and never really spoke on our little episode.

I had seen her out a few times and we always spoke, but not much more. Then late in November when my mom and little brother were over chilling and smoking a blunt with me, something crazy took place as my brother played outside in the courtyard. I had left my screen door unlocked and my front door open so I could keep an eye on them, when all of a sudden both doors swung open with a bunch of officers screaming, "Get the fuck on the floor! Now!"

They had their guns drawn and were ready for action if necessary. Everyone in the house froze as the officers who were wearing mask, cuffed us and put us in restraints. Once we were calm and they had control they explained that they wanted the guns and drugs and if I told them where they were, they wouldn't tear the apartment up. So to save myself from having to pay for any more damage I showed them where the drugs were hidden. In my closet I grabbed the shoebox that had eighteen ounces pre-bagged and a .38 snub with the serial numbers scratched off.

They asked me was that it and I told them, "yes." They explained to me that someone had turned them on to me, etc. I just knew I was going to jail but after a few minutes of talking, they let me go. They took the gun and drugs then spoke to my mom and her friend. The nosy neighbors watched with the apartment manager. I just shook my head.

Later on, the manager told me that they told him that they had only found a small amount of weed. This was strange to me, on top of the fact that they hadn't taken me to jail and said someone told on me. I was cool with the whole building because they all smoked, so I was thrown off, but I knew I had to move ASAP.

Three days later, Rochelle and I talked about moving back together because of the extra attention and my lack of security that I felt I needed. She decided to keep her apartment and would join me later. I pulled all my resources and took my money that was stashed and found another place on Six Mile and

Telegraph called the Avon Manor. My stacks were still growing at a rapid speed so I made my transition easily to this new apartment and hopefully a new experience. It was time to move and do me!

CHAPTER 16
TIME TO UPGRADE

Once I'd moved to my new one bedroom, third floor apartment it was time to get focused. Jay and Will helped me move in so they were the first to see the new crib. At this spot there were more perks than none. Here I didn't have to worry about Rochelle watching my every move and she also had more freedom at her own apartment. I was still only ten minutes away from work and one of the hottest clubs was directly behind my building, called Millennium A.D.

All the doors to the apartment stayed locked and you had to be buzzed in to enter. The only down falls were the landlord lived on the first floor and stayed in her window watching the parking lot. I was also on the border of Redford Township and since the apartments were so close, the smoking and partying had to be kept to a bare minimum. Picture a college dorm setting with an all glass entry way.

Rochelle finally made her way down to check out the new crib and she liked it a lot, but not enough to move in. I guess she liked the freedom she had at her own place more. I had started to furnish the place. I bought a king sized bedroom set that was gator print. It had a large mirrored headboard. Then I got a small fish tank for my room with a few Hammerhead sharks. Then I grabbed a large aquarium for the living room and placed an Iguana named Pona in it.

The apartment was ready for show. All my boys and my uncles loved it. My mom had moved back to Kentucky to change her life for the better and Granny came over to check out my new place and gave me the thumbs up. I added a small mini-bar in the living room and kept it stocked with all the top shelf liquor. Then I had an alarm from ADT installed for my security.

REGGIE GIST

I met a few people that lived in the building, after a few weeks of settling. A guy named Sherm, lived there with his baby momma and child. They smoked weed and played the video game so we got cool real quick. He lived directly across the hall from me and soon became as close and Jay and Will to me. From his apartment you could see the parking lot so I told him what kind of truck Rochelle had so he was always on alert. He also hipped me to the back exit that I could use and no one would see me come and go.

My other neighbors looked at me like a drug dealer even though I worked every day. It was mid-February so I wore a Black Diamond Mink with the hat to match and a Rolex that I had bought from Gary at the Plaza, so I guess I stood out a bit.

After a few months of living at the apartment Sherm's baby momma introduced me to her friend that came over sometimes. Nisha had a man and was cool with my Rochelle issue so a lot of times we smoked or just chilled playing the game and watching movies.

After a while we became a cute secret couple which meant no tripping in public and mostly we only met over Sherm's house when she got away from her boyfriend. Once we started having sex, which was great by the way, things got deeper. Like if I didn't know she was at Sherm's and I brought another female over she would act out. I had a full roster at the time so trust me she was tripping a lot.

The more Tashaun and I hung out and partied the more women I met. We would hang out at the River Rock on Two Dollar Tuesdays and the Millennium on Friday's. On Saturday's we went to Club 2000 and on Monday's we hung at the Michigan Inn in Southfield behind Northland. All the clubs were hot spots where all the hustlers hung out to show out.

I had even dated Tashaun's little sister for a minute, but being the player I was I didn't feel it was fair to her. She understood and we became even cooler friends. The hanging out gave Rochelle more opportunity to distance herself, but I was never lonely. I was still dealing with most of the same women and meeting new ones every week.

Tashaun and I settled into a routine, eating breakfast every day at Arkbar's or Connie and Barbara's on Six Mile. Then we would head to the mall. We spent between $500 and $1000 a day shopping. Iceberg, Coogi, Willie Esco or Sean John were the picks of the day and the shoes ranged from Kenneth Coles and Gucci to Gators depending on the outfit and occasion. We rocked Cartier glasses blinged out with diamonds and the Rolex watch I wore had a five karat diamond bezel laced with Princess cut diamonds. From the looks of things, we were on our "A" game.

I started losing contact with a few people that couldn't keep up with my lifestyle. Trice had faded out along with Hank, Twin and several others. My Uncle Cody had fallen to a new low by getting locked up for a few months, so I passed him in the street game. Back in the hood I had caught back up with Dean, who was living on Mark Twain with a roommate from Chicago named Big Mack. After we connected, I started hanging over their house and eventually made it a stash house to store more pounds. See there was always someone there plus where they lived allowed me quick access to the underworld.

I didn't have to travel far from Redford to make a big sell as long as I kept this house and Jay and Will at the complex loaded. It was enough weed to go around and I never ran out.

Dean was a long-time friend so I trusted him a lot. He worked down at 36th District court and was a good father to his daughter. I had his back and everyone else in my circle.

Rook and I had started getting closer due to him working and plus my boy's shit was crazy. He was still living on Stoepel with his girlfriend and had started a new job at Chrysler. Once we linked back up we grew close quickly and he played his role in my circle. He allowed me to stash work at his house, but the traffic had to be kept at a low. This was my bro and I had to protect him a little more because he wasn't really about the street life, like me and the others.

Through all this maneuvering I had stumbled across a new plug for my supply, by pure luck. I had an Arab friend named Mel that I was cool with who trusted and loved me from the start. He spoiled me by giving me my product cheaper than Tashaun, E, Twin or anyone else. I would get fifty-sixty pounds for 700-800 apiece and sell them third hand for $1000 to everyone. By the prices being so low and me having three different connects that flooded me with work. I never ran out and stayed making money.

Yes, I was moving fast and making every second count. It was only May and it seemed like a year had gone past. Rochelle had started missing me so I would allow her to spend a few nights with me with hopes that Nisha wouldn't act out if she found out that Rochelle was there. My relationship with Rochelle was still being worked on and she remained my main focus. I would only fuck with other women if she wasn't around or available. I would stop everything else I was doing if she called or needed me because she was my woman and I was her man. At all family outings and special event we were present as a couple. A few months earlier CB and her mom had gotten married and I attended the wedding as her date, of course.

At this point Rochelle and I were cool and even though our time spent was limited, we were still going strong. Back at work things were getting a little hairy because they wouldn't hire me in as an employee after my six months of consistent good work. This wasn't sitting well with me so I left the job to focus on my other hustles. The women at my job who I still kicked it with occasionally were sad to see me leave. I promised that I would keep in touch and visit when I could. After I left they would jockey for position and settle for what little time I could offer them.

Now that I wasn't working, my main focus was building an empire. I had let Dean drive my Blazer because his car was down. I had cashed out on a 2000 Lincoln that I kept parked at the apartment. But since I only had so many spaces at the apartment I let Granny drive the Lincoln and would switch with her whenever I needed to switch cars for the day.

I was still meeting other women on a daily basis. My phone and two-way Timeport pager stayed jumping with action. There were so many new women in my life that I easily lost count and contact. If they weren't saying what I wanted to hear, they fell off to the wayside and were never missed. Even though I made it a point to never leave a woman on a bad note, at least I tried. So that way when I saw them again, most times it would be cool to rekindle with no problem.

I had bumped back into a few old hustlers and a few new up and coming, like my homie Boat and my coworker 'E1C' who introduced me to Que and his crew. All of us were street niggas who stayed in touch with each other even though we were all on different levels. It was important to me to stay connected with the streets and who was hot and who was not. Que was a local rapper and "Boat" was a lot like me. We had met back in 99' through a connect and became cool trust worthy friends.

In mid-June I started planning for my birthday events. I finally got a call from Tee-Tee who hadn't called me for a week to check in or grab a few bags. I thought that maybe she was copping from Jay or Will and avoiding seeing me. It was nice to hear from her because she was a cool person to hang around. We spoke for a few minutes and she told me she and her friend were bored. I invited them over, since I knew everything was in control in the streets.

It was around 9 p.m. when they got there. We started getting high and playing the game. The weed had me blown and I started to get horny and wanted to fuck Tee-Tee. We had only fucked once and it was a quick thrill, I wanted to go all the way with her little ass. They had a different plan as we all moved into my bedroom and I watched them go at it for a few minutes. You could tell they were rookies, but that shit had me so turned on that I had to join in and take control of the situation. I had my way with the both of them and was impressed with my newest sexual experience, the threesome.

This showed me a new side of Tee-Tee that I liked. She was adventurous and it excited me. They asked if they could spend the night and that was fine with me. I was so into it that I lost track of time and lost track of Rochelle in the process. I had ignored all of her calls all night and all the warning signs she was sending. The next morning I woke up to two sexy women and a hard on. I only fucked Tee-Tee that morning and once we were done, she cooked breakfast before they left.

While they were cooking, I returned some of my missed calls from my phone and pager. Tashaun, Jay and Rochelle had called, I reached out to them all except Rochelle who wasn't answering and I assumed she was at work. Tee needed to go to her car for something so I made a call to Sherm, just to be on the safe side. He didn't answer so Tee headed out to the car and not a minute later she was running back into the house.

"Rome, I think Rochelle is outside. I saw her truck parked out there next to my car," Tee-Tee said looking a little shaken. We both knew that Rochelle was crazy and not to be fucked with.

"Fuck!" I yelled calling Sherm again for confirmation. He didn't answer, but I didn't need his confirmation anyway because simultaneously my cell phone and apartment buzzer started ringing like crazy. It was Rochelle and she wanted in and no one was going to stop her.

It would only be a matter of time before some asshole trying to be a Good Samaritan let her in. Once she got in she was kicking and banging at my door to let her in. I told the girls to be quiet and we pretended that I wasn't there.

"I'll tell her I was with Tashaun, or something," I thought to myself. I replayed the lie over and over in my head. Eventually she left, but not before she keyed Tee-Tee's car and busted all her tires.

Once they left through the back exit, I did the same and went to meet Tashaun and Boat at Connie and Barbara's. I told them what happened as we smoked and laughed about the situation.

A day later I had saw Rochelle and buttered her up. Since she had never really seen Tee-Tee up close. She'd only seen her entering my section from a distance. So she really couldn't be certain that she was really coming to my crib. We talked about it for a while and decided we had to earn each other's trust back. Our sex life was always awesome and I think that's what our foundation was built on. It takes time for old wounds to heal, but I kept buying band aids to reseal my emotions. Only one person had my heart at this time, but a lot of females had my attention. So after Rochelle and I made up things were still rocky but acceptable.

The next day I went and visited Rook on Lyndon, where he was chilling with an old friend named, Lyve Wire. Lyve Wire was a cool ass dude who came through and played PlayStation or brought a few bags to smoke with Rook. Rapping was his other passion. Once he found out I was about to start a record label and was looking for new artist, he became a loyal member of "Ineffable Records."

The record label consisted of Rook and I, who were good rappers since we were kids, Lyve and Rock who I had met at a S.A. class earlier in the year. I had started building the studio upstairs at Rook's house. Our dreams were coming true and all we had to do was push towards them. Everyone had faith as we created music and became known for many things throughout the hood.

Our team was starting to rise as my Arab connect kept me flooded with work along with several other connects. Tashaun had done the usual and grabbed him a 2000 Suburban Truck with the wet bar in the back and TV's in the headrest. He still came through as we hung out all over the city and tag teamed groupies and potential future wifey's.

My brother and Dean's houses became the local hangout and meeting places. All members of the group had to hustle to eat or get extra's so I tried my best to guide us on the straight, yet illegal path.

Tashaun and I would cruise through BrightMo to chill and collect money from his friends who quickly became my friends after we met. Friends like Fred a.k.a. Benzo, Leon a.k.a. Bo-Ski, Keith a.k.a. Big Ugly and many more hood cats who were part of the hustle.

BrightMo was where we all started from so it was our place of safety or comfort zone. On several occasions we would all hook up on club nights and party until we fell out. Life was moving so fast for all of us.

Over the next few months things got hectic and sometimes scary. One day Tashaun and I were getting ready to go to Club Nickel's for Monday Night Football like we always did. So we got dressed out in our newest Iceberg outfits with our mink coats and iced out glasses and watches. We hit the club scene like superstars as women flocked and jockeyed for our attention. I had at least three or four women that had a crush on me and a few whom I'd slept with over the course of a few weeks. So my presence was noticed as soon as we entered the club and hit the bar to grab a few bottles of Moet.

I bumped into a girl named Leona who lived in Oak Park and was extra beautiful and loved me like crazy after only three weeks of chilling. She had a cute little friend that Tashaun had hit, but really didn't have time for, as his roster was full. So we were all at the bar drinking and shit then it got late and we all headed to the parking lot. We were going to Rod Sherman's after hours in BrightMo to catch a fish or two, but as we pulled out the parking lot and turned onto Greenfield we bumped into Leona and her girl again and we decided to meet up at the Coney Island on Seven Mile to make plans for the night.

Unfortunately, Tashaun already had some other girl in mind, but was cool with me hooking up with Leona and heading towards my crib on Telegraph. So I jumped out at the Coney Island to kick it with Leona who pulled up in the rental car that she was driving. The restaurant was getting crowded from the club crowd. As I talked to Leona, Tashaun got a call from his freak so I told him to go pick her up since she was close by.

I jumped into the back seat of their car while I waited for him to get back. Leona said they were hungry so we decided to hit the drive thru because the inside was crowded as hell.

Cody and Granny stayed a few blocks away so I felt safe without my gun in this hood. When we pulled into the drive thru, I figured a few guys had seen me pull up all flashy in the big truck and the mink, or saw me at the bar and wanted to make trouble.

As I sat in the drive thru I noticed a small framed guy coming from the alley headed towards the Coney Island, or so I thought. But when he got closer he pulled out a big ass .357 and demanded I open the door to the car. Now I was in the back seat with a child proof lock on it so I couldn't move or open the door. The women in the car froze as they looked for advice from me and I had none.

The gunman walked around and checked the other doors with gun in hand as he told her friend to open the driver's side door. Her window was rolled down because she was about to order the food, so he just reached in and pulled her out. She screamed and Leona took that opportunity to open her door and run. This left me sitting face to face in a small ass car with a dude with a gun.

The young dude demanded that I give all that I had or he would shoot. I'm thinking it was a hit on me, but if it was why was he talking and not shooting? All types of shit ran through my mind like, where is Tashaun? No one sees this nigga robbing me? Two girls just ran out of the car screaming and no one noticed?

I handed over my Rolex watch and iced out glasses, then the three karat ring and bracelet and my gold chain with the iced out silver dollar piece. He took that, but wanted more.

"Give me all your money and that coat, nigga!"

It was by God's grace, and some other unfortunate niggas luck that he happened to be getting robbed too, but shots were fired and it scared my robber off. He made away with just my jewelry.

A few minutes later Tashaun pulled back up and we linked up and started searching the neighborhood for the nigga that robbed me. No luck finding him or the girls that we were with so I swallowed my pride and called it a night.

The next morning Leona called me crying and explaining why she left. She was afraid that he was going to kill me. I told her I was straight. Her friend, who happened to be married, wanted her husband to come and pick up the rental car, which was fine with me too.

I called Rochelle to check on her to make sure she didn't need anything. She was cool and wanted to come over later so I called all my other females to warn them off. I was kinda down so I decided to do something nice for myself. I picked up Sherm and we headed over to Granny's to pick up the Lincoln. I laid my head back, activated the heated seats while Sherm rolled a blunt.

We headed to Greenfield Plaza to see Gary. I told him that I had gotten robbed of my Rolex and he showed me a sixty thousand dollar Rolex that he was making for Tashaun's boy, Twizzy. I told him I wanted to spend a couple dollars so he took me to the back to show me some new pieces he had just gotten in. There was a stainless steel Rolex with the black face and bezel laced in diamonds. I had to have it. After negotiating, we settled at fifty five hundred dollars. Then he hooked me up with the chain, charm, ring and bracelet to match the Rolex. They were in white gold, which had just started getting popular. While regular niggas were rocking gold and Techno watches, the ballers had switched over to white gold and platinum.

I ended up dishing out another seventy-five hundred for the set. Now all I needed were my Carti's and I would be set. I shot across the street to Northland mall and parked at the D.O.C. door. Sherm and I blew a blunt then went in and I bought my first pair of wire framed Cartier glasses with the traditional lenses. Another $750 and then we went off into the city to get my day started.

On the way home I shot by Tashaun's crib to show him the shit I bought the day after the jack took place. Ironically he was telling Twizzy the story as I pulled up to his crib then they saw me with my new shit and figured I had a little more money stacked then they originally thought.

We chilled for a second but my phone was on fire with sales that needed to be met and females checking in on me. So I made a few quick stops to let everyone know that I was ok. The story of my robbery had spread all through the city so I had to prove that it hadn't hurt my pockets.

REGGIE GIST

I went to Rochelle's job to take her to lunch and reminded her to come by early to get the key because I was coming in later that evening. She was happy to see me so I let her show me off to a few co-workers and gave her $500 to get her layaway out at JC Penny's.

Jay had called with Lyve Wire to check about some studio time. He was going to be moving with his mom this week and Will was moving since he and his girlfriend had recently broken up. Around 9 p.m. Rochelle came through and I cancelled all my plans for the night to spend a little quality time with her.

The next morning she left for work then it was time for me to catch up. As soon as I jumped out the shower Tashaun pulled up to check on me. We headed out to IHOP to have breakfast, then to bend a couple corners in the hood. He had to pick up his son so I told him to drop me off at Rock's house because the studio and everyone else would fall through. Sure enough Lyve and Rell were in the lab doing what they do with my cousin Darcell helping on the tracks. He started me in the studio game and we supported each other on the quest to be the best.

About an hour or two later Tashaun called and told me he had something for me which usually meant a female he thought was my type. I had Lyve drop me off at my crib to change, and I waited for Tashaun to scoop me up. As soon I jumped in the truck he told me the scoop on this chick he had met named, Kerisha. When he had gone over her crib to blow a blunt, she had a friend over there that just my type and he needed me to play wing man.

Tashaun had never failed me before, so I was cool with that. We were always in a friendly competition. Once we bet on who could get the most girls to tattoo our names on them. Then we bet who could make the most home pornos. Then we bet who had the most females inside the hair show, in a magazine, at the club. Everything was a competition.

OPTIONS

When we pulled up to Kerisha apartment she came out looking like Lisa Raye and dripping with diamonds like Trina. She was a cool babe, no lie. After we picked her up we drove to her girl's house named Seta, who was definitely a sight to see.

We pulled up and Kerisha jumped out the truck I figured to give the scoop on me. She came back out looking pretty as hell. She was maybe 5'5 and a curvy 125 pounds with long silky hair and a gap like Tee-Tee's. She was dressed sweet with jewels and a Timeport two-way like mine. Kerisha made the introductions and I could tell she liked what she saw.

We stopped at the store and got a few bottles of Moet and rolled a few J's of some hydro they had. We drove around the city showing them off. We talked about a lot of shit and I soon saw that they were street smart like Tashaun and I. I had to have her on my team because she not only cute but connected as well.

Throughout the night we got so high that Tashaun decided to stop by his crib to chill for a second to see if we could liven the party up. We pulled to his crib and started smoking and drinking, then he shot a move by putting on a porno. A few minutes later the girls started laughing at the actors like they were amateurs.

"Yeah, I'm way better than he is," Tashaun said to Kerisha.

"Oh, yeah?" she said as grabbing his hand as he led her upstairs to his room.

A few minutes later Seta and I ended up in the kitchen with her bent over a chair doggie style with me pounding her little pussy. Not long after Tashaun came downstairs and signaled that it was time to drop them off. I enjoyed my time with Seta and knew that I had to fuck her again. The pussy was worth the chase, but next time it would be on my terms and my turf, for sure. We beamed each other our contact information and promised to keep in touch.

Time went on like usual. Tee-Tee had drawn back into her shell and it took some coaxing for me to get her out sometimes. Every so often she would call or stop by the studio, and if I caught her in a good mood she would let me fuck her in the bathroom at my Bro's crib. I loved to sneak and fuck. It gave me a rush, especially if the pussy was good. Tee-Tee was in my Top five with room for advancement, definitely.

The Auto Show was in town and even though I didn't go, Tashaun and I hung around downtown and cruised the club scene. While riding in his truck we bumped into Twizzy who had just gotten his Rolex from Gary. He was driving around too. Since we were three deep in Tashaun's truck I jumped into Twizzy's ride with him.

I wore my mink coat and hat and my Pluto Australian outfit that had hit me for $750. Inside my coat I stashed my 9mm that I had in case of another jack move. I was still on edge leaving out of clubs being that it had only been a few weeks since I had been robbed.

As a unit we drove past the River Rock and Captain's Bar to catch a few females in the parking lot. Then we drove to the gas station on Jefferson following Tashaun where we bumped into Boat and Fade. We spoke and exchanged numbers with our two-way then he pulled off.

Tashaun was kicking it with a chick at the gas station when the narcos pulled in and demanded everyone clear out of the gas station if you weren't getting gas. But before Twizzy could pull off the police jumped out the car to inspect the new Suburban that Twizzy had just got.

"Whose truck is this?" one officer asked. "Show me your license."

I sat quietly, trying to avoid eye contact as the officers stood by each door. I figured that we would be ok since our licenses were straight. That thought immediately evaporated as soon as they asked, "Are there any guns or drugs in the car?"

"Shit," I mumbled.

"Do you mind if we search the car?" the officer asked Twizzy.

I had tried to slide the gun from out of my coat to the floor to kick it under the seat, but at the same time the officers opened the doors to pull us out to be searched. The gun hit the concrete right at the foot of the officer with a sound that echoed in my head like an explosion. He grabbed me and cuffed me, then picked up the gun as evidence. Like a man, I owned up to the gun, but that wasn't good enough for them. Off to 1300 we went.

They drove Twizzy's truck to the precinct and booked us. We were thrown into a cell until the next morning when we would be arraigned. The next morning after laying on a cold slab of concrete without a cover, they came and told us that court would be at 11a.m. since we had money on us and no hold's we could be released until then.

I used the jail phone to call Rochelle and let her know I was ok, but there was no answer. Then I called Granny's house only to hear a slew of people in the background. Once they put me through I heard my mom's voice and I knew something was wrong.

My mom was living in Kentucky so for her to be here was another sign that something was wrong. I told her I was in jail and she started crying. But she wasn't crying for me, she was crying because my Granny had passed away that night.

My heart dropped as I let the phone hang while I cried for the first time since David had been killed. "What the fuck happened?" I screamed into the phone.

Mom explained that Granny had chest pains and they called 911 and the EMS came, but she passed away. The entire family was devastated and folks began to painstakingly make funeral arrangements.

Later that morning I went to video court and was given a personal bond for the gun charge of CCW (carrying a concealed weapon). Twizzy had not been charged since I confessed that he had no idea that the gun was in his car. We were released with all of our money still intact as I headed home to shower and rush to Granny's house.

I had to multitask while trying to get dressed and call and check on all my stash houses and workers. I also had to call Rochelle and my boys to let them know I would be with the family for a few hours. I picked up Jay we went back to Granny's to support the family.

It was chaos everywhere and everyone was unstable. Granny was the root of our family, our foundation. Her home was always open for any of us that ever needed it. She had been my living angel.

My Uncle Cody was still in jail doing a small bit as we tried to pay for him to come to the funeral. I talked to him a few hours on the phone and decided I would leave and let them plan things. But before I left, I pulled my Granddad to the side and gave him some money to cover the cost of the tombstone, which her insurance didn't cover. We hugged and comforted each other in one of the hardest times in either of our lives.

Several days flew by and Monday, Tashaun and I stepped out to Club Nickels. The scene was live as a few people came by to chat with us to get the latest news. Since it was my first appearance since the robbery everyone was observing me to see how I was reacting. Even Leona, in her sassy voice came up to me and said, "Damn, didn't you get robbed? I mean, I haven't heard from you. What you think I set you up or something?"

I ignored her as another female walked up and said, "Damn Rome, you shining baby!"

I guess since the robbery people assumed I would be down about losing some of my shit, but I wasn't fazed. My Coogi outfit and shining Rolex were speaking volumes. "Yeah, I got robbed a few weeks ago, but it ain't shit. I'm right back out here on my A-game," I replied to Leona who was still standing there gawking.

This was a major statement that had to be made to show all the other hustlers like Fade, Boat, Pop, Rock and several others that I had to ability to bounce back quickly. This meant that I had more money put away than everyone thought.

That night we met a lot of new dudes like Mark, The Watson crew and a couple other rappers that were local but hot. I also saw Seta and Kerisha stroll through the large club with a trail of nigga's chasing behind them as they sported their Rolex's and diamond rings. I waved but didn't intrude on their stardom at all. A simple gesture letting Seta know that I had played by the rules of the game and I would get with her later.

That night I had Nisha come over to Sherm's apartment for a quickie before her boyfriend came home. She left around 2:30 and then I called this new chick that I had met a few weeks ago to come through and stay until the morning. I was still down from losing Granny and tried to stay as busy as possible to avoid thinking about it.

The funeral was in a few days so I laid low from the studio and the circle until then. The day of the funeral came and Rochelle, Jay and Will wanted to come. Despite our relationship issues, she still had enough love for me to want to come comfort me and be by my side.

It was a wonderful Home Going Celebration held at her church, Peter Rock Baptist Church. The church was filled with loved ones and friends who spoke with compassion and sincerity about my grandmother. Even some of the young children spoke while others praised her lifelong accomplishments. My heart was broken as I stared down at the casket at my angel. I wasn't there, my soul was trying to pump life back into her. My mind was numb from pain and weed smoke as I drifted to another place

After it was over I hopped into the Lincoln and headed home to let Rochelle help make me feel better. It took weeks for me to get back in the right state of mind. It just wasn't the same without Granny. She was a key part of my motivation to succeed in life. It was Granny and my mom that who had made me the man I am today. I strived to make them proud every day. Now I had to switch gears to fill a void with a different kind of love. The love from the streets.

As time passed things began to get back to normal with me. My connects were still dropping what I needed. Tashaun and I were still in the mix of making money. Tee-Tee and I had fucked at the studio and began talking a little deeper. I finally got a chance to fuck Seta at her apartment. Rochelle and I were still off and on, but stable.

I was still dealing with a bunch of other women that all had their own life or a man, but whenever they were with me, the sky was the limit and they felt like they were number one. Each female had a unique quality about themselves and variety was always my fetish. Some had different sexual positions that they loved, different smiles, different attitudes and styles of dress. Each one had a different story to tell.

Over the months many would lose their spot only because I had so many options every day. Women like Jazzy, Leona, Joy, Zane and Cheryl would fall down several slots due to their lack of commitment to my cause. I still would pick up the phone every now and then to check on them to keep us on good terms. My rule was if you left on good terms it was easier to return on good terms. You never knew when one of them may come in handy.

It was close to Christmas and I was getting ready and stacking money for extra gifts. Mom had gone back to Kentucky and the family was scattered since Granddad had sold the house to move into another with his new friend. It was sad, but true. I moved throughout the small apartment bagging ounces and making calls to a few clients. Sherm knocked on the door to let me know he was leaving for a few, so be on alert. So I chilled playing NBA 2K by myself until Jay and two guys from the apartment came to join me.

I was waiting on my boy Rocky to come through with a pound of Hydro that he had tried to sell, but it was short due to a few people handling it prior to him. Patiently we chatted and smoked a blunt while I waited. I heard the buzzer buzz and got up to let him in.

I heard him screaming into the intercom, "Rome! Rome! The raid van just pulled up. The SWAT team is down here about to come into the building!"

My guest heard the commotion and I told them it might be a raid coming my way. I immediately grabbed all the money I had on me and hidden in the kitchen and gave it to Jay. I told him to run down the back stairs to the hidden exit in the back and wait until I called him to come back. He ran with his pockets stuffed while the other guys ran behind him. Then I ran down the hall to see if the SWAT team were coming in the building yet. It didn't look like it so I ran to Sherm's apartment and knocked on the door, but I forgot he told me he was leaving. So I either had to run back to my apartment and grab the key or run down the back exit like the rest. I quickly tried to run across the hall to my apartment, but noticed a trail of weed coming from Sherm's apartment to mine. Damn! It was too late to try to get it up because I could hear the building door opening up fast with a lot of voices coming up the stairs. I made a dash for my apartment, but it was too late.

"Get on the floor and show me your fucking hands!" a big burly white dude screamed at me. He was backed by about six other dudes just like him so I complied. Once I was restrained they asked me to show them where the drugs were at. I only had a pound in my room and a few ounces on the stove. They were not happy as they tore up my shit looking for more. It was only a one bedroom, but the search took forever. They even found my .45 Taurus in the fish tank base. I knew it was over and I was out on bond for the CCW charge, oh it was curtains for me, for sure.

To my surprise another huge officer had followed the trail of weed to Sherm's apartment and came back and asked me did I have keys. I told them I didn't know who lived there and pointed to my key ring on the table. The officer laughed and said, "Yes, you do."

A minute later I heard them kicking in Sherm's door with no warrant and rambling through his shit. They brought fourteen pounds back to my apartment and told me to lay claim to them. That's when I noticed that these looked like the same cops from the first raid. They talked to each other then wrote me a citation and uncuffed me.

"What the fuck?" I said out loud as all my neighbors stood outside their doors being nosy. I was pissed I had just lost eighteen thousand worth of product.

A few minutes later, Jay came back to check on me. He had the nine thousand I had given him in his pockets still. We figured the landlord had called on us and we found out later on that was true. I couldn't retaliate against her so I had to move. Besides she had given me a thirty day notice.

The next few days, I hustled hard to make up for the lost product and tried to find somewhere to live. I stayed with Rochelle for a few days until one of my boys offered me a crib on Colfax and Vancouver. It was a two family flat and his sister stayed upstairs. It needed some work but for $2000 he said I could get it. I gave him $4000 and told him to lay some carpet, get a new toilet and bathtub and we could take the overage out of the rent. No rent for four or five months was what I needed to help catch up.

Until the house was completed, I enjoyed my stay at Rochelle's. When it was done I offered to let her move in and as usual she said, "Not yet."

The house was ready and looked great and there were no nosy people looking at me. My landlord was a friend who knew what was up and was sometimes a client. I bought all new furniture and a few old things from the other apartment. Jay helped me moved and moved in with me to help keep me sane.

I soon found out that Sharice's big sister lived a few blocks over which meant that she could visit her and sneak away from her man without a trace.

"This was the life," I thought each night as Rochelle, Sharice, Tee-Tee and a few others took turns helping me break in my new home. This time I vowed not to handle my business where I laid my head. Even though Twizzy would come through, he was the only nigga outside of my circle that knew where I laid my head.

Tashaun unfortunately got locked up on an old case and had to do six months in the county. So I laid low from the hood and hanging out. However I made sure his spots were cool and his main chick was alright. I did what any real nigga would do and never crossed the sacred line.

Christmas was even closer and I had to get ready to get everyone's gifts. I was missing Granny like crazy so my spirits were down. The only thing that could bring them up was weed, money and sex. So I did it by fucking more and taking on more projects daily. It was a rush to me and since Twizzy started showing me love and a new lifestyle because he was loaded with cash, I had to set my goals to higher standard. His crew was all paid. Dudes like Big B, Wayne and etc. They all owned houses and businesses of all sorts. I learned there was much more to the game than to just being in it. It was how much you got out of it that mattered. So I watched and learned and became a solider for him and them while I stayed true to my own connects.

My life had taken on new meaning and I was still in my prime. In January, shit had taken a quick turn when my friend, Boat, had been shot in the head at a club. Thank God he survived. Then Sharice had gotten pregnant and I had to make her get an abortion, against her will. Then I had been given two years' probation for my CCW and lastly my new house caught fire one morning when my neighbor left her damn iron on and it caught fire.

Luckily, I was able to get out safely but a lot of my stuff was damaged and the house was no longer safe to live in. I had to put my stuff in storage and stayed with Rook and Rochelle until I made my next move. Twizzy gave me $2000 back for my trouble so now all I needed was to find another pad to lay my head in.

"No apartments" was my motto and no more flats. Until then I would enjoy a few more nights at the studio that we were adding on to and I could always get a quickie in. Then I would enjoy a few nights at Rochelle's apartment where the sex each night was live as hell. It would be crazy because some nights Jazzy would have a fit if she saw me and her together but she had to keep it to herself or she would get in trouble with both her crazy ass man and Rochelle.

All day I would make my rounds looking for a new crib and would stop by Dean's on Mark Twain where I would meet Nisha and a few others or Rook's where I would meet Tee-Tee, Sharice and Seta occasionally. It was cold outside and shit was moving slow, but at least it was moving. It was time to start to the new year off better than ever because this past year was jammed pack with ups and downs. "To live is to learn," I would always say because once you stopped learning then you stopped living!

CHAPTER 17

2001 and It Don't Stop

Snow falls at a slow pace onto the slush covered streets of the city. Cars and trucks drive around slowly trying not to slide of the road. I was still trying to find a balance in life after the holidays and I enjoyed the random visits and gifts I gave and received. Since I was staying with Rochelle we were able to get closer and that made a lot of the extra females fell off.

We talked about her moving in with me again and she still was unsure about that move. I couldn't peg our problem or decide why her fear of commitment was so high. Maybe it was because she didn't want to move with me out of fear that I would put her out or dog her out. Then she would have to rebuild her independence again. Or was she afraid of the "raids" and all that my lifestyle had to bring. Or maybe she just needed freedom to roam and to live a separate life. Whatever the reason, I wasn't going to allow her or her emotions to hinder my goals.

In February I searched extra hard for a place to live with Lyve Wire by my side. We located a nice condo in Dearborn that was clean, huge and available. I contacted the landlord who agreed to see me and show me the condo. She only lived a few condos down and was at least 70 years old. She asked a few questions as I told her I did music and worked for Ford. My display of fake check stubs and cash in hand was enough to get me the condo. Trust me, she was not an easy person to convince either. I would be the only black person in a five mile radius so that meant all eyes on me in this predominately Arab community.

Once I told her I had the deposit and two months' rent, she agreed to rent me the nice fourth floor condo. Moving in would be easy one. I found Jay and a few others to help grab my stuff out of storage. After a few calls to track down my helpers, I was told that Jay had gotten locked up for probation violation, and was in the County jail. Damn! I needed him so bad, because I trusted him to keep my location a secret from the streets. I had made a vow to never let a street nigga know where I laid my head in order to avoid anymore "raids" in the future, only family and a few women. The job was finally done with the help of my little cousin Ray. The move took a few hours but the results were wonderful.

I loved the new house and couldn't wait to show it off. A few days later I got a call from Tashaun and Uncle Cody and to my surprise, they had both gotten out of jail on the same day. I rushed to check on Tashaun who was getting shit back on track. Then I raced to see Cody who was doing the same thing. Out of love, I took him to Northland Mall and let him get a few things on my account. We shopped a little then I dropped him back off and got my day started.

The winter allowed us to stack more money. It was cold outside so the stash spots and the studio became the hangouts. We hung out there and smoked, made music, talked shit and showed off our latest girls. After a while I allowed Tashaun and Rook to visit my new place and everyone was impressed with the condo. It definitely upgraded my status.

Since Rochelle had declined to move in, a few other girls were special guest at my place. When I wasn't hanging with them I frequented the topless bars and searched for new prospects to entertain. I became a regular at the Brass Key, City Heat, le'Elegance, AllStar's, Grind, 747, BT's and a few others throughout the city.

I enjoyed the view at the bars and the confident dancers. Dom P with orange juice was my drink of choice with an energy drink as a chaser. The women came in groups and one by one I knocked them down, making them trophies under my belt. Rochelle couldn't stand this new fetish of mine so I had to keep a low profile by not driving to any of the bars.

I met a lot of women in the bars. Like a chick named Nicole. She was a half breed with long pretty hair. She was cool and understood my lifestyle which allowed her to become top ranked. As the cold days came and went, so did the women and people I encountered. Some just faded into the back of my mind.

At the studio things were moving along. My brother's friend Dris who looked more like a boxer than a promoter, was trying to get his crew's record label and ours up and out. With him, Lyve and Rock we were getting a lot of extra attention as we learned more about the music industry. I was introduced to a female rapper named, Shakun, who also joined the label and played her part. She became one of my favorite partners. Things were still cramped up in my life and every day was different. My circle was tight and everyone lived their life and experienced new shit every day.

Dean and his girlfriend had fallen in love and she moved in so Mark Twain was in the process of slowing down. Lyve Wire had become a loyal friend and road dog to me. I put a lot of trust in him and allowed him to see a lot more of me than the average. My dog CB had come back into the picture after getting settled in his new marriage and home in Southfield. I had missed him a lot so we played the catch up game every day and grew from friends to family.

It was early spring and a lot of shit was popping off. Nisha told me she was pregnant and the baby could possibly be mine. Since she lived with her boyfriend, the chances were slim in my mind. She refused to get an abortion because she felt that would ruin her relationship, so we waited.

Tashaun had called me for another co-pilot mission and of course I was down. My last hook, Seta was still in place but she was about that money. She was deep in the game with her girl Kerisha and they had become a hot commodity in the streets on all levels. I had much respect for her because she was all business when it came to the money and stayed true to our friendship. So when Tashaun, called I came with no hesitation.

He introduced me to his girl's sister named Mary. Mary reminded me of Seta and Sharice because she was about her money. She was 5'2, 135 pounds, light skinned with long black hair. This chick was cold to the bone. She even wore a Rolex and two-way and the latest Gator gym shoes. Our first date was a smash as we ate at East Franklin's soul food restaurant. We exchanged info and set up a one on one date for later. Eventually we linked up and became partners. I liked her for a few reasons, but mostly because she loved to fuck.

My hustle was great and everyone was eating on a major scale. In May I went to Cancun with Fade, Boat and a few other "Hood Stars." I left the city without a trace and brought my road dog "Q" with me. It was a wonderful trip as we took boat rides and snorkeled with the baddest women they could provide. We shopped like crazy and hit the night life like Superstars. We hit the outskirts of the resort and grabbed a few ounces of the best weed.

I would call back to the states to keep my squad on their toes. I pretended that I was sick because I didn't want anyone to know I was out of the county. The trip was great and as soon as we got back I jumped directly into my routine to catch up. Everyone missed me and I had to fuck extra hours in order to keep everyone satisfied.

The first two days home I had sex with Rochelle, Nicole, Seta, Sharice, Shakun, Alaya, Mary, Rhonda P and Trice. Damn! I was so tired and still had to hustle and run the studio at the same time. My life was exciting and the chances that I took made me a Champion according to me.

Once shit got back on track a few weeks later, I got invited to the Carabana Festival in Canada with Boat and a few other Detroit Hustlers. I really didn't want to go so I told him I would play it by ear. I had a lot to cover and plus a lot of product that needed to be moved in order to turn my profit to pay bills, etc.

While doing so much moving around, I noticed that it had been a while since I had seen or talked to Tee-Tee's little ass, so I reached out to a couple sources and to my surprise, nothing. I was worried about her and had no idea what had happened to make her go away. A lot of times I would lose contact with females because I lost my phone or just doing too much, but I usually kept track of Tee-Tee. Everything else was in place despite the fact that Tee-Tee wasn't around. So I decided to take the trip.

My mom had surprised the family by coming into town and introduced her new friend to the family. He seemed cool to us and easy to chill with. I had missed her so much and it was always a beautiful time when she was around. Too bad that I had already made plans to leave, but she understood as I gave her a few hundred bucks and an ounce of weed, along with the keys to my condo if she wanted to stay there.

I then called Vaughn and Shakun who had another friend with her and invited then to drive to the event with me. I would pay for everything and supply the smoke for the entire weekend. We all met up at my crib and packed for the trip. I sported my new black gator gym shoes, and a Fubu Platinum outfit to match.

I had told Rochelle about the trip. I left her my car and a thousand dollars to enjoy her weekend, so she was fine. The trip was great as we drove the seven hours to our hotel, sat our bags down and hit the strip. The setting was like Mardi gras as peopled filled the packed streets and partied into the wee hours of the morning.

Of course I bumped into Boat and Fade and we drank and smoked and got laid. Everyone was happy to see a nigga outside of the city limits and all the niggas wanted to fuck the two women that I sported as company. We partied with the likes of Vince Carter, Shaq and went to a small island party hosted by LL Cool J. Tired and restless we headed back to Detroit to continue the hustle.

Once we got back we headed to the studio. I talked to Dris and my brother about the trip, our new plans and how to elevate our lives and the label. As I soon as I headed home to check on Mom and my sis, my two-way went off. It was Nisha saying she was about to have the baby.

The moment of truth was finally here. I texted her Congratulations and told her to call me when he boyfriend wasn't around and I could see the baby. That was the longest drive home ever. I had a lot on my mind. I wasn't ready for any kids and I didn't want to hurt Rochelle with the irresponsible decisions I had made. This one could lead to us breaking up forever. I knew she couldn't have kids because she'd had her tubes tied, plus this blow would kill her. All I could do now was pray for the best results.

After several weeks of trying to recuperate from the trips and the fast life, I was spent. Mom had gone back to Kentucky, Rochelle was still front and center as my main chick, Tee-Tee was still MIA and my relationship with Mary had grown a bit. I figured it was because she didn't have a boyfriend like most of my female friends so she had time to put forth a little more compassion towards our friendship.

In June, Nisha allowed me to come see the baby girl that she'd had. I couldn't tell either way, but she told me that she'd had a blood test and it was her boyfriend's anyway. That was a close call and I let her know that I was cool with that. I would keep her secret and still be there for her and the baby in a limited capacity, of course.

I went back to the hood to celebrate. Tashaun had recently installed a wet bar in the back of his Suburban so we sat in the driveway and got blowed, then went to Floods to hang out for the night.

I bumped into Nicole, who I hadn't seen in a few weeks and she was looking good. So I bought her a few drinks and told her to meet me at my house after the club, to which she agreed. We fucked until 5a.m. before she had to get up to let her sister in out in Canton.

Things were back on track for me. My biggest problem wasn't the game or money, it was the multiple relationships that I had going on at the same time. Each woman played a specific role in my life, but I just couldn't be loyal to one. Maybe because I needed to feed my big ego or maybe I was a sex addict. Whichever it was, it was causing all kinds of problems in my life, but I never seemed to slow down.

A few weeks later I was standing outside of the barbershop that Rook worked at smoking a blunt and a car drove by honking the horn. It was group of females who were trying to get my attention. One of the girls got out and started walking towards me. To my surprise, it was Tee-Tee.

"Girl! Where have you been?" I asked her giving her a hug.

She explained that she had moved to Flint with her family and had actually been sick with a stomach ailment. Now that she was better she had decided to come back to the city. It was good to see her, but I made sure not to show any extra emotion as I gave her my number. I told her the studio was still the hangout and she should fall through later. She agreed and got back in the car with her girls.

Since my birthday was around the corner I had made plans to spend it with Rochelle that night and make my rounds earlier in the day. It was hard only because a lot of the girls didn't know I had a main chick and expected me to spend my birthday with them. I was used to avoiding these situations on the holidays like Valentine's Day, Sweetest Day etc. But birthdays were a lot harder because you had to choose to be with the person unlike the other days when they could choose to be with you. Rochelle was my girl and every event or family function we showed up as a couple despite our status at the time. Her family was my family and they treated me like I belonged.

Fortunately my plans played out like they were supposed to. Before I hooked up with Rochelle I visited everybody else and picked up my gifts and promised to hook up with them later after me and the crew finished at the "topless bar," or so they thought.

Instead that night Rochelle and I went to the Maxwell concert at the Fox, then out to dinner. We spent the night at her house, even though she didn't want to, and had great sex for several hours. I figured she didn't want to stay at her house because of the late night calls and drive-bys and I'm sure she was thinking I was trying to avoid the same problems. Anyway, the night went perfect and she even did the trick that I like.

The next morning she got up and went to work, but not before I gave her the business to keep a little something on her mind. The whole reason I fucked with her so long and so many times was because I knew she had other dudes on the side and I wanted to leave a hole in her that they couldn't fill. While she was at work, I took my time and looked through her stuff for evidence of another man. I found several things including a box of condoms with two missing out of it. I was mad as hell as I wrote my name on the box for her to find and a $20 bill and a note that said, "Need a refill for a cheap thrill. Rome was here." Then I left the apartment and called Rook for a haircut. I knew she would find the note, but would never tell me. That's just fueled me to continue to do me.

A few days later I was chilling at the studio when Tashaun, Dris and Lyve wanted to go to the Platinum on Six Mile. We were high as hell and I wanted to go, but I had just got a two-way alert from Big Booty Mary to fall through her crib for a booty call. She only lived five minutes from the studio in the same direction as my condo. So I told Tashaun I would get back with him tomorrow.

I was knee deep in the pussy when my phone started ringing off the hook. It was Tashaun's main chick telling me that he had been shot and to go to his house to make sure everything was straight. I jumped up and headed to his house in a panic.

The house was safe and locked up. I called her back to let her know and she told me that someone had tried to carjack him. He saw them coming and tried to get away and they shot up the truck to stop him. He managed to get away, but he had been shot in the arm, leg and wrist a few times. I was happy to hear that he was ok.

I headed back to my house to wait until morning to go check on him. When I awoke to my surprise, Tashaun was at my door in a rental Lexus with our homeboy driving him around. I let them in, we smoked and talked about what happened. I got dressed and rode with them to see the truck that was in the shop getting worked on. I couldn't believe all the bullet holes that had come through the windshield and had left holes all in the passenger seat and headrest. If had gone to the club with him, it was no question that I would have been dead. Yes, God was on my side when he allowed me to make the right move this time, for sure.

The next few days, I stayed close to Tashaun, riding with him as much as possible taking care of business. I helped him as much as I could then I had to drift away to fulfill my own business and personal obligations, one of them being Tee-Tee.

She had called me and said she was coming through the studio. It was cool because no one was there. Rook was cutting hair and his girl was at work for a few more hours. We ordered some food and talked for a while. Then she gave me what she know I wanted. It had been a minute since I had had her and I was anxious. Every time I fucked her it felt like I was fucking a virgin. She knew exactly how far to go up when she rode me and didn't mind me pushing her off me before I came. She would be all into it and wouldn't mind if I came inside of her. Yeah, I had missed that pussy. We fucked for a half hour and washed up before Rook got home.

Rochelle's birthday was in August and so was Tee-Tee's so I had to do some extra planning. There was no limit to what I could do, but there was a limit on quality time. I loved all the women in my life on different levels. However Tee-Tee just had a down to earth vibe and a "snapper" that I enjoyed. A snapper was what we called a tight pussy. A pussy so tight that when you exited from any position, you could actually hear a snapping sound. Only a few women could achieve this level of tightness and Tee-Tee had it literally on lock.

Tee-Tee knew my time was limited on her birthday, but I made sure she enjoyed it. Rochelle's birthday was strictly about her so I gave her money, fucked her steadily and let her enjoy her day with her friends, male or female. It was only mandatory that her ass be at my house no later than 2:30 a.m. or all hell would break loose and she knew it. She made it so I felt like nothing else mattered at all.

A few days after the birthdays were done and over it was business as usual. I got a call from Dris who told me to call his cousin "Kato" cause he needed to holla at me. "Cool!" I was familiar with who he was and had dealt with him on several occasions. We talked on the phone and he had set up a deal for us in Warren for some product since it was the beginning of drought season and he couldn't produce enough to fill the order.

That was cool, but I only had enough for half the order. I called Tashaun for some assistance and he agreed to lend a hand. A few days later we set the deal up and all followed each other to the set location. I rode with Kato and Tashaun rode with his driver, as his arm was still in the sling. We were a little late and when we got there we realized there was another person in control of the deal. In all we had four people and a fifth person who we never knew selling forty-five pounds of weed to an unknown source.

As we waited for the buyers to come to the location on Nine mile and Gratiot things got a little scary. The guy who was the fifth wheel started acting strange and trying to back out of the deal. Shit! We had rode outside of the city with all this work and now we had to drive back with it! Luckily a few minutes later I got a chirp on my Nextel that the buyers were ready.

The crew gathered our stuff and me and Kato drove to the location to show the buyers a sample of the product and to see the money before the rest came. Everything checked out, but it was a little tense as we waited with the fifth person to introduce the buyers. Since we were late it took them a few minutes to double back and get ready.

While we sat at the bowling alley, Tashaun sat at the Rite Aid waiting on the signal to proceed. A few minutes flew by and still no sign of them but I did notice a few police cars driving by. Maybe it because we were black in a white neighborhood or maybe it was just the police doing their round, I tried to rationalize. They never knew what kind of car we were in, they only knew the fifth guys Durango from previous sells. He decided he wanted to go inside the bowling alley so I went with him and Kato stayed in the truck to wait for them.

Tashaun chirped me and said he saw several police coming in our direction looking at us, so I told him to pick me up and abort the plan. I came out of the bowling alley by myself and headed for the car Tashaun was in. I jumped in the back seat of the Neon and told the driver to "Pull the fuck off!"

It was too late. As soon as I got in the small Neon's back seat we were surrounded by five police cars. The big white officers jumped out with their guns drawn and ready to shoot. The driver threw the car in park and we put out hands up in the air super quick except for Tashaun because of the sling.

They dragged us out of the car and placed us under arrest with Kato who was sitting in the Durango by himself. We were hauled off to the Warren police station. We knew it was a set up because the fifth guy who was supposed to be Kato's cousin, was nowhere to be found.

This situation was all fucked up and I knew I had messed up by not doing my due diligence on the clients or the deal beforehand. Now I was sitting in a cell with my boy facing several charges plus I was on probation for the CCW that I had caught with Twizzy downtown.

The entire precinct told us that it was sting that was set up several weeks ago by the fifth guy and the Warren police department. He was a rat that was trying to get off of some other minor charges by setting up his cousin Kato. Kato had no idea of this and had sold several pounds to the police through his cousin. They had asked him for a bigger load and he called me to assist in the matter not knowing that it was a set up. They had gotten three extra dudes in on a deal that they only expected to get two.

So we were processed and booked for possession and delivery charges, coupled with CCW and felony firearm. Since they had found the gun in the front seat of the Neon's armrest, they charged all three of us with it. Then since the drugs were in the trunk of the car that wasn't Tashaun's, or my name they charged us with intent to distribute.

The next day we were made examples of by being beaten and pepper sprayed by the police. We had to go to court and be arraigned and set a bond. That day everyone bonded out except me due to my probation hold from Wayne County, so I was sent to Macomb County jail with a Hold and $50,000 bond.

I hated this shit, but I had to adjust so I could figure my way out of this situation. I called Rook to give him direction on how to run the circle and had Rochelle check on the condo and etc. Since she didn't have keys to the place I had to release my personal stuff to her on the visit. This meant my cell phone, keys, wallet and jewelry was all available to her. The only good thing was Tashaun had an extra set and I had him go clear the condo of anything pertaining to another woman. I told Rochelle to contact my landlord and tell her the situation without the details. The rent would still be on time until I was released.

The entire hood had caught wind of what had happened and was pretty upset that I was the only one still in jail. After a few days in jail several letters came in for support by Nicole, Trice, Mary and Nisha. I had access to call collect and write as much as I needed. I would be in jail until my next court date which was in October. I had started letting my hair grow into braids. Rochelle was supporting me to by sending letters and pictures each week and by coming to see me on my visiting days.

September 11th came and shocked the world by the World Trade Center terrorist attacks. Shit was crazy in jail and out! Security was tightened while we were on lock down and everyone's bond was raised to the maximum amount. So I sat and waited for my lawyer who informed me that the case was weak due to me not having any contact with the police at all that day and no one knew my name or how I was involved. In the report my name never was mentioned except for me being in the back seat of the car that wasn't mine.

This was good news as I prepared to go to trial if necessary. Meanwhile, Rochelle was starting to act a little strange during my brief stint away. Like once I called her at night to talk and she picked up the phone. We talked for about five minutes then I heard a knock at the door.

"Who is that?" I questioned her.

"Just my friend coming over," she said calmly.

I heard a male voice and her telling him to talk quietly and I flew off the handle. She played it cool and told me to call her back.

I hung up the phone filled with rage. I placed those feelings and thoughts of murder in my memory bank. I never called back, but a few days later she came to visit me. She was looking beautiful as usual, but she was wearing a turtleneck in September. I told her to let me see her neck and she hesitated. I got up to leave and she stopped me to show me. As I suspected she had passion marks all over her neck. She swore she loved me and I talked over her.

"It's cool. Just check on my house for me," I said and blew her a kiss and left the booth to return to my pod. I wasn't really hurt that day, because the night I cried when she had company was the last day I would submit my emotions to anyone.

My court date came and they postponed it until November and I was pissed but my lawyer told me the case might be thrown out and to chill. Rochelle came to visit and sent a few letters that month and before I knew it, my court date had come up again.

The process was quick and my attorney did all the talking. They reduced my bond down to 10% of 50,000 and I headed back to the County after a few calls to my connect and Uncle and the money was given to Rook who came a day later to bail me out.

"Thank God," was all I could think while being processed out of the County jail.

At the last minute there was a problem. I just knew that my warrant for my probation had come up. I waited silently for the bad news, but it was that warrant it was one for a traffic ticket in Canton. I was transferred to the Canton police station when I saw a judge who gave me time served and a fine of $200 which was paid and finally I was released after ninety days in the belly of the beast.

The drive home was calm as we fired up a blunt and headed to Rook's house to drop off his girl before heading to my crib. I explained to him why I had to have someone else pay the bond money and how Rochelle played me in the County. I told him about the money that was put up in my home and I had another place where I kept twenty thousand stashed for emergencies. Since I didn't want to expose my secrets yet, I decided to go another route. He understood and gave me the latest on the circle and the hood.

Tashaun had tried to help him out when it came to placing orders. I called Rochelle at work and made arrangements to pick up my personal shit. I had had my phone turned off while I was in jail, but she still had access to my phone book and call logs. She was scared to bring my stuff to me, but I convinced her to bring it later that day.

Our history was so up and down that I never really knew when it was over. She came over that night and brought my stuff. She didn't stay or give me any sex, we just talked. She said that before I left we had been on shaky ground. This was new to me, but I let her continue. She said she was seeing a guy named Ted and that was who I had heard at her house the night I called. I wanted to shoot her in the face and dump the body, but instead I got up and walked away. She let herself out and I got in my ride and headed to the hood.

Yes, I was hurt because she was my girl, but since I lived a player's lifestyle I had to stay focused on myself and revenge. I continued to make my rounds and calls as I caught up with Tashaun, Live and Dris and told them what happened in court and etc. I checked on Nisha and the baby, called Seta, Trice, Alaya, Sharice, Nicole and a few others. My final stop was at

Mary's. She came out and sat in the car talking for a few. She dropped a bomb on me by telling me that while I was gone, she found out she was pregnant and had an abortion because she couldn't find me. She though that I had been locked up and wasn't coming home. I had to respect that. She had done what she felt needed to be done. We chilled for a little while longer then I made up a reason as to why I had to leave.

Being home for a week and trying to catch up and restore my position in everyone's life was exhausting. Since Rochelle and I had taken a break again and I knew she was fucking, I had to click into my zone to avoid the hurt and emotions. I called Tee-Tee, not only to fuck but to talk because she knew Rochelle and understood me. Luckily she picked up and told me that she had moved again and to meet her at the studio.

We met up and then she followed me to my condo for the first time. That night we talked, smoked and fucked until the morning. She cooked me breakfast and left me alone in awe. Even though I enjoyed myself, my mind was still wandering and thinking about Rochelle.

The only person that could relate to me was Rook, but he didn't care too much for Rochelle and would bash her until I got defensive. So I called him to talk, but like before he never got involved with our problems.

So my Thanksgiving was spent alone and I had to prepare for Christmas and the New Year. The next few weeks all my girls were on their best behavior trying to get a good gift. I had fucked so many of them trying to forget about Rochelle that they all blended together. The funny thing is that I had to tell them pussy wasn't a Christmas gift. They all agreed so I spent a few dollars trying to play Santa.

A few days before Christmas Rochelle called. I was surprised to hear her voice as she expressed that she missed and loved me. I figured her new fuck partner hadn't worked out or wasn't on my level. That's how it usually starts out and ends. After chatting and realizing that the power had shifted I talked her into coming over.

She was still kinda scared that I was going to flip on her, but she came over anyway. I couldn't get the thought of her giving up the pussy out of my head. All the jail phone calls and visits floated around in my mind. Instead of acting like an animal I decided to coax her into the bedroom where I would fuck her brains out. That night we fucked for an hour and a half straight. Every position was open game and even when I came in her and on her, my erection wouldn't go away. I kept thinking about the next nigga who was getting this good sex. All through the night her phone kept ringing and I would just roll over and fuck her some more to take away some of the pain inside of me.

The next morning we talked a little more about our future. I. personally was cool after a few nuts and looked at her like any other female. Rochelle had lost her rank, but still had my heart. I knew she loved me and I also knew she was hurt from all my prior indiscretions. I lived more than a double life and if I thought that she hadn't noticed a change in me, then I was a fool. I assumed she had fallen for this dude because he was the opposite of me and could be controlled.

Before she left she said she was going to leave him alone, but after Christmas. She figured since they had consummated their relationship, she was owed what was coming to her.

"Typical Rochelle," I thought as I let her out. Her actions were crazy, but since she was a square to the game, she actually thought she was running shit. My feelings for her weren't as strong as before because I knew she could jump ship at any time. This didn't sit well with me at all.

As the days passed moving closer to Christmas I felt a bit off, like something was wrong with my life. I was in constant contact with all the women in my life, except Tee-Tee who had done a disappearing act on me again. As I lied in my lavish bed, all alone, I realized that David was gone, my mom and siblings were scattered everywhere and I was searching for affection. How could I have everything I ever wanted, but still be alone at the end of the day?

On Christmas day, I chilled at home all day. Rochelle was out with Ted and her family for dinner. That killed me to know that her family had accepted another man into their family. We spoke briefly and she told me that she would come over later on. I was stuck watching movies all day while everyone else was enjoying the holiday with friends and family.

She came over later and we exchanged gifts, then made love. She didn't stay the night and I found myself once again alone. This gave me time to reflect on my life and my plans for the New Year.

On New Year's Eve I chilled at the studio and a few guys and girls came by. We smoked and drank but I left a little before midnight, to avoid the celebratory shooting. I got home poured myself and drink and watched as the big ball fell from the sky signaling a new year. I threw a couple thousand in the air, screaming, "Happy New Year to Me!"

My phone rang and it was Rochelle wishing me a Happy New Year. I just laughed and said, "Enjoy your night with your man and family. Trust me I'm used to being alone." Then I hung up and turned my phone off. Time for a better me and a better year!

CHAPTER 18

2002 – Role Play

The wind blew hard and the snowflakes fell to the earth's surface causing a slushy mess all over the ground. I sat at my kitchen table staring out the window day dreaming about my next move. I had just gotten off the phone with Sharice who was in Atlanta, then followed that up with a phone call to my lawyer about the Macomb County case. He told me that the case would go back to court in February and my chances of escaping prison time seemed good. Since I knew that some time would be required, I prayed for time served.

My thoughts were everywhere as my phone rang again and it was Rochelle letting me know she was on her way over to spend the night. Yeah, things were different but my heart was still the same. She had finally broken off the relationship with Ted, but the mere thought of her allowing him to get close enough to fuck her threw me for a loop. I'm a strong person and I know the rules of the game, shit, I had even help make a few over the years. But that was a pill that was hard to swallow.

I still kicked it with several other women. I guess as I safety net for when and if Rochelle decided to do her thing. But like the women, I lot of my friends came and went in and out of my life. As I conquered levels in the streets, my surrounding circle would change. Jay, Will, Dean, David, Chris, Hank and Twin and a few others exited my life. I had learned to never become attached anyway so it was pretty easy to adjust.

When she got there we talked about my court date and I asked her if I could depend on her to handle some things while I was gone. She said she would do anything that it took to help me and CB would also help her if necessary. I felt good about that so now I had to get the rest of my affairs in order.

Tashaun and I still played in the streets and I spent most of my time at the studio and playing video games with Lyve and Dris until Rook came home from work.

Valentine's Day was around the corner and I was ready for my court date. My plans for Valentine's Day were simple, drop off flowers or send them to their jobs with a few extras. Then Rochelle would take me out later. This worked because all of the other chicks had main men, so they would be spending time with them.

Sharice had called me a few days earlier and said she would be moving back from Atlanta, so I sent her some money through Western Union. I had also rode by a few of Tee-Tee's old hang outs. This girl would always dip in and out of my life. Strangely, it killed me and thrilled me at the same time. It was something about her that stood out from all the other women. I think it was her shyness and insecurities about our relationship. She wouldn't get too close because she knew Rochelle and wanted to protect her own feelings. The thrill in the chase was real with Tee-Tee, plus I wanted her. I knew she would come back around eventually after she finished playing the field.

Valentine's Day went as planned with Rochelle, and we had a good night. I loved when we were on the same page because our chemistry was at an extremely high voltage. Sometimes I wished our past wasn't so tainted. She wasn't a bad person all the time she just seemed to be a little immature. She wanted her cake and wanted to eat it too.

On the 23rd I went to court with Tashaun, Kato and Bird, the driver of the Neon. Rook had driven me out to Macomb for support to help me avoid getting pulled over on bond. The process was quick for us all. I was ten minutes late because of the roads and soon as I walked in my lawyer told me to wait in the hall with Rook. They took a brief recess and had a sidebar as we waited. Then he came and told me the agreement that had been offered by the Court. They wanted us all to take a cop for six months in the county with no probation.

Their case was so screwed up that they had to offer us something and plus we found out their informant had disappeared. So, we all had to agree to the cop in order for it to stand. We all did and then they gave us a court date for two weeks later to be sentenced. Before I left I asked my lawyer to ask the judge for time served which meant I only had to do seventy four days in the county. After a few minutes he came out and told me it was all good!

Tashaun was upset that Kato had gotten probation because this was his first felony ever. This meant that Tashaun would have to do five and a half months in the county, but he knew I had his back. He could trust me and it was mostly my fault that he was even in this situation.

Rochelle came over that night and we talked about our next move. I told her to move into the condo while I was away and if she stayed loyal we could start over fresh. She finally agreed, reluctantly. She was still concerned about losing her independence and submitting to me by moving there. In her mind it gave me too much control over her. I knew that she felt this way and I knew that a lot of things would have to change and I was willing to make those changes to make it work. I knew it was a big step for her so I tried to make it as easy as possible.

A few days later we moved all her clothes in and gave her furniture away to a few friends. I introduced her to my landlord and paid the rent up for three months. Since I knew I only had a week before I turned myself in I visited all my female friends and told them I was going away and embellished the story by saying my mom would be staying at the condo so it was no longer a hanging pad. Only a few had been there anyway so that made the transition easier.

Rochelle and I went over the rules and back up plans together like no company except family, no late nights out. She agreed to get a house phone so I could call whenever I wanted. I gave her money to hold her over while I was away, plus I had money hidden all over the house so she would be straight if an emergency came up.

The next forty-eight hours I got high as a kite with Tashaun, Lyve, Dris and Rook. I couldn't help it, I visited some of my "friends" to chill with or get a quick fuck before I left. I spent my last twenty-four hours out with Rochelle. We sipped Moet and fucked ourselves into a coma. The next day she swore to be true to me and I sent her off to work with a smile on her face.

Rook drove me to the jail as I prepared to turn myself in. I hated going through this process. I knew the routine like the back of my hand and I had to switch into convict mode. Tashaun hadn't turned himself in yet because he postponed his sentencing for a few weeks after mine.

My stay in jail would be easy because I knew the layout and the routine from my prior stay. I was stripped searched and then moved to my rock upstairs where I would spend the next fifty-seventy days. My Bunkie was cool. He was a young dude who was doing a year because of a DUI. We got along good and that was a good thing.

Once I got settled, time seemed to fly by. My hair was getting longer and I gained a little weight. I did push up's every day to get my strength up. I called home twice a day to check on Rochelle. I got mail every day from everybody except Tee-Tee and I really missed her.

My heart would beat faster when I questioned my level of trust for Rochelle. In jail you have a lot of time to analyze your past, present and future. I thought about how my lifestyle would have to change since Rochelle had moved in with me. I was actually happy about it and wanted it to work. She had to prove that she could be loyal and dependable on every level in order for me to fully release my safety net.

The future would be ok, but I first had to make it through the next seventy days, focused and strong. I did that by taking time to read all kinds of books. I decided to change the name of the record label to FlatLine Records or F.L.R. This time I would make it a legal company recognized by the state and registered as an LLC.

I couldn't wait to call Rook and let him know what was up now. He could spread the word to the rest of the crew eventually. Everyone liked the idea and moving forward and FLR was an official operating business.

My time flew by and before I knew I had three days left and Tashaun was just coming in to do his five and a half months. I called Lyve, Rook, Rochelle and my mom to prepare them for the new focused Rome. The day of my departure I was excited as Rook and Rochelle picked me up in the morning to take me to my castle.

Rochelle looked great as we hugged and kissed while Rook rolled up a blunt to celebrate my return. We drove and talked about things until we dropped him off then it was home to reunite. The house looked the same as I checked around for any signs of a nigga having been there. There were none, but as we sat down to talk she appeared to be nervous. I didn't say anything, but made a mental note then did my usual and fucked her until I was satisfied.

When she went to work I called Rook to come get me since he had my phone and car keys. He did, and as soon as my phone was in my possession I called everyone to check on them and to set up a meeting at the studio. Everyone showed up and to my surprise Lyve had bought a new white Monte Carlo and moved into a house on Schoolcraft and Ward. I explained to everyone about the label and that I would be moving the studio to Dearborn and buying all new equipment. The hood was excited to see us growing as a team.

I contacted all my connects and set up another meeting to get the product I needed to supply my clientele. Once I had this set up I hit a few local hot spots with the squad since Tashaun was locked up in the county. This is where I would network and let everyone know that I was home and business was open and ready.

I called all my ladies and made my playa rounds to ease the stress of me being gone. Things had gotten really tricky and complicated because a lot of them wanted to spend the night or wanted me to stay the night with them and this was impossible now that Rochelle had moved in. So out of respect, I tried to be home before 2 a.m. every night. I was cool with it since a lot of my time was spent at home rebuilding, stacking money and playing video games until Rochelle came home.

Our relationship wasn't bad and our time spent at home was special especially since she had held me down while I was in jail. As time went on she started to change her ways and slowly but surely started acting out of character. So I had to keep an eye on her and check her trail more carefully. Whenever she left for work I checked to see what color panties or thongs she had on. I also checked her phone and messages. She thought I didn't know her password, but I resolved that one day when she checked her messages on the house phone and I pushed redial on the phone and her password popped up. I saved it in my memory and would check her shit every day.

The first couple of days she was slick by erasing the messages as soon as she checked them. But while she was at work guys could call her job or come there and that would allow me to use special tactics. For a few weeks I acted like I trusted her as usual while I returned to my own life.

OPTIONS

Honestly my female rotation had slowed down sexually, but I would still hang out and chill with several of them. Then one day Rook called me and told me that Tee-Tee had come by the shop and asked him for my number. He was leery about giving out my number since he knew Rochelle lived with me now. It was cool to me since I had been looking for her again. A few hours later she called while I was in the hood and we chatted for a few trying to catch up. When she told me that she had moved in with her girlfriend on Joy Rd. and American I decided to fall through since it was close to my house.

I pulled up and she was sitting on the porch awaiting my arrival so that she could jump in the car to talk and smoke. We watched "Pimps up Hoes Down," on my car TV screen. The conversation was everywhere as I explained to her that Rochelle had moved in recently. Her entire mood changed but she remained calm. After we finished the movie, we promised to stay on track and I left on a good note.

As I drove home buzzed as fuck, I admitted to myself that I really missed her and I knew that we would be fucking real soon. When I pulled up to the house I had an uneasy feeling. I walked in quietly and could hear Rochelle talking in the back bedroom. I sat on the stairs and listened to her talked to Ted and several other niggas. It reminded me of the closet situation with her which was precisely why I always checked my closet when I entered the room.

Once she finished her conversation I acted like I had just gotten there and greeted her like normal. We cooked and ate like normal and when we put a movie on I checked her voicemail. There were several messages from different guys talking about sex and how they either missed it or liked it. It was cool. I didn't trip. I just moved to Plan B. Then we fucked all night then slept until the morning.

When she got up to get ready for work I called Lyve to come through in his car. He did and we rolled a few blunts while

I had him drive me to her job. We sat in the parking lot of the plaza on Inkster and Michigan. She never saw Lyve's new Monte so we could blend in discreetly outside the clothing store she worked at. We smoked and talked as I made phone calls to make sure the hood was in order. Then an hour and a half later a strange black car pulled up and parked next to her car. It was crazy because a man was driving, but he got out and went into the women's store. He walked in and talked to the other girls that were working then Rochelle came out.

"Ok, cool. Don't panic," I thought to myself.

They walked outside to his car and hugged, kissed and talked for a few. I called her cell and of course she didn't answer. I called inside the store and surprisingly they told me she as with a customer. Once he pulled off I got out and went to the Subway next door and got her lunch. I walked into her store and the look on everyone's face was priceless. I played it calm and hugged her, but no kiss was exchanged as I told her I was making a drop close by. She was a good actor but I was better as I laughed and walked out.

"See ya later baby," I said leaving out the door.

She knew that cat was out of the bag, but she didn't know what to do because I hadn't said anything. Since I knew she was up to her old tricks I started to get back into my old ways and played the game too. See, I could have been mean and put her out or treated her like she did me when we lived in the apartments. Instead, I allowed her to hang herself each night until she couldn't breathe any longer.

Meanwhile, my hustle got back on track and my playa rounds did too. My time with my other chicks was pleasurable and I still kicked it with Seta because she stayed connected to the underworld. This was a turn on to me. Even though we weren't fucking each time she visited, through her I learned a little bit more about the streets. She and Sharice were connected to major ballers in many different ways and they stayed up on the latest fashion and jewels. Niggas spoiled them because their high level of beauty and understanding of the game. These type of females inspired me to stay focused and be successful. I didn't care who they were fucking as long as we could remain friends then I was cool with it. A lot of women were a part of my life for different reasons, like these two.

My appetite for women was huge. I could never find all I wanted in just one woman so I had several to make one complete woman. Kinda like Voltron or the Fantastic Four, when together their power was at its highest and when separate the power was still there but not as strong. Many understood my reasoning and some didn't.

During this point in my life Tee and I had become so close it was crazy. I could talk to her about all my women and Rochelle and she wouldn't get mad. Actually I think it turned her on. Sometimes we would talk on for hours or even spy on Rochelle together while she noted to herself all the do's and don'ts of relationships. I was actually building her up by showing her the strengths of women. She learned a lot about them and me at the same time. Only because I was a major player and she knew it and accepted it.

One day we were chilling at her crib, after we had just taken my hair down and washed it. We had sex upstairs while her roommate was downstairs. The sex was extra special since it had been a while since we had been intimate. My favorite part was her doggie style position and the way she looked at me like she knew it was the best I'd ever had.

Anyhow, after we finished and washed up we headed for the car to smoke before I left because the kids were home. She didn't want me to leave. I thought it was kinda cute and wished that she could stay with me for the rest of the day. Seeing that I had a gang of girls that I had to visit that wasn't possible, or so I thought.

I figured if she was strong enough to accept me for who I was then maybe she could let me step my game up a little. "Tee, dig this. How about you ride with me and play like you are my cousin?" I said with a serious face.

"What? You silly, Rome," she replied.

"This way you can get up close and personal with my lifestyle and witness me in action."

"This is crazy Rome. I ain't trying to get in no sticky situations," she said shaking her head.

"That's cool. I understand. You just have to set the emotions aside and trust me. A lot of women have love for me and if you get emotional it will only cause issues," I said looking into her eyes.

Her eyes always told her true intentions just like when she looked at me when we were having sex. Since she had been around for a few years, I thought she could handle this situation. We had had threesomes and she knew a lot about me and my lifestyle. This would be the ultimate test of loyalty and trust and would allow her to move up in ranking amongst the top five women in my life.

So we went to visit a few of my female friends and I introduced Tee as my cousin and allowed each one to interact with each other. They all liked her and accepted her as my family, but only if they knew the truth! Over the next few weeks we stuck to our secret and I watched closely to see if anything had changed. It didn't take long for things to go awry. The fact that I had so many women in love made her see my power over the mind. The fact that I had sex with all of them made her jealous and upset at times.

Once Sharice came back from Atlanta and we started hanging out you could really start to see the change in Tee, especially with the cousin scheme. If she knew you were part of my Top five then she would try anything in her power to bump you down including Rochelle.

Back at home things were getting worse with Rochelle since I knew her little secrets. She never knew that I had her password to her cell, so she was more reckless than ever. Instead of treating her like an enemy or trying to make her miserable or kick her out, I just did what I needed to do in order to live my life.

She would always say things like, "You cheating on me or you don't love me, Rome." My favorite one was, "You'll miss me when I'm gone."

But to stop from killing her I would look her in the eyes and say, "I do love, just not your actions."

See deep inside I knew that she wasn't happy and wanted her freedom to roam the streets even though I took good care of her. Some females just like to be desired by many men like strippers. She loved the money and special treatment but she didn't love being tied to me. I understood the game and was learning how to understand the love portion of it, kinda like Tee was doing, I guess.

One night I was out making moves and I got a text from my neighbor telling me that my girlfriend was moving out. I was pissed and stopped what I was doing to rush home to catch her. Driving down Schaefer faster than ever allowed me to get home in minutes, but I was too late. She didn't have much to pack as when she moved in the condo was fully furnished. With just her clothes and personal items it didn't take long. She left a note saying that our relationship wasn't working. My heart dropped to the floor.

My thoughts were all over the place, but deep inside I knew that she had to be set free to be the person that she wanted to be and not the person I needed her to be. I tried to call her, but she wouldn't pick up the phone at all. I called CB, her sister and friends and everyone said they didn't know where she was. I could have waited and gone to her job to plead my case but instead I did nothing.

Her sister's boyfriend who was one of my customers eventually told me that she was staying in Westland hiding out from me. I guess she had found some old pictures and went crazy. She also told them that she had my voicemail code and had heard several disrespectful messages.

Cool, I'll let that be the reason for her departure, but both she and I knew the truth. Once she had time to explore her freedom if it was meant to be then she would be back. Until then my life had to move forward and my bills had to get paid.

The first few nights it was hard on me coming home knowing my in-house wasn't around. I would think about who she was fucking and get mad until I was bored and sleepy, plus she still wasn't answering the phone and never called me to talk.

Thank God for my circle because they stayed around to help me get over the hurt inside. Lyve would become more loyal and closer to me, along with Uncle Cody, D-Maz and Tee-Tee. Rook always stayed by my side whenever he wasn't working and Tashaun was still locked up for a few more weeks. Now it was time to take a step forward on many levels and since the weed game was at a major stand still due to the drought, I had to multiple my hustles.

I still had a few weed sales, but it so expensive and only a few guys had access to a small quantity. Hustlers like Fade, Boat, Rellee and Kato were among the few who could still fill my orders. Pounds were 16-18 hundred dollars while ounces were in the $200 range.

Damn! Ever since Wacky Wayne and a few members of the local rap group "Street Mob" got pinched, shit had been crazy. Niggas had to buy high price exotic weed just to support their own habits. Connects like Seta and Sharice always knew a few dope boys who had a major supply of that, so it was good to know who you knew at this point.

After getting used to Rochelle being gone I started letting Lyve and Tee-Tee stay around a lot more. Especially since everyone knew her as my little cousin and accepted her as that. Lyve had signed with a local management company and they had a project for him to work on. He came to me and asked me to sign on as his head manager and handle the event with him.

"Cool," I told him and they set us up a show in North Carolina for the weekend. It was a much needed break from the city and my high maintenance lifestyle. We packed up our clothes and camcorders along with Lyve's demo of instrumentals and prepared for the quick vacation.

Before we left, I let Rook know to check on the condo over the weekend and to watch out for Rochelle because she still had a key to the house. Then I called a few of my females, including Tee to let them know I would be gone for the weekend. Before we headed out I contacted Dris for Key's new cell number to go shopping for the trip. Key's agreed to meet me at his mother's house to show me his goods. We kicked it about the case that we had caught and I bought an ounce to take with us on the trip.

We boarded the Greyhound bus as we rode with Ms. Cain the manager and CEO of the company and a few other artists. We arrived at the hotel eighteen hours later and couldn't wait to check into our room to get high and practice for the show.

We walked around the hotel complex and found a Waffle House and sat down for a quick bite to eat. A few of the other artist were still arriving at the hotel. I noticed a slim female looking and pointing at me like she knew me or something. I was wearing a Maurice Malone jumpsuit with the gym shoes and extra jewelry. Maybe I was looking like a rapper or maybe she wanted to meet me. However, once we finished eating we started walking back towards our room for a smoke and for me to learn the songs Lyve was going to perform. A few seconds after we rolled the blunt there was a knock at the door.

"Oh, shit! Damn, that might be the hotel security," I said putting the blunt out. I went to the door and opened it up slowly and to my surprise it was the two females from the Waffle House.

"Rome, why you acting like you don't know me?" the tall one said.

"Damn, I'm high as hell, baby. Who are you?" I asked her.

"You can't remember who you fucked several times and got caught by your wifey in the process?" she whispered in my ear.

My high ass mind still wouldn't let me process who she was. She could tell by the look on my face that I was sincere so she finally told me her name.

"It's me, Jamie, nigga," she said hitting me softly on my shoulder.

I remembered her when she told me her name, "Damn, it's been a while," I said as Lyve approached her friend.

"Yeah, it's crazy bumping into your ass down here," she said accepting Lyve's invitation to come in.

She told us that she was on the same showcase as us and drove down to Fayetteville because she missed the bus. I slowly began to remember the full incident from my apartment on Telegraph. I had almost got caught fucking her when Rochelle popped up uninvited and tried to kick the door down. Jamie was naked and had to hide in the closet until the manager asked Rochelle to leave.

OPTIONS

Jamie worked at Ford and was trying to get her music career on track. After the incident we stopped talking because she said I came with good dick, but extra drama. To see her again was cool and we had a blast over the weekend catching up.

The day we performed, Lyve and I were ready. Right before we hit the stage, my cell and two-way went off several times. I snuck a quick call in before my cue to hit the stage came. It was Dris telling me that Kato had been killed a few hours earlier. They had found him in his driveway.

My entire vibe was changed because Kato was a cool dude who didn't deserve that. I hung up from Dris and hit the stage to do what I can do best. After the show I told Lyve the situation and we went back to the hotel to pack up to leave the next day. We blazed a blunt and talked about Kato and the times we had shared. It was crazy because before we had left I told Kato to be careful out in these streets. It was drought season and niggas were thirsty.

He always stayed to himself and hung with his girlfriend. It wasn't safe bringing people to the house. It was a sad moment as we prepared to leave for the city. We drove back with Jamie and her girl to help them get home safe and quicker. We arrived back at home around 3:30 a.m. so I allowed them to stay at my house until the morning.

We unpacked, smoked a blunt and fucked until we fell asleep. The next morning we all exchanged numbers and I told her my studio would be up and running in a few weeks after we transferred the equipment to the new location.

The following day Rook came over to check on me and give me the 411 on Key and the streets. I called everyone to let them know I was back and safe then we watched the video of our performance from the trip. We discussed the future of FLR, while Rook and Lyve played PlayStation.

I walked upstairs to call Rochelle, but still no answer. Then I called everyone else in my circle to see what my next move would be. Later my nigga Rellee came through to join us and showed us the latest skit from his TV show, "7 to the Isle." Then Dris came over to talk about the funeral for Kato and what really happened.

Since my crib was full and the streets were crazy, I decided to chill for a few days and lay low. Finally, Rochelle called me and told me and she was staying with her sister over in Westland which I already knew. Briefly, we talked and since I did miss her, I told her whenever she felt like talking to call me. I knew she wasn't happy staying there and wanted her own place, but she had made this move on her own.

Eventually, she would agree to meet with me and show me where she was staying and to also tell me that her sister was leaving and wanted her to take over the lease. Our relationship was crazy no doubt, but something about her kept me crawling back.

Days after Kato's funeral I felt a little low so I called Tee to chill with me. She told me to fall through and smoke a blunt to ease my mind and I did. Once she told me that shit was crazy at her crib and that she had to move out soon because her roommate was getting evicted. I knew Tee had a job and was waiting to get a better position at D.M.C. downtown and all she needed was a little help to get her on her feet.

My life was so crazy at this time that I considered letting her move in with me. My hustle was stunted a little because shit was so crazy in the street, plus I had taken a lot of losses and my monthly bills were high, so we decided that she would move in so that we both could save some money.

This was going to be difficult because if Rochelle and I decided to get back together, shit would be crazy. Then a lot of females knew Tee as my cousin and accepted that but the emotions could come in and crash and burn by me dealing with so many women. So we agreed on certain ground rules. Tee knew her position and promised to control her emotions in order to make this work. I could still have my friends and she would still continue to play as my cousin whenever they were around. She would also pay her part of the bills and keep up her part of the house.

After finalizing our understanding, Tee was up to the challenge and planned to move in by the weekend. We never discussed the amount of time she would stay, so we left that option open.

The transition wasn't as bad as I thought it would be. It actually went well for the first few weeks. My squad and family adored her and understood our position in each other's lives. Having her around was not like having Rochelle there. Tee had value in women skills such as cooking three meals a day, cleaning every day, grocery shopping and allowing me to do me. Her only concern was me coming home every night and to not let any females stay the night.

We would chill with my crew and my other females while she played the role of my cousin. Many like Sharice, Alaya, Nisha and Trice really enjoyed her company as well. Yes, we had a few ups and downs. I had started building the new studio by purchasing thousands of dollar's worth of equipment. So a lot of my time was spent there.

Then Rochelle and I started spending time again and that made it really hard for Tee. By her living with me, her feelings had grown deeply for me and she wanted me to herself. The mere thought of Rochelle and some of the others would send her on an emotional roller coaster. My actions were not changed and I had to remain strong and emotionless in order to stay in control.

Tee tried everything to keep me close. One day she even surprised me with a tattoo of my name on her lower back. Then she would pay extra bills and buy me things with each check. Shit, I'll give it to her she gave me 110%, but it couldn't change my feelings for Rochelle.

Once Rochelle and I started getting closer I had to switch up my routine to avoid any drama. It was crazy because some nights when she wanted to come over and spend the night, I would convince her to stay at her sister's house instead. Rochelle never suspected this because if she had all hell would have broken out. Some days Tee would spend the night at hotels or at my family's house just to avoid a confrontation. Tee hated this option and voiced her hatred for it every time it occurred.

It was hard for me because Rochelle could pop up at the condo anytime and catch Tee there. Since they knew each other the affect would be horrible. Rochelle's family was still like my family even though we had several problems in our relationship. The pressure was building up inside Tee and my relationship, but we could overcome anything if we stayed on the same page.

Some nights Tee and I would stay up talking and listening to Twista's 'Emotions,' song and plan for the future and what direction to take. I knew it was hard for her to be in the situation, but she just didn't know it was hard for me too. I didn't want to lose either of them and it took a lot out of me to hide my feelings. Things weren't always bad or so serious at the home-front during her stay. Only when it came time for me to spend time with Rochelle, did we have problems. Everyone else didn't matter or allow Tee to feel threatened.

For example, one day Tee and I were sleep upstairs at the condo, Lyve who often stayed nights to work in the studio or act as my side kick had left early in the morning to take his children to school and left the back door cracked so he could reenter without waking us. Wrong move, because while we were sleep, all hugged up, I heard the stairs creaking and footsteps approaching. Seeing that no one came to this level in my house, I grabbed my .45 Cali that I kept close to my bed. I quickly aimed at the door, only to see a set of wandering eyes looking directly at me. I jumped up and so did Tee as the person ran back down the stairs quickly. Once I caught up with the intruder I was surprised to see it was Alaya who immediately apologized.

"Sorry Rome for popping up, but I was on my way to school and wanted to check on you beforehand," she said nervously. "Who you in the bed with?"

I just smiled and asked how she got into my house. I really didn't care, I was just happy she wasn't Rochelle. She explained that the door was open and she was worried but when she saw another person in bed she got scared and ran.

Damn! Now I had an option to either tell her the truth or lie as she waited for an answer. So I just told her that it wasn't anybody to worry about and to go to school.

"Yeah, ok, but when I get out of school she better be gone," she said as she turned around and walked her big booty ass back to her car.

Tee came downstairs after she heard the door close to see if the coast was clear. She laughed out loud after I told her who it was, thinking she had knocked one of the out of the circle. If only she knew.

We chilled around the house for a few hours and eventually Lyve came back and we started playing Madden on the PlayStation. We all froze when we heard a knock at the door. I looked out and saw it was Alaya, as promised she had come back after school.

"What up Rome? Is she gone or what?" she asked angrily.

"Let me talk to you for a minute," I said as I closed the door to hide our conversation. We talked while I explained the current situation and who Tee really was in my life. She was hurt but had enough love for me to at least try to understand. We talked about it a little more.

She calmly said, "I'm not leaving, Rome."

"Neither is she, Alaya," I said with a blank expression on my face.

Then she moved me out of the way and went into the house and sat at the dining room table to roll a blunt up. Tee and Lyve were upstairs with the camcorder laughing because I had got caught up. I yelled at them to stop bullshitting only because it could get ugly dealing with females. They did as I said and I continued to talk to Alaya trying to calm her down.

After a few puffs of the weed she said, "I'll be back." She headed for my room where Tee-Tee was. Lyve came downstairs and looked crazy as I followed him to the basement to have a drink from the miniature wet bar in my studio. I was kinda scared hoping that they wouldn't start fighting in Dearborn because if the police came out we would all be fucked.

After several minutes nobody showed up and there was no arguing to be heard so I figured they were talking. They did know each other well since she was my so-called cousin first. I got my nerves together and went upstairs to check on them. To my surprise the both of them were sitting on the edge of the bed smoking and talking. Slowly I walked into the room.

Tee-Tee said, "Don't be so scary. We worked it out."

"Yeah, we both good and we both staying here, "Alaya said holding the blunt.

"Game time," I thought to myself as I hit the blunt for some extra energy. Before long we were engaged in a beautiful threesome. We tried everything like me watching them go at it, to me fucking one doggie style while she ate the other one's pussy. They both were beautiful and the fact they both loved me gave me an erection that could break a door down.

OPTIONS

It was wonderful to experience this with these two sexy ass women. The entire night we sucked and fucked our way into a deep sleep but before we did, I had to watch them both give me head as a team until I came one last time before bed.

The next morning Alaya had to leave, but before she did I had to give her a quick one on one while Tee made breakfast for all of us. See sometimes when faced with adversity as a man we must look the situation in the face and take control of the leverage that'll give us the outcome that we want. From that night forward they both were happy with their role in my life and the position they had to play in order to get the results they wanted.

Life with Tee wasn't all bad, but teaching her how to control her emotions was a task to reckon with. Over the next few months many more obstacles came and left and Rochelle was still deep in the picture. The holidays were fast approaching and I knew that only presented another set of issues I would have to conquer. I would deal with them as they came. But for now it was time to play Santa. Ho! Ho! Ho!

CHAPTER 19

2003 Boomerang

I was grateful to see the New Year come and even more grateful that I was around to see it. Things went surprisingly well for Christmas and my cover with Tee-Tee hadn't been blown. I was actually enjoying my double life and the pleasures that came along with it.

Having Tee as a live-in girlfriend was stirring up a lot of emotions and controversy. Only a few understood the level of commitment that we shared for each other. We still had a few bumps in the road that needed to be smoothed out, but we addressed them as they affected us.

Things like Rochelle wanting more time or when I wanted to play the field would always start the bullshit. I knew Tee loved me on an entirely different level than the other girls because of her loyalty and the sacrifices that she made.

Her bond that she had with Alaya was beginning to grow which only made her hate all the other women. So she would sometimes do silly things to destroy my relationships or get me caught up. She would call Rochelle and play on her phone or stomp around the house if I had another female in the house. She enticed me to fuck her every day so that the other chicks only got a quickie.

I didn't mind her attempts and just found a better way to maneuver around the obstacles. Rochelle was staying at her new apartment and our relationship was still the same. She loved her freedom and her new location only because it was harder for me to travel down Michigan Ave. only because I wanted to avoid the police at all cost. Since I kept a gun with me at all times I couldn't risk getting caught in Inkster with one, plus she knew this and was happy about it.

Her job was only a mile away from her apartment so she hardly ever came into Dearborn, so Tee was nice and tucked away. In a week's time I could split up my time evenly at home and with Rochelle.

The drought in the city was ending and my connects were moving product rapidly. During the drought season a lot of players had gotten killed or locked up, but Tashaun and I had survived.

My hair was long in length and I wore it in crazy braids. My clientele was coming back into play and all the women were still hanging around and I was meeting more by the day. I got my hair braided along with Rook and Tashaun who had grown theirs out too, at my friend's shop called 5th Ave on Fenkell. This shop was live as hell and featured beautiful women of all sorts. Within a few weeks I had fucked at least four of the stylist at this shop. This gave me the idea to start my own shop for Rook and I in the future.

The studio was starting to become more advanced as I spent countless hours and money trying to build my brand. A lot of my friends would support and hangout at the lab to inspire me to stay focus.

Tashaun was still getting money and buying a different car every other month. My Uncle Cody was still hanging around, but not making any power moves at this time. My other uncle had moved into his new house on the west side and was closer to me. He was older and married, but still loved the street game and the benefits it came with. So a lot of times I would fall through his crib to smoke or conduct a deal in an environment that I felt safe in.

Other cats like Lyve, CB, Darcell and Rook were still cool and close to me and played a major role in my life daily. At home Tee was still taking care of business and she proved time and time again that she wanted to be with me. My money was starting to look good again and all my ducks were lined in a row.

I had started hanging with my boy Rellee and his crew who were a part of Comcast Network Team. They were hosting their own TV show about Detroit and its talent, called Seven to the Isle and The Glove is Dirty. We interviewed several artists, major and minor industry folks like Bun B., Luda, Scarface, Lil John, Lil Scrappy and Special Ed and more. I was blessed to be in the presence of great artists and as usual my product was also in high demand amongst them.

My street status was growing and it was time for me to take my life to another level or at least try. Being that things were casual at home with Tee, I started taking her for granted and became a little sloppy with my pimping. The pressure was building up as we argued over several in house issues. So I started hinting on the subject of her moving out to get her life in order. Deep down inside I knew this couldn't last forever and if we got caught the pain would be unbearable to us all.

She never liked the idea and would brush me off by doing everything that I wanted and needed from the heart. Like one day I had been out all day and had come home late with a new pair of turn tables and needles. Once she saw this she automatically assumed that a girl paid for the stuff and began to go crazy. So I kindly walked out the house to cool off by driving around until she calmed down.

I had picked Rook and Lyve up to show them the new addition to the studio and how to work the new system. We pulled back up to the house and entered the lab in the basement filled with excitement and motivation. I turned the DJ equipment on and placed several records on the turn tables but no sound came out of the speakers! We couldn't figure out what was wrong with the $2000 system. Then something told me to check the needles which cost me $300 apiece. To my surprise there were no needles! They were gone completely and I knew just who had them.

I stormed upstairs only to find Tee looking crazy like she didn't know what I was talking about. When she saw that I was seriously mad, she gave them back to me, but they were broken. I wanted to kill her ass, but instead I made her pay for them out of her next pay check.

Things like this happened a few more times. Like the time she kicked out my basement window because she thought I had locked her out because I had a girl in the house. Tee was small but where she lacked in size she made up for in attitude and aggression.

I had taken on a lot trying to rebuild my empire and control multiple women at the same time. However, I stayed focused and shifted into high gear. Since Granny had died my vision for success had become even stronger and more vivid. My mom and siblings were still far away and I missed them as well.

I needed to make some changes that would alter my stride for the best. Rochelle was still my main chick and Alaya, Sharice, Nicole and Parish, a new chick I had added to my roster, still played their role in my world as usual. One time I brought Sharice to the condo to smoke and chill with Tee and things changed real quick. See, Tee didn't like Sharice and had only accepted Alaya into our circle. So once she thought that Sharice had fucked me in our room when she dozed off on the couch, it was all over.

From that point I knew that she wanted out and couldn't handle our arrangement anymore. A few months later she had devised a plan to disappear without a trace, again. I wasn't surprised, but I was hurt only because I wanted her to myself. I came home and relived that entire Rochelle situation all over again. Damn. Twice this shit had happened to me and both times I never knew what had gone wrong.

I had to stay strong and focus because Rochelle would be coming around more now that she was gone. But where had she gone? Why did she leave like this? So many thoughts ran through my mind and it killed me not to hear from her.

Several weeks went by and still no word from her and my heart was so confused. I knew she loved my uncle and aunt so I spent a lot of time over there, hoping she would stop by or at least let them know where she was. Their house became a hangout and the entire block became loyal customers of mine.

A month went by and I still hadn't heard from Tee so my focus had to change. I concentrated on building my label and making money on the streets. Tashaun and I would still hang out at the local clubs like Captains or the Dynasty and then Chuck's on the weekends. He was still my Ace and even though our business wasn't the same our loyalty and trust always stayed the same. The next few weeks I spent a lot of time with networking in the streets and with Rochelle in the sheets.

Did I miss Tee-Tee? Of course, so I was so happy when she called me about half way through the summer and gave me her new number, but not her address. We would talk briefly and she would tell me about the new relationship that she was in which killed me inside. I tried to push her out of my mind and life out of anger and regret so I built mental blocks to avoid being hurt and distracted.

So to take my mind off of Tee, Rochelle and I started doing all types of shit. We went to comedy shows, plays, concerts and basketball games at the Palace. Her favorite spots to chill at were at Dave and Busters or the Casino where she loved to play Blackjack.

Our relationship wasn't the best, but we managed. Her family still supported us and CB was my main man. Of course I still had a full roster of women that I could have divided my time between. Instead I stayed focused and I balanced the studio and the game. My new motto was, "You can't have both. Either you'll have a lot of time or a lot of money." I preferred to have a lot of money and no kids. Dealing with so many women I had to make sure that I avoided that at all cost, even though I hated condoms.

I guess I hated being alone because it reminded me of the lonely nights I had in prison. So I vowed to never sleep alone, unless it was by my own choice.

My Uncle Lee helped me appreciate my idle time when it was slow in the streets. I chilled with him at his house all the time with hopes that maybe Tee would fall through. I still made my money, but my mind and heart where searching for Tee.

One night I was really missing her, so Rook and I were leaving the Topless bar I decided to give her a call. We were driving down Eight Mile headed home as the phone rang. It was late as hell so I half way didn't expect her to answer. "She may have had company or something," I thought.

I was so happy when she answered sounding sleepy and tired. Her guard must have been lowered because I was able to convince her to let me come over.

When she gave me the address I was shocked to know that she had been hiding in plain sight. She had moved to the Grayton Park apartments where Rochelle and I had lived years before. As a matter of fact from Tee-Tee's window you could see the entrance to the apartment that we had shared. How crazy was that?

She hesitantly let me in as I was more than a little buzzed from the excessive drinking and the funny pills I had taken. I could tell she was a little worried about how I would react to her just up and leaving, but little did she know all those feeling went out the door when I saw her sexy ass in her pajamas. The wind from the early morning breeze blew her bottoms just enough for me to see the gap between her legs.

OPTIONS

My mind went into overdrive as I scanned the one bedroom apartment for the first time. I liked the set up. It was really nice and smelled like passion fruit. We sat and talked for a few minutes while she rolled up a blunt of Hydro that I had with me in a small jar.

Once she knew that I still loved her and missed her she became relaxed and led me to her bedroom. I couldn't resist the temptation to fuck this good little pussy despite the emotional connection that would come later. So once we hit the room it was on to the max! All I can remember is that she was on top of me riding me and taking control. My hands moved all over her silky body, rubbing her large breast and landing on her nice round ass. The more she moved and grinned the quicker it made me want to cum. The next thing I knew I pushed down on her shoulders so she couldn't really move and pulled her close to me as I pumped harder until I came all inside her little pussy. Damn!

"You caught some of that," I said to her in the moment of lust and passion.

She just smile and continued to move her pussy muscles squeezing out any cum that was left over. Shortly, after the sex session I tried to fall asleep but to my surprise she asked me to leave. I was shocked but I did what she asked. Then I drove back to Dearborn at 5 a.m. and got a few more hours of sleep.

The next day she called and we agreed to just stay friends to avoid the emotional rollercoaster. It was cool with me as I kept my focus on the streets and the studio, but I was a little shook though because she had some good pussy.

Over on my uncle's street, his neighbor was about to move so I asked her could I rent her house since I needed somewhere to serve my clientele. I promised to take care of the place but she said, no. After a few days of persuasive talking and me flashing a few thousand dollars in her face she finally agreed. This house would be used as my local trap to provide product to the public twenty-four hours a day. Eventually I would open up selling $10 bags of hydro at 0.8 grams per bag. I would also use the house to conduct the majority of my big sells as well.

Lea and her friend Pooh, were two young girls from the Mile that would become loyal workers and playmates at the same time. The first few weeks the trap was moving slow as I networked through the hood to create a buzz. After the first month things picked up as the word spread around that I had the best shit around. I was paying $2200 for a pound of hydro and my Uncle Slybone would front me four to five pounds on consignment. The profit was out the roof.

In the meantime, my Arab connect was still on deck and kept me with major units of the mid's. Money was getting better since the drought and my vision of the studio and the barbershop was coming into view. All I had to do was focus, save up and keep things in line with my squad. Rook was my main man and guys like Dris, Lyve, Rellee, Lil Damien and Duke were all prepared to hustle hard. We had to move as a unit in order to get the best results.

My Uncle Lee had become a team player as well and he made sure my back was covered at all times. Uncle Cody was still around, but not as involved as before. Something was up with him and sooner or later he would come around, so I had to win in order to provide for my family. Someone had to take a stand to be above average and that somebody was me.

My life was like a movie with several guest appearances and no doubt I was in the starring role. Now that the world was mine for the taking nothing could get in the way of my success. Or at least that's what I thought.

My phone rang one day and when I checked the caller ID I saw it was Tee.

"What up, baby?" I said calmly

OPTIONS

"I'm pregnant and I'm keeping the baby."

"Oh, shit! What am I going to do now?" was my first thought. My second, "What about Rochelle?"

CHAPTER 20
2004

After talking to Tee about the baby, things went sour. We argued constantly, that is whenever we would talk, which was rare. My life was good in every other area, except here. The studio was up and running and we were putting out demos every other week. The trap house was moving major weight and making me a major profit. I was making 6-8 thousand a week. At home, Rochelle was still around and we were spending a lot of time together.

However, I still tried to convince Tee-Tee not to have the baby because of all the consequences that would follow. She was friends with Rochelle's sister and as soon as she found out, that would be the end of us. I still loved Rochelle and I knew that as soon as she found out about the baby, she would be gone for good.

Rochelle had been pregnant by me before and I asked her to get an abortion. After the abortion she got her tubes tied, so this would absolutely devastate her.

Meanwhile, I kept trying to convince myself that a baby would slow my hustle down and take away from my personal time. I wasn't ready to be a daddy, I kept telling myself. But who was I fooling? I had come inside of Tee on purpose and really didn't mind her having my baby. Since Rochelle couldn't have any more children, I secretly yearned for a child of my own. But how could I pull this off without causing major pain and an emotional breakdown?

Tee had her mind made up and since she knew I really didn't support the baby idea, she completely shut down on me. She wouldn't answer my calls or call me back. I would try to call her from different numbers then hang up once she answered. Damn, I can't lie I still loved her and I was concerned about her.

Life was about to change once the baby was born and as a man I wasn't ready for the pressure. I tried to question whether or not she really would have it, or if I was even the father. But I knew I had to get ready one way or the other.

Back at the trap, shit was looking great! I had a swell team, with my uncle watching over the girls that worked the trap for me and Lyve and Damien making sure the block runs were on point. Rook stayed at my side making sure I was straight, I was good.

I had bought a few items from my profits like another Rolex, a few other watches by Ice Man and Jacob. I bought a Rover truck that had two sunroofs and pecan leather seats. I added the sound system and TV's and a PlayStation for entertainment. My home was refurnished from the top to the bottom and the studio was fully upgraded to unlimited tracks.

With money coming in like that I also made sure Wifey had her share of things that she needed. The entire crew was getting love and playing their part to the max. Everyone ate off the same plate and shared the same spoon. My reputation had grown to another level and so had my pockets.

On the other side of town, my nigga Tashaun was making big moves in the city. He had introduced me to a few older guys that were all about making money. His boys Red, Mickey B, and Big Darryl all had businesses and money as long as I-96. They accepted me as a team player and friend as we all hung out and lived the lifestyle of made men. Once I saw how they opened their clubs and stores it made me feel like this was the level I needed to be on. A lot of things made sense, but I needed them to make dollars.

Meeting and greeting was a part of my everyday life and it had its benefits. With the trap doing numbers, all types of women came around to buy those $10 bags of hydro. Some days I would give the girls the day off and work the door myself just to meet the different dolls that would fall through there. Each woman had a unique personality and swag about themselves. Candy was light skinned and in school and had a smile out of this world, while Nikki was short thick and pretty as hell. I kept my roster full but there was always room for a team player.

Tee was still on my mind and we hadn't seen or talked to each other in a while. There was so much shit going on in my life that I stayed busy. My plan was to have my business established by the summer. So to stay on track I expanded on every level from taking trips out of town to dealing with the major players. By me hanging with Rellee my name started to ring in heads of a lot of superstars. Now I needed to explore more options and be known for my body of work. At the label we added cats like Elc, Worth the Don, Scurve, Duke, Astro, Rock, Xo, while Rook and I would drop a few bars ever so often.

I also had Shakun and a few others who still represented the label at all times. Since the movement was creating a buzz in the city, Rook and I started a clothing line to promote the label. We had our logo designed and put it on jackets, shirts and even cars. We also had flyers made and passed them out throughout the city. I was happy about the feedback and results so the next thing we did was grabbed a few guest appearances and also tried to get features on other labels tracks. We hooked up with Dope Boy Records out of Flint through my ace Joey who had a few hot local artists. My favorite was 1000 bars and Sho who were his main acts.

Our buzz was on fire when we added cats like Herk, Duke and M. Porter. With hard work and determination I felt like this was a chance to work on the other plans at hand.

I managed to still make time for my women. Rochelle was enjoying the spoils of being my main chick and I didn't really have much trouble from her. Candy with her fine ass had multiple tattoos and liked girls so she shot way up in the ranks. She was also cool and sexy and loved to be around me in my grind mode. Then I had Nikki who I had fallen head first for because of her calm demeanor. She was a hot commodity and thought I didn't know she was playing a few different niggas at the same time. We were still tight and she moved up on the roster too, plus, Sharice, Alaya, Nicole, Parish and Rhonda P from my old job were still around and playing their role in my life.

The more money I made, the less sleep I got. So my new mantra was, "I'll sleep when I'm dead." There was so much going on as I multi-tasked my life and the events in it. It wouldn't be long before Tee had the baby, so I prepared to lose the woman I loved.

Meanwhile as the block pumped more each day the unexpected happened. In April the house got raided. Rochelle's other sister's boyfriend Redderick had got caught up doing some stupid shit in the suburbs and lead the police directly to me. Damn, I thought he was cool and part of the family.

When the police kicked the door in and found me, Rook, Tim and Damien inside all hell broke loose. They found drugs, money and weapons then questioned everyone. They let everyone go except me. They figured I was the ringleader and they took me to jail and charged me with it all. Once my appointed lawyer came in to see me I was released on a $100,000 bond. They posted 10% and I was released. I knew where the heat had come from so my next mission was to handle that and rebuild the trap.

Here we were again with charges pending having to avoid the police and earn for myself at the same time. When I went to the trap I was surprised to see it up and running at full pace. While I was locked up for a day Uncle Slybone and Damien had kept the shit going and closed down the old house.

Supply and demand was the name of the movement. We relocated a few cribs down and continued to make the money. I moved further away to lower my risk of violating my bond. My squad would have to step up in order to let me rest and focus on the hidden rat.

Since I was out on bond a lot of my time was spent in the studio or being chased by the women in my life. I had to find a way to rebuild and prepare for the future. My mind would wander as it forced me to submit and bow to Allah in prayer. I needed advice and guidance before my life spiraled out of control.

After several weeks of stacking money and leaving the lime light alone, I had been approached with a great opportunity to open my own business. A close friend of the family had heard about my plan to expand and go legit and offered me to buy him out of the barbershop game. I was happy for the leverage and called Rook to see if wanted to manage it for me. He agreed and I bought the building and upgraded the shop on Joy Rd.

I finally became the business owner and real boss that I had aspired to be. I started hiring employees and bringing the business to life. We changed the name to The Fam and with Rook at the lead, we made legal money look good. It only took a few weeks to get things together and it was pretty easy since it was already an established shop.

At home, Rochelle saw a change in my attitude and knew that I was focused on life and success. The shop had given me new benefits and allowed me to merge the studio and business along with it. I would sell F.L.R. products like the t-shirt's, cd's and DVD's to the local clients for profits.

I had five barbers and one nail tech at the shop, who all had become like family to me. With things falling into place I needed to place certain people in certain positions to help aid me as my connect had moved to Cali and left me in control of a small portion of his contacts. My Uncle JR, Cody, Tim, Damien and my younger cousin T.B. and his girlfriend Teri had all become team players. T.B. and Teri were the closest because they loved me like true family members and were always available if I needed them.

The shop was our hangout. Tashaun would fall through every day in a new Vette or truck as we catered to the entire west side and represented the business world proudly. Once we got on a roll everyone came through even artist like Special Ed, Lil Scrappy, Scarface, Bun B, Jagged Edge and Spanky Hayes from Wild-N-Out.

I had to keep things in order and proved to the courts that I was a legit business man who paid taxes. I had a court date soon and needed to get prepared for battle. I was stressed out as I navigated through the crap. That summer, Usher had put out a song called Confessions and it hit me straight in my heart.

I was doing so much and had so much bottled up inside regarding the baby situation that I panicked. Tee and I weren't beefing but we weren't really talking either. In fact, I hadn't seen her at all during the whole nine months that she had been pregnant. So every time I would listen to the album it would remind me of my life as well. In fact I think I played that cd so much that one day Rochelle asked me was I trying to tell her something.

I just smiled and said, "No, the beats are just nice."

The look in her eyes told me that she was noticing a change in my world, but couldn't figure it out. As the days passed my court date got closer and my lawyer called to tell me he needed five grand down on my twelve grand legal bill. I met him a few hours later at J. Alexander's to give him the money. Once that was done, I made my way back to the trap to make up the money I had just given out.

Being around my family during stressful times really helped keep me focused. Uncle JR, T.B. and Teri would hang out with me or handle the block business so that I could rest or relax and think. Sometimes I would go out to eat by myself to get away from it all. My favorite spots were Starter's, Beans and Cornbread, Arkbar's, Mama's Kitchen and sometimes Uptown BBQ on Livernois. This gave me time to think about what I had to do.

I was really uneasy because I hated doing time. Then one day Teri told me that she had someone she wanted to meet that would change my life. I had to chuckle at the thought. Who did she know that could change my life? I needed a miracle right now, not another woman.

A few days later I had to go to court so I had my new chic Tiffany drive me down to the court house for a quick pre-trial motion. That day, Rook and Dris had met us down there to support me on the case. I sat down next to my lawyer and proceeded with the routine only to hear that the state was dropping the case! I couldn't believe my ears.

Then the Judge spoke again. "But, Mr. Giles the Feds would like to talk to you," he said nodding towards to suited gentlemen at the back of the court. The Feds were picking up the dropped case.

My heart dropped to the floor as two plain clothes agents grabbed me and searched my pockets before detaining me. They pulled out eight grand in cash that I was about to pay my lawyer. My lawyer instructed me to keep quiet and that though he could no longer represent me, he would call someone that could.

The Feds took me to the county jail to be booked under federal charges. I called Rook and told him not to panic. He picked up the cash and keys from Tiffany and chilled until I could give him further instruction. My lawyer called and gave Rook the number of a federal attorney who was good but expensive.

"Cool, let's go to court," he whispered to me and hung up.

The next day the same agents came to get me for court and I noticed they were the same dudes from the raid. After several hours in the holding cell it was time to face the judge. I had been briefed by several other prisoners who were back on appeal like T. Stuckey and Bird on the process of bond. The process was quick as my lawyer argued about the bail, which lead me to being placed on the tether until trial started.

I was released the next day when Rochelle came to pick me up. Man, shit was crazy. I was on tether by the Feds so all eyes were on me. Once the entire hood heard about the tether I decided to lay low not to spook anyone or give the thought that I would start snitching. My involvement on the block was limited as I utilized T.B., Teri and the squad to pick up the slack.

The barbershop was my headquarters and I only dealt with a few street niggas in case them folks were watching. Being on bond allowed me to stack major money and to get plenty of rest. Rochelle also enjoyed me being on tether because she knew I would be home before 2 a.m. and that my popping up at her apartment wasn't happening. I hated the fact that my restriction kept me at home but allowed me to catch up with my music. I needed that relaxation with a federal case pending and a baby on the way.

On the block Lea and Pooh had to step down since their house was no longer the trap. However they stayed close like sisters, and were definitely team players. Being in control of my life was great but not knowing how long wasn't.

I had tried to reach out to Tee-Tee several times only to find myself hanging up when she answered. My mom would call to check on me or to give me advice about the baby situation even though she only knew the surface of the problem. I was in the middle of a triangle of sin and wanted out! Only time would predict the outcome so patience was necessary.

OPTIONS

Several months passed and I was still on a self-inflicted house arrest. It was the studio, shop and home for me most of the time. Occasionally, I would step out with Tashaun and the crew to Club Dynasty for a few drinks. We stayed in VIP and met and mingled with the women. This is where I met Adriana. This chick stood out amongst all the beauties in the club. She stood at a regal 5'11, 160 pounds with long black hair. She also had on a full body suit that showed off her shape and curves.

"This is just what the doctor ordered," I thought to myself as I approached her drunk off the bottles of Moet we had consumed.

The entire club watched as I macked her and we exchanged numbers and smiles until later. Tashaun and the crew couldn't believe that I had scored so quickly. Damn, she was ice cold and soon she would be a part of my everyday life.

It took her a few days to call me, but eventually that call came and I had her meet up with me at the shop. The entire squad's mouth dropped when she got out of the car. I smiled as she walked over and greeted us. We were going to Red Lobster, so I pushed the automatic start on my truck and we headed off to get to know each other better.

The date was great and afterwards we kissed good-bye with promises to talk or hook up later. This chick reminded me of J-Lo just a little bit thicker. Since I was still on tether my playtime was pretty hectic. All the women wanted to stay over and it just wasn't possible. I had them in rotation on the hour. We would chill, fuck, talk, get high all in an hour and I would send them on their way and repeat the process with the next one.

In June, around the 7th I got a call from my Mom and Aunt letting me know that I was a father. I had no idea how they knew before I did. I didn't think they even knew Tee like that but come to find out they had been in touch with her throughout her entire pregnancy. My aunt was even there when the baby was born.

Once I heard it was a boy I was tripping. I felt lightheaded and woozy. Rook sat there waiting for the announcement like he already knew what I was about to say. Once I told him he gave me a long speech about manning up and being a real father.

A few days later I finally called Tee and arranged a time for me to meet up to see the baby. Rook went with me and Tee-Tee was nice as she gave me directions on what to do and not to do around the newborn baby. We took our shoes off and I looked around the apartment. She looked like she had never been pregnant. She was back down to her small petite size already. It had been a while since I'd seen her and I immediately wanted her back to myself.

She went back to into the room and brought out the tiny baby. Rook and I looked at him and he said, "Rome, he looks like you."

I looked down to see him looking up at me and my heart drifted to another place that gave me a feeling I'd never experienced before. Fighting back the tears, I realized Jay was my son. I just held him and kissed him while Tee explained that she didn't need or want anything from me. That made me feel bad because I wanted to be there for my son, no matter what she and I had going on. There was no way that I was going to be a bad father or leave her alone especially after seeing how my father's absence from my life had affected me. I let her talk but told her I had her back.

Rook played with his nephew as Tee and I went into the kitchen to talk. We covered a lot of ground and she told me that she would pay for the blood test if needed. A few minutes later my phone went off and it was time to go back to the shop. I hated to leave my family so I told her to stop by anytime to bring him to see me.

The ride to the shop was cool while Rook and I smoked and laughed at the fact that the player Rome was a proud father. To me the hard part wasn't over until Rochelle found out.

The next few days Tee and I would talk and then I would fall through to let the crew meet Jay. He was too small for us to take out the house plus this allowed me to spend time with both of them. This time spent with them kept my mind off the streets and the bracelet around my ankle.

Being a father was new to me and I talked to Tashaun and Rook a lot for advice. They always gave me good advice on fatherhood. Despite the relationship that Tee and I had as partners the baby would always be the foundation. I learned that quick when I found out she was dating other men.

Things moved forward and being a parent was a work in progress. Over the next few months I would visit Jay and play my part in raising him. Rochelle had yet to find out about him but CB knew from the jump. He was my boy and I needed his advice on how to tell Rochelle about the newest addition to the family. It was going to be extra hard and I knew once the word got out that I had a child by Tee-Tee shit would get crazy quickly. So I decided to keep it to myself and swore everybody around me to silence. Hurting Rochelle wasn't intended to be done on purpose, trust me.

I had a lot on my mind with the baby and court coming up. Facing twenty years wasn't an easy pill to swallow. Throughout the days and months my visits to Tee's house stayed regular and sometimes they would come over to the condo to chill. Our bond was strengthened as we raised our baby together. Eventually we started having sex again, but she soon drew the line there. She was upset that I hadn't told Rochelle about our son.

One day in September I knew something was wrong. I just had a bad feeling. I had just come back from seeing my probation officer. My vibe was off due to me dropping a dirty urine and my PO told me I had one more time to drop dirty and I would be in jail until my court date. I wasn't about to stop smoking so I decided what better time than now, to tell Rochelle about Jay.

She came over looking good as usual and we sipped on some Moet and orange juice her reaction was what I expected.

"A MOTHERFUCKING BABY ROME?" she screamed as her eyes welled up with tears. "By who and when?" she demanded to know.

I lied and told her that it was someone I had met while visiting Atlanta and it was during the time when she and I hadn't been on the same page. I wanted her to at least know about the baby. I couldn't go to jail for twenty years and let the streets tell her. Since her past wasn't squeaky clean she decided to let it go until I had a blood test or until she met the mystery woman.

My mom came into town and visited Tee and the baby. She and Tee had a really close relationship and she enjoyed spending time with her grandson.

I kept Rochelle at bay by telling her that I hadn't talked to her or that I didn't have pictures of the baby yet. But the truth was Tee-Tee had given me a small scrap book filled with pictures of Jay with my mom and siblings. I had hid the book in my basement inside the washer that didn't work, only because Rochelle would sweep the condo for any trace of female evidence. The washer didn't work so I figured she would never find the pictures.

In October, Lyve and I were driving in my boys Corvette when my cell rang with a call from Rochelle at my house. She sounded sad and was crying then she told me she was leaving. I had no idea what had happened so I jumped on the Southfield

Freeway to head back home. Once we pulled up I noticed the screen door was open and her truck running in the drive-way. She waited for me to enter then headed to the basement. I followed her asking what was wrong. When we got down the stairs pictures of Jay were thrown all over the floor.

"You have been lying all this time, Rome. Everybody knows about this baby, but me. Even your mom is in some of these pictures," she cried.

I felt terrible as I reached out to try to hold her and she snatched away.

"Who is the mother and why have you been lying about taking care of the baby?" she asked.

Words can't express the pain and hurt in her face. I knew that she was gone for real this time. Since there was really no way to calm her down, I said, "I'm so sorry baby. But I have to be a better father than mine was to me. I love you and we can work this out if we try."

Tears fell down my cheeks as I lost the love of one to gain the love of another that would be unconditional for life. After the conversation she walked out as I stayed home with Lyve and thought about how my life would change.

The next few weeks were rough then finally a break came that could put me back on the right track. I got a call from my lawyer asking me to bring him ten of the thirty grand for taking the case. He told me to meet him at the Hut in Westland ASAP and to put the money into a western union envelope. I did as I was told and met him at the restaurant. He took the money without giving me a receipt and told me to leave before the judge came in with his family to eat.

I left and met up with Rochelle who was still upset, but still hanging around. I was enjoying being a father. There was something about the way that he looked at me that made me keep moving forward.

A few days later I got a call from my PO telling me to report on Monday. All I could think of was that I was going to jail for dropping dirty. My entire weekend was fucked up as I was on pins and needles.

On Monday I went to the probation office and Nikki came with me just in case what I thought was going to happen, actually happened. Rook was on standby, he had all the directions on what to do to handle my business while I was gone. When I walked into his office he sent me to the back room, where he gave me a huge pair of scissors and asked me to cut off the bracelet around my ankle. I did what he said wondering what the hell was going on.

He handed me an envelope and said, "You are a part of the 1% of guys that beat a Fed Case. Your case was dismissed. You are free to go, Mr. Giles."

I couldn't believe what I had just heard. I got the fuck out of there and ran downstairs to the car where Nikki was waiting for me. I must have made fifty calls telling everyone of my good fortune. The entire hood and squad couldn't wait for me to get back to my business and be stress free.

That weekend we partied like some real rock stars with no limits. Every topless bar, club and woman was hit. I was free with no warrants or cases pending just in time for Christmas.

My cousin T.B. had planned a little get together for his birthday at the pool hall and invited me to come. I thought about being that Rochelle was over I didn't really want to leave her alone. Then Duke my homeboy convinced me to go have a little fun for a few hours. While I stalled or tried to see what kind of mood she was in, I remembered that Teri told me that her cousin Carlin was in town.

"What the hell?" I thought as I headed for the door and yelled to Rochelle, "I'll be back in an hour."

Duke and I headed for the pool hall on I-96 and entered to greet the family. The place was live even though it wasn't packed. I located Tub and his crew and Teri and her girls. We all drank and played pool at our own table. Teri saw me looking at the girls about to make my move and she motioned for one female in particular to come over to my table.

This chick was 5'7 with hips and ass out of this world. She walked over to our table and started messing up our game by rolling the balls around. Me and Duke just looked at her like she was crazy, trying to figure out her angle.

"Dig Shorty, what's up with you?" I asked knowing Teri had sent her my way.

"I'm Teri's cousin and I'm here visiting from college. My name is Len," she said in a very sexy voice.

She had my attention. We talked for a while and ordered a few more drinks. Before we left we exchanged numbers and she told me she would be in town for the weekend and to give her a call. I promised to set something up before she left. Truthfully I wanted to set something up now. Afterwards, Duke and I left the pool hall and drove downtown before returning home to chill with Rochelle.

That Saturday, Carlin and I agreed to hook up and go eat with T.B. and Teri. At the restaurant, I learned that she was really cool and had just had a little girl and had a few years left to go in school. That was pretty sexy to me so we kicked off into a deep conversation in which I told her that I was the proud father of a handsome baby boy. The entire date was wonderful and just from this date I knew that she had to be ranked without even trying her sex game. After she left, we continued to keep in touch until her next visit to the city.

Back at the crib it was getting closer to Christmas so I took Rochelle on a major shopping spree. I took fourteen grand from my private stash and treated the whole crew to a great Christmas. We bought everything from jewelry to TVs and clothes for them. I made sure that my son who was too young to really get the experience still was taken care of. All of my special girl-friends each got a little something too. Their gifts ranged from earrings and necklaces to trips around the world. Rochelle had gotten so many gifts that the money couldn't be counted or matched.

I was so happy to be off the tether that my life had to be celebrated. Before the holidays, I had two meetings with my two main connects to be sure that we were on the same page. Once this was done I stayed giving out priceless advice to my friends and family like my mantra's "The only way a relationship can work is if the woman loves your hustle and respects your pimping." Or "The difference between a made nigga and a paid nigga is paid nigga can buy whatever he wants and a made nigga can get it for free." Then my favorite one was G.F.G.D "God forgives, Gangsta's don't."

Over the next couple of weeks between Christmas and the New Year this phrases would be a part of the oath to all my nigga who wanted to get money on a major level. Trust me, more will come when the time is right, but until then I just enjoyed the blessings that Allah was giving us and brought the New Year in ballin'!

CHAPTER 21
2005- NO LIMIT

When the New Year rang in I was happy that my son was in good health. Not very happy that Tee had a new boyfriend, but what could I say? Rochelle was still hanging around, but who knew for how long. This would be the first year that I was free from all warrants, tickets and court cases. My money was stacking and it felt good to be able to live without limits.

It was still cold outside and I spent most of my time at the studio or the barbershop. The block was still pumping and my mind told me it was time for a change. I would start planning my next great move when the time was right. Until then my focus was strictly on doing me. I surrounded myself with all my homies that were not in the game for the simple fact that my risk would be lowered in the game.

Sho, Rock, Lyve, Damien, Duke and Tic became my closest friends and hangout partners. They weren't concerned about the street life like my original squad and when I'm with them the stress wasn't as high. My status was still highly recognized in the streets so all the perks still came with my presence. VIPs, free drinks and plenty of women were always at our disposal.

We would hang out at Studio 51, Stinky Rose, The Dynasty and other major topless bars in search of women and fun times. The streets had fallen in love with artists such as Young Jeezy, Gucci man and G-Unit. Every club or car system blasted their hottest songs. I personally admired the Gucci man trap movement because we shared the same lifestyle and a lot of the same experiences.

The New Year meant no mistakes and no breaks. I was taking no shorts and giving no loans. I still had a gang of women and they were all cool, but I was always prepared for the bridge to break with Rochelle. She was always on edge, especially since she knew I was in contact with the baby and his mother. I tried to at least make her adjust so she could meet my son but she never budged.

My son was the world to me and no relationship not even the one I had with his mom mattered more than that. Even with Tee having a man I could use my power to my advantage. Since she seemed happy with the dude, I became more distant to avoid problems. We talked when I visited, but it was still always brief. I would pick him up several times a week or they would come by the shop so that we could spend time without Rochelle surprising us. They could never meet up because if they did shit would be crazy.

While the weather was trying to warm up, so was I and the rest of the squad. Adriana had been coming around and as expected we had sex at her crib on 94 and Cadieux. She was well-grounded and knew how to let me take control of the session. Trust me by her being so thick it was a lot of work required. The only thing that bothered me about her was her crazy ass uncle who played the daddy/man role in her life. He looked out for her because she wasn't from the city. He would call or come by since he had a key to her apartment. He didn't like me because I was a doughboy and he hated them.

Because of him we didn't spend too much time at her house. That wasn't good for me because Rochelle could do a drive by any time since she had keys to my player pad. Adriana was cool and our relationship was just as great as the rest, plus she loved me like crazy.

On the other side of the coin my relationship with T.B., Teri and Carlin had grown even deeper. Whenever I came out the house or went to the shop they were there and willing to pull their weight. This meant a lot to me because their hearts stayed in the right place.

After several trips back and forth from school, Carlin became one of my top ranked females faster than I expected. She was a great person and we had so much fun together. The time we spent kept a smile on my face and she was a wonderful parent to her baby and that was definitely something I could appreciate.

The entire crew loved her and encouraged me to make her above everyone else on the roster. To me she had to prove that she was able to handle and produce like I needed. My lifestyle was hard to handle and many had fallen to the wayside because they didn't have what it took. However, whenever she was in town she definitely held all of my attention.

One day she finally gave in and allowed me to have sex with her. It was kinda warm outside and she wanted to stay the night after chilling all day. I knew it was time to see how good she really was. So we talked for a while then headed upstairs to my room to play. My bed was five feet off the ground because I had two quality mattresses and the box springs for support. My quilt was made by Coogi and my bed was layered with decorative pillows. The room was always appealing to women.

We lied down as we kissed and undressed to perform. Once she took off her clothes I could have passed out. Her body was perfect and since she had just had a baby, Carlin was extra thick and soft. Before I touched her she demanded that I use a condom. I didn't have any but she insisted, "Rome, I just had a baby. I'm ripe and I'll get pregnant fast."

I could respect that and as much as I hated the rubber ducks – to the store I went. Still in my robe and slippers I headed to the local gas station and grabbed a three pack. Then I rushed back as she lied in the bed looking too damn good. I ran up the stairs because new pussy could do that to you. Then I jumped on the bed to embrace in a small kiss to reheat things up. Boy, was she ready. Her nipples slowly dripped milk and her pussy quickly dripped wetness. I licked her all over until I got to her secret spot. Once I was there, the battle started to heat up as I licked and sucked on her entire pussy. While my show was being put on her reaction was moaning so loud that I could tell that she was ready to cum. So I grabbed her arms by the wrist and ate her pussy until she came all over my face and then kept doing it until she came again. I was trying for a third time as she climbed the wall trying to get away. She begged me to stop after the last time she came, but since she couldn't move, she had to take it like a big girl.

Once this was done, the room looked different as she laid half way off the bed with her head almost touching the floor. The more she ran the more my bed on wheels moved into another location. When I came up for air to begin to enter her I noticed the bed was way over by the bedroom door. Damn! She got the biz! Now it was time to fill her up with Stanley, my nickname for my dick (as in Stanley the power drill).

I put the condom on then entered her tight pussy and after five deep strokes, the condom came off. After several attempts to keep the condom on they all failed. I assured her that I was completely disease free and safe to have sex with unprotected. She made me swear to pull out, I agreed and we continued to have sex for forty five minutes. Doggie style was my favorite position and she represented well. Her hips and ass was so cute and round that from behind she looked like a 79 Chevy Malibu with 36 inch rims on the back and 24 inch rims in the front.

The sex was well worth the wait as we continued to bond on many levels. The one thing that was unlike the rest of the women on my team was she didn't have a boyfriend or man. I was the closest to her on that level for a while. Plus she was like family since my cousin and hers were lovers.

Whenever she was in town my time was dedicated to her. Meanwhile, life was exciting as my every day routine was to explore all that I could. Damien, Lyve and Sho always stayed close as Rook worked his job and ran the shop. Rook was my right hand man and at the end of each night we would hang out at the shop or our houses just to catch up while smoking a few blunts. Even though he was my brother he always stayed on top of my actions. Every so often after talking to him I would call mom to vent or to check on her and my siblings. Being that they were so far away I missed them. I made it a point to call and send them money to let them know they were loved. Whenever she got a chance she would visit for the weekend and stay at my place.

Love was always around in my life even though I was not used to showing emotions towards the world. Deep inside ever since Granny and David had passed away, I had built a wall around my feeling to block away any pain. This is why the street life was an outlet for me. Making money gave me a sense of relief and multiple women catered to my ego. I had a lot of friends but only a few appreciated me for who I was.

It was getting hot outside as we prepared for the summer. So much was happening I could hardly keep up. My dude Herk used to come around and rap at special events. My comrade in the game Fade had been brutally murdered in his car and several months before that Boat had been shot but luckily had survived. This was going to be a wild summer and I really wanted to live through it and not just in it.

All my plans were in the works while my relationship was being worked on. With so many females in my life it seemed unreal to spectators. How could I manage to control so many emotions without getting caught or hurt for that matter? I realized that everything in life had a purpose or it wouldn't have been created. My purpose was to create harmony within GOD's most sacred creation –The Woman, the mothers of the universe.

Being desired, respected and in control always turned me on. So to feed my hunger I chose to nibble on multiple desserts. Being in love hurts and I did everything I could do to not feel that pain again. So in all, I figured that spreading myself thin wouldn't allow me to focus on just one. One woman would never handle the type of love that I could display so I ran from that to avoid the inevitable hurt that I had been programmed to expect. I vowed to live my life with no limits and to live it to the fullest for Granny and David. The summer would be mine and everything in it.

While the weather reached the warmer temps everyone came back around like Dean, Dmac, Twin and Herbie and my block and business was still doing big numbers. My mid sells were creating a buzz as my clientele grew. Tashaun was on the other side of the set still making power moves and would still fall through to blow a few or patrol the hood. He was my dude and we would just sit some days and compare notes on the women we had or the money we were making.

A few weeks into summer I decided to upgrade a little so the trap switched places until I could make my power move. I had bought Uncle Lee out of his house contract which was a few cribs down from my current location. He had seen a house on Seven Mile that he wanted, so I helped him get it to profit from the trap until the power move. Then once that was done I went and grabbed some more chairs and an awning for the shop. As for myself I went to the plaza and had Gary make me an iced out dog tag. He was happy to see me and started showing me special dog tags from out the back. I ended up cashing out $5500 for the charm and chain. After I left him, I headed to Hamtramck to get a ring and watch set. The store owner was also happy to see me as he buzzed me into the store. I copped an iced out Iceman watch with interchangeable bands, a 2 karat pinkie ring and a pair of platinum wire Cartier glasses with transitional lenses. This set me back close to $7000. The jewelry upgrade would complement the collection I already had.

I went to the mall and got Little Jay some shoes. He was so small but growing fast. His birthday was close so I figured that I should do a little something for him too. While in route I came up on Davison to grab some gas and a box of blunts, when

I noticed a sexy female inside the gas station. She was brown skinned, a little thick with nice juicy lips. I quickly grabbed a flyer for the barbershop and studio that had my number and picture on it. Walking up to her car she looked me up and down as I presented the flyer to her. This was my strategy with approaching girls, if they weren't interested I could use the business as Plan B.

"What's up sexy? My name is Rome," I said handing her the flyer.

"My name is Angie," she said with a smile.

Bingo! I had her so I continued to charm her for a few, then told her to call me that night. I started getting crazy looks from al the dudes at the gas station being that I was in a shiny Rover by myself. I quickly flashed back to Tashaun and me in the past, when my stupid ass got robbed at the Coney Island. It was time to go. I said my goodbye's and continued on my mission.

Successfully, the completed trip to the mall had me exhausted, so I sent for Lyve to help take over the block. Days went without any major setbacks, though Rochelle had started to act strange. She was still hurt and all the money in the world couldn't heal her heart. It reminded me of R. Kelly's song, 'When a Woman's Fed up.' So I played my role and decided not to trip and just enjoy it while it lasted.

With my focus still on my money a vision came to me in my sleep and it showed me that it was time to relocate the trap. I followed my vision even with the trap only had been moved for three weeks to its new location. I transferred to the Schoolcraft area. I let go of the contract my uncle and I shared to lower my risk of being raided. A few phone calls later and my new trap was set up with a drive through window. The hood was crazy so I instilled the help of new workers to protect the trap. Uncle Cody would oversee the house while doing small shifts but

Damien, Gee and Black would rotate the main shifts. I had to bring in larger muscle and security especially after being there only two days and Damien got robbed. They almost killed him and set the house on fire.

The trap had kept its pace being that my clientele didn't mind the extra five minute trip to shop. Once word got out in the neighborhood, hounds came growling. Not paying attention to my strict orders Damien got caught slipping and learned a valuable lesson in the process. Now everyone had to be alert until the Schoolcraft leaders knew that this was my shit. It took several days but eventually things went well.

The summer had paid off and really started moving fast. It stayed extra hot while I enjoyed all its benefits. I had met a slew of new women from hanging out and trapping on the Craft. Lyve and Damien started growing in the studio and on the streets as they branched off into their player node. My stable of main chicks stayed steady, but for some reason it wasn't complete without Tee-Tee. Yeah, I knew she had a man, but my son not being around wasn't cool to me. She would not let me fuck her or stay nights over her crib. She was a good mother, despite the fact that she didn't love me anymore. So to avoid being hurt I redirected the energy into everything else.

By winter, I tried to have enough money put up to start on my new business venture. I had to expand and open up a club or topless bar, so I had to start my research. That was my main focus, but along with money on my mind there was always women. I had a plethora of women around me and whenever the holidays came around they were all extra nice. They wanted good gifts and I had the money, power and resources to fulfill all request. A lot of cats call this portion of the game, tricking. I didn't give a damn. I call it an investment. I'm not paying for the pussy, I'm paying her to leave. Plus, giving a woman money before sex was considered tricking to me. Giving it to them after was called gratitude. They all had someone else in their life, but when they were with me, they were with me. Shit, even Rochelle had someone else.

Angie, one of my main chicks, only stayed a minute from the trap so we spent a lot of time together. She wasn't afraid to meet on the block or at the trap so she gained hella points for that. Once we started fucking she quickly became pregnant and you guessed it…I was a contestant in the Who Is the Baby Daddy contest.

She had started feeling different around New Years and couldn't figure out what it was. Once she found out she could be pregnant, she was honest and told me about the dude that she had been fucking for years. Her baby father had given her another child and stayed around even though they weren't together. She wasn't a wild chick. She had only slept with me and him. So because we were so cool anyway, I started spending even more time when I found out she could possibly be pregnant by me.

My life was on a roll now, but I had to remain focused. The year was almost over and it was time to get ready for 2006, the year the Superbowl would be held in Detroit. Things had to be on point for me by then. This would be the year that Rochelle would either make it or break it because dead weight and emotions made your balance unsteady, if it was too heavy.

"Oh Allah, lead me on the path of those of whom you owe favors and not on the path of those thy wrath shall be brought down on." I recited this every night until the New Year came in. Let's get it!

CHAPTER 22

2006 – CAN'T BE LIFE

Christmas was live as usual. A few of my females had treated me really well and Adriana had performed the best. Her gift was a Techno-Master with two bezels full of diamonds that had cost $3500. She instantly rose to the top of my roster with this action. In all every gift was special because to me the thought meant everything.

I spent a lot of time at home since it was so cold. Rook ran the shop and Uncle Cody handled the block. We had no more problems from the Schoolcraft hounds once they figured out whose trap it was, so business flowed like water and money stacked as usual.

At home Rochelle still played her role as the leading lady even though she was still distant. Her family had started to look at me different, but only if they know some of the shit she had put me through. CB had kept things strictly between us and always showed a high level of respect towards me. To kill time, whenever Rochelle was at work, I would chill with a variety of women in the studio or at the crib.

Nikki would fall through each day but since she had gotten caught up through the grapevine, she had started changing. I knew she had a secret man so I played along with her until the streets caught up with her.

Len was still in school and we would talk every day or send cute pictures through the phone to stay in touch. She was sweet as cherry pie and whenever she came to town it went down.

Candy had made herself know again as we heated our relationship by spending more time together. Sharice, Alaya, Angie and Beana would come through a few times a week, but they all had men so the time I got with them was limited.

Seta had come back around, but only as a loyal friend. Her street cred was still up and since she had become a mother a lot of her time was spent with her baby daddy and son. Her family had love for me so it was cool to be able to hang out with her on any level. Trust me, I did want to fuck her little ass but she was too focused to give in. However she, Kerisha and Tee would fall through as sisters to the squad and everyone knew they were off limits.

Since Angie was pregnant and didn't know by who, she always told me that she hoped I was the father. I kept her around just in case I was and watched her every move. Being a major player, this took a lot of energy especially in the winter. My movement was not limited, I just chose to sit idle during the cold winter.

In January, Len had gone back to college after spending her birthday weekend in the city. We had a great time hanging out with T.B. and Teri for a few days. My body was exhausted from smoking, fucking and lack of sleep, so I decided to chill for the day.

A few days later I called my nigga Joey from DBR to fall through and listen to a few new beats that I made for several for his artist. He did so as Rook took a break from the shop to come play a few games of Madden. Sharice had just left the condo after a quickie and a few blunts before she went to work. The day was slowing down as we sat in the lab smoking and talking. Several minutes later Duke showed up to pick up a few personal bags since he was in the area. He and Rook played a few games then they headed to the shop to close up. Before they left something told me to ask Duke to hold several pistols that were new and still in their cases until later that night. He agreed, then they both left.

Shortly after Joey and I played a few beats off the Motif 8 while he rolled up a bag of hydro to stay in our zone. Suddenly through the window in the basement I noticed several sets of feet moving around quickly. I got his attention as we noticed whoever it was had dogs with them too.

My first thought was the "Jack Boys" were coming to get me. Then I remembered I lived in the suburbs and that was pretty unlikely. Then my second thought was, it was the police. I wasn't sure whether or not to run to grab the .45 Lima in its carrying case which was upstairs in my room, four flights up or try to get to the .357 I kept in the kitchen behind the stove in case of emergencies.

I usually would have a .45 on me or in its carrying case but since Joey was the only one there with me and I trusted him, I didn't. I made up my mind to get the .357 from the kitchen. Joey looked surprised because he wasn't sure if it was setup on him by me or if it was a raid. Before my feet could hit the first step up to the kitchen, they were running through the house, screaming "Police! Police! Put your hands up! Show me your mother fuckin' hands!"

Joey was dumping the weed into the toilet. They warned us again to show them our hands to which we complied. There were several masked agents and officers that rushed down the stairs. Seconds later, we were in custody. I couldn't believe this shit. This couldn't be my life.

They searched around the condo and found 6.5 pounds of high grade hydro called AK 47 and several thousands of dollars of cash. While talking to me and Joey the officers came across my .45 carrying case and started to look even harder for the missing weapon. I explained to the officers that marijuana was for persona l use. I also told them to let Joey go since he didn't have anything to do with me, he was just a business man. Eventually they did and moments later they found the .45 Lima under my mattress.

It was time to lock the place down and head to jail to start this process all over again. My landlord had seen all the cop cars and rushed down to secure my home until I contacted her. They took me to the Brownstown Police station and booked me on several charges including possession of a weapon. I spent a few hours at that station until they transferred me to the county jail for more processing.

I called Rochelle to let her know I was gone until my court date and she seemed not to care. The Superbowl was around the corner and the city was on fire. The Feds had done a sweep to clean the streets and help keep crime low and the visitors safer. The raid on my home was considered a "No Knock" which meant that since I had a Fed case before I was considered a high risk to society. My record showed that I was a gangster on paper. So they set my bond sky high to try to keep me out of the way and off the streets.

I spent two weeks in jail then bonded out once the bond was lowered. Rook and Tee-Tee had come to get me after court and posted my bond. My money was scattered everywhere in the streets because I had been gone. Thank God Tee-Tee had money put up to help until I was released and could pay her back.

When I got home I called Rochelle, only to find her out in the clubs partying. I tried to call a few other chicks, but it was Friday night and I was unsuccessful. No sex for me on my homecoming so far.

Rook and I headed to the block only to find shit in an uproar. My team had failed to keep things in order. Since I had been locked up people thought I wasn't ever getting out. Surprise! When they saw me they panicked. The trap had several women and guys chilling in it at no cost. At least three different workers had their own hydro and to my surprise T.B. and Teri were there also.

Man, I was pissed as I kicked everyone out of the house except my one faithful worker Turk who was a close friend of T.B.'s. Before they left, I set an example by making everyone break themselves of all drugs and money ASAP. This was my shit and all proceeds had to come to me regardless of whose it was and how they got it. Then once that was done I had a serious one on one with Turk and T.B. about loyalty.

Rook rolled a blunt as I let them have it, then we left to check out my crib. In the morning, things would be back on track after I talked to my connect and Uncle Woodro. I needed some pussy and some real sleep. A few calls later I found Adriana around 1:30 and she came through to put me back in touch with reality. I had wondered why Tee-Tee didn't want to spend the night, but I just brushed it off to avoid getting upset.

Now I was back out on bond and trying to move through the streets to make up for another major loss. The bust yielded six pounds of hydro at $2000 a piece which meant a street value of $30,000 or $36,000 if broken down retail. Not to mention that fact that I had lost a new .45 Lima and $11,000 in cash! The good thing was the trap wasn't hit or the shop so making the money back wouldn't be a problem.

Once my day got started everyone came back around, even Joey to check on me and to see what my next move would be. I had to start looking for another trap spot to shake the police and snitches.

Then Rochelle finally came around but it wasn't nice at all. I was so stressed and pissed that once she came over the fighting started quickly. Out of anger I ended up choking her until she almost passed out. I knew she was cheating and I knew she wanted to leave me but out of fear she chose to stay until the time was right. If she left, I would find her. She knew I was connected and respected and she didn't want to chance it.

When I got my swagger back the women started coming back around and Angie was the first to step up. I had called Tee-Tee to check on my son and to have her visit me on the block since she had been acting funny. Whenever she came around and saw me with other females she wouldn't trip in front of them, but the look in her eyes said that she still had strong feelings for me. Maybe she still wanted to be with me or maybe things weren't going good in her relationship. It took me a while to get used to her mood swings but I adjusted.

Like one time she came to visit me with Jay at the condo while T.B. was over chilling. We chilled, smoked a few blunts then my phone rang with a call from Rochelle and she went crazy. The next thing I knew she had packed Jay up and rushed out to her car that was parked next to my truck. Before she stormed out she asked or demanded that I give her the money I borrowed from her for my bond. I had it, no doubt, but because of her attitude she wasn't getting it now.

When she heard that she really started acting out and I had to rush outside to calm her crazy little ass down. She jumped in her car and tried to back out quickly but I was quicker and opened the driver's side door to stop her. She put the car in reverse and slammed on the gas almost knocking me down and running me over. Thank God my truck was there to stop the door from knocking me down. The bad part was her car damaged my car and there was a huge dent in my door. I could have killed her, but I looked at my son in the back seat and told her to just leave. She wasn't a bad person, she just wanted what she wanted. I let a few days past and things with her went back to normal.

In my life dealing with multiple women came natural, so I was able to benefit from my talent. Since I was out on bond I was stressed out so I would do different shit to ease my mind like, hang out at different topless bars since I had a fan base there. I also went to clubs like Studio 51, Captains or Celebrities and chill out with Sho or Rook playing video games.

My Aunt Tina would start to come back around after leaving the party life alone to get her life in order. Tina was always fun to be around and since her birthday was the day before mine, we started planning to celebrate together. One thing about Tina was all my boys wanted her and all her girls wanted me. Whenever we were together it was a blast.

In April my nigga Tashaun dropped the new 745 BMW and had a case pending for weapons. He never gave a fuck about the law so he just kept balling out of control. We still hung out at Mickey B's club and played the streets as usual.

Since the weather was warming up everyone had their eyes on the prize. Damien had started getting his hustle on with his young crew and started making extra cash doing the snatch and run trick. They would hit several jewelry stores for thousands of dollar's worth of rings and watches. Then they would resale the items to the local money makers like myself, at a lower ticket. It wasn't right, but it wasn't wrong either so I encouraged them to make the best of it and invest the profits.

The entire squad was all about making money on some level which me proud to be a leader of example. Even Lyve had started working a job while on the block. I had also started looking for another location for the trap. My theory was, if you build it they would come. So my goals were set at new heights. By June, everything would be in motion.

I had a new crib on Ardmore that suited my purposes and would be ready to rent in a few days. It was clean and Angie only lived a few blocks away. This was also Lyve's hood that he had grown up in so rival beef would be to a minimum. My clientele would follow so the transition would be easy and smooth.

My birthday was coming and since Tina and Rook's birthdays were also in July we were going to have a big party. The only issue was if I had a party like this, the whole roster would show and that wouldn't be a good thing. The planning had to be specific and several women could not know about it.

Rochelle would be in the blind and Len wouldn't be in town that weekend. The rest of the ladies would be invited but with caution and at their own risk. We had paid for flyers and catering along with a special DJ and guest performers. Herk, 1000 Bars, M. Porter and many more made the list of elite acts to entertain me on my special day. We had passed out so many invites from the trap to the local hot spots. I expected several hundred people to attend, so I had to represent FLR to the fullest.

Rook and I bought our outfits for the party ahead of time to speed up the process. I had decided on a light brown linen short set with a matching t-shirt. Then I went to City Slicker and grabbed a pair of gator gym shoes that ran me $1200. Then I laid low until the hall we rented was ready to be decorated.

My cousin Ray had come up from Kentucky to help out on the block. He was cool but cold blooded when it came to loyalty. We had a bad history because he was the same cousin that I had caught a case with back in 92. He had stolen from me on multiple occasions from money to jewelry, but because he was my cousin I always found a way to forgive him. He was interested in making music, so I let him stay around but I kept my eye on him.

A few days before the party, my lawyer called and told me the plea that the prosecutor was offering. It was their one and only offer and I had twenty four hours to accept it. They wanted to give me five years flat and agreed to drop the other charges. If I didn't accept the plea and went to trial my sentencing guidelines would be eight to twenty years.

I was disappointed that I was facing another jail term when I was at my peak. It was final. I would be going away for five years. It was like my entire life flashed before my eyes and my heart dropped to my feet. The next day I had to go sign the plea agreement to seal the deal and I had Angie drive me since my license were bold.

Ray had spent the night in the studio, I told him to take out the trash then leave since he didn't want to ride to court with us. I locked the doors after he left out then went to see the judge.

It took five minutes to sign my life away as the female judge explained that she didn't want to send me to prison for such a petty crime. I listened with Angie who sat next to me uncomfortable from her pregnancy.

Several people knew about the time as I prepared the squad, family, and myself for the sixty month journey. The court had given me until September 29th to turn myself in so I had about sixty days to live it up.

When Angie dropped me back off at home, I entered to find my jewelry missing and a hand written note from a stranger. The note wasn't making sense however, I knew the handwriting was Ray's. I ran through the house looking for my money stash, weapons and product that I had hidden throughout the condo. Everything was still in place except for five watches, three pairs of Cartier glasses, two chains with charms and several pinkie rings. In all, he had taken over $40,000 in jewelry.

All this happened a day before my party and plus I was on my way to prison. As I went to leave the condo my neighbor confirmed what I already knew, Ray was the thief. He had tried to call me but I was in court. He didn't want to call the police and cause another scene over there, and I understood that. I was pissed as I called around to my family to see if anyone had seen him. This was the last time that he was going to fuck over me and think he was going to get away with it. I was going to catch his ass before he ran back down south and tried to sell my shit.

But the show must go on, so I prepared for the birthday celebration the next day. Everything went smooth all the way up to the party time. Rochelle had no idea of the party location and Len had called earlier to send me her birthday wishes. Before the party, everyone met at my crib to ride together for a grand entrance.

When we pulled up the crowd was nice and the hall was packed as Danger hosted the red carpet event. All my family and loyal friends showed up. A few of my females came out to support regardless of the risk. Even Dean had showed up out of nowhere to show his support. Tashaun couldn't make it due to some prior business arrangements and Nikki chose to stay home too. It was cool with me as several hundred people came out to have a good time with the three of us.

All the performances went well and I ended up drunk off of hydro and Moet by the cases. When the party was over I was so drunk that I had forgotten to line me up a playmate for the night. One of Tina's friends that I had fucked before, Kim, offered to stay and entertain me, but I was so drunk I passed out several times before the show. I woke up on a neighbor's lawn and was found by T.B. and Teri. They told me I was off the hook and had pictures to prove it. Hey, I was on my way to prison so I didn't give a fuck. Every day until I left was going to be a party day!

The next day I called a meeting to let everyone know I would be leaving and that announcement changed the whole mood of the room. Now it was time to tell Tee-Tee, Rochelle and Len that life must go one without me. I already knew when I left, many would fall including Rochelle. Len had become my favorite and truthfully deep inside I hoped she would be the strongest. Alaya, Candy or Angie would push a strong second place.

A lot of the girls had other men in their lives so they would move on as normal. I figured they would at least remain pen pals and try to stay in touch because they had love for me.

In August, time was closing in on me. My son was getting older and looking more and more like me every day. I tried to see him every day before I had to leave. Tee had taken the news ok. I guess since she had a man, I was just her baby daddy. Angie had vowed to stay true and tried her best to have the baby before I left. She didn't stay far from the trap that was still doing numbers, so I spent a lot of evenings at her place.

I hadn't found Ray yet but I had offered a reward for anyone that could catch up with him. Tina had my back and was there to help with anything I needed from her. Nate had picked up the pace and starting helping to control the block with T.B. and Teri.

A few days later, my nigga Boat had gotten killed on the west side and that broke my heart. I was beginning to believe that saying that "life for a hustler always ended in jail or death."

I had 45 days of freedom so I tried to spread myself thin to please everyone. At the same time everyone knew my time was limited so my boys off Linwood got together to throw me a going away party at Club 2281 a few days before I had to turn myself in. Rook stayed glued to my hip as he had to take over and run the trap and shop while I was gone.

I still had to talk to Rochelle to get a few things straight so I invited her out to dinner to talk. We met at Friday's at 8 p.m. I was tired from packing and moving my stuff to storage. It didn't make sense to hold on to the condo, so I took a loss and let it go. I rented a room in Dearborn with a Jacuzzi in the room for my last fourteen days. So it felt good to see Rochelle as she looked beautiful as usual.

She had already ordered my favorite meal before I arrived. This kinda reminded me of our first date. During dinner we covered a lot of ground about certain issues that had affected us in the past. We talked about the baby and me going to jail. She already knew from CB, who had told her mother. I told her that I knew she had another dude or two on the side and that her actions gave it away. She never denied my allegations instead she just sat there quietly with her hands on the table and tears in her eyes.

I grabbed her hands and said, "I know that once I'm gone you will take this opportunity to leave me. Yes, it will hurt because this is when I need you the most. I never meant to hurt you or involve you in the baby situation. We've been through a lot Rochelle and I never turned my back on you."

She looked at me through the tears and said, "Rome, I love you and even though you did a lot of wrong things, I wasn't always an angel."

I listened to her as she spoke and knew that she had just been freed from the prison of the lifestyle of a hustler. We continued to eat and talk then parted ways until later.

Carlin called concerned about me the next day. She wanted to know if I needed her to sneak into town to visit for a day before I went to court. She had a lot to do for school and work so she treated me to personal visit without letting her family know. Of course I agreed and prepared to spend the day with her as soon as she touched down, only because I had crazy feelings for her. I was 100% sure that if I wasn't going to jail we would be a couple. She had all that a man needed and wanted, such as an education, looks, personality, one child and she was self-driven.

Once she arrived in town I got her set up at my room while my block runs were done and the shop was secured. I was a little behind schedule getting back to the room and she was upset with me. When I came into the room she had a major attitude and actually cursed me out about leaving her by herself. I felt bad, especially when I looked around and saw the water ready and food on the table.

She was ready to leave but I bent down and kissed her face and apologized profusely. As tears filled her eyes she forgave me and we finished our night. The sex had heated up after we smoked a blunt and sipped on a fifth of Remy. I tasted her as usual then she rode me for a few, before my favorite position, doggie style. This was the last time I would probably ever see her so I fucked her good. I observed every inch of her body as we played together. The crazy thing was at this moment I realized how much I loved her, and she didn't even know it.

I had to convince myself, not to plead with her to stay by my side through this over and over again. I just enjoyed her presence and remained silent. After we finished we slept until morning then prepared to say our goodbyes. She was dropping me off at the condo and had to be back to school so she didn't have time to fuck again. We kissed and I told her, "I love you and don't leave me."

She replied, "I won't, Rome." This was the last time I saw her before I left.

I spent the next couple of days catching up with all my other "friends" and saying my farewells. A few of them took it hard like Nisha. Her daughter loved me and no matter who else she dealt with I was always number one to her. Alaya was upset because we had some good times together. I saw Seta and tried to get at her, but she was faithful to her baby daddy. So we hugged it out while I snuck in a quick squeeze on that ass.

Rochelle had called a few times but I was still avoiding her. Once she told me that she was on her period, she was pushed all the way to the bottom of people to visit. Tee-Tee wasn't having it either since she had a man, so I tried to see everybody else I could.

When the time came to a day or two before I left, I started having suicidal thoughts. The thought of becoming a slave to another man's idea of punishment drove me crazy. Thoughts of my Granny and David and the love I lost brought me to tears each second of the day, but I needed to be strong for myself.

My phone rang in the middle of my thoughts and it was my mom telling me that Angie had had the baby. Lyve and I quickly jumped in the ride to see the baby. She had been in the hospital for a few days, but had waited until her baby daddy was gone to call and tell us to come down. I looked at the baby boy lying in her arms and I couldn't tell if he looked like me or not. But I knew that I didn't get the same feeling like I had when I'd held Jay for the first time. I knew that we would get a blood test so I would just hold out until then.

The next day at my party I was dressed in Evisu from head to toe. I had cut my braids off to everyone's surprise into a clean cut fade. The party was packed from wall to wall with people from everywhere. Tina and her crew were there, Rook, Lyve, Sho, Red Dog, Tashaun, Big Dave, Herk, M. Porter and a list of elite individuals had showed up to see me off.

Several girls from my roster had shown up to get their last glimpse of a pimp and maybe be lucky enough for a sleep over. We drank and smoked and danced to all my favorite songs. At midnight my label performed and several other major acts blessed the stage.

I felt like a King being sent off by the Linwood squad, Mr. Maggie, Herk, Rock, Bookey and etc. Hours had passed and it was time to leave the club after I had bought the bar out for $3000. We decided then to cruise Jefferson and go eat at IHOP.

I had about four girls with me and Rook, Tashaun, Lyve and Big Dave as we ate and drove the place into the ground. I decided to take Candy back to the room with me and Herk took her friend. The room was cleaned by housekeeping so we entered and got straight to it. Candy was a cute sweet girl that had been on my team for a while. I knew she loved me by her actions like hanging on the block with me, participating in a threesome she had put together and by not leaving my sight at the party. The sex was wonderful as we went through several positions. She cried the whole time we were having sex so I knew I had some type of effect on her. By the morning she would leave to go home in tears and made me promise to visit before I went in the next day.

I had less than 24 hours of freedom so I jammed all my goodbyes together. I visited Rochelle, Tee-Tee and Jay and all my niggas on my team then went to eat with a few more at Nicola's. I called everyone I knew to say goodbye and to get personal information for me to take with me to court. We rode around my last few hours, exhausted from all the drinking and smoking and ended up at the Sting, a topless bar, and made it rain one last time.

I had a few unreleased tracks that I had made in the studio. Dris paid the DJ to play them and the crowd's reaction made me smile. Niggas were screaming "Flatline," and pouring money until 2 am.

Candy surprised me at the room when I pulled up. She was there to fuck me one more time before I left. In the morning she left in a cab because I had to be a court at 9 a.m. She made me promise to stop by her house before I went to court. So I showered and smoked and cried until a knock on the door came unexpected. I first thought it was Rochelle or the police but it was Nikki. She was looking so cute crying asking me to not turn myself in. I explained to her that I didn't have a choice then I kissed her tears and told her life would go on.

I had told Tee-Tee's mother that I would meet her at the condo so on my way there I talked to Rochelle, Carlin and Little Erica on the phone. My phone had rang a thousand times with everyone calling to say goodbye. When I pulled up to meet Tee's mom, she gave me a beautiful Quran to take with me to prison. She wanted to ride with me to court, but I told her I needed to go alone in order to avoid an emotional breakdown.

I drove to Candy's house before I met up with Rook, Lyve, Sho and Dris. They had called trying to see where I was but I told them a lie too, I didn't want to see them before I left. It would be too hard. When I pulled up at Candy's she led me straight to her room and gave me some head. Then I got it doggie style and came all over her back and ass. I could tell she wanted me to leave it in, but I had enough problems.

Then I heard some loud male voices. I stopped in the middle of round two and got dressed. When we went upstairs all my boys were standing in the kitchen. I had forgotten that Lyve was fucking Candy's roommate and she had told them where I was. I wasn't mad but was sad because leaving them behind would cause a break down in court for sure. Before I had to pull off Candy ran to the truck in tears begging me to stay. I kissed her forehead and told her, "I'll never forget you and I promise I'll be back soon."

I pulled off with the whole team following behind me to Rook's crib. Once we pulled up, Rook had a blunt rolled and waiting for me while he puffed on another one. He looked sad as hell, but tried his best to be strong for me. We all stood outside talking while I ordered me a chicken and waffle meal from the restaurant down the street. His neighbor, Beana came outside looking sexy as usual to see me off. She was slim and tall, light skinned with short hair. Our relationship had grown to a good level and she was sad to see me go. I gave her a hug and kiss as she quietly cried. I told her I was going to be ok and if she loved me she would stay in touch. She promised and then I jumped in the truck with Rook.

I had one more stop before we hit that freeway and that was to see my little niece Rizzy. She was at the day care so we stopped by and the day care worker took us to the back where she was sleep with a few other kids. When she woke up and saw me she ran and jumped in my arms.

"Rizzy, I have to go away for a little while but know that I am always going to be watching you so be good ok."

She held my face with her little hands and I couldn't hold it back anymore. The tears streamed down my face. Rook took her and told her it was time to go back to sleep. She understood and wiped my tears away.

I was late getting to court but my lawyer and the judge understood. I had thirty minutes before my life was in the hands of the judicial system again. I ran outside to smoke a blunt and called Tee-Tee who didn't answer and Rochelle who did.

"Rome, I'm not going anywhere. I love you, you are a part of me," she said.

"I love you too. I just wanted to her your voice one last time," I said. Then we said our goodbyes and I changed my voicemail on my phone to a farewell message.

Rook would control the family business and use my phone for contacts. It was time to give my last speech as a free man to my boys encouraging them to be the best in life at life. After a short personal conversation we all headed back into the court room. I sat next to my lawyer and before long I was headed back into the system.

The judge asked me a few questions and then the bailiff came over to haul me off to jail for sixty months. I threw up the special Flatline hand signal to Rook and the few real friends that I did have. They signed back and that was that. It was jail time. In my mind I said, "I'll go, but believe me this, the next time I won't lose and the world would be mine!"

EPILOQUE

Well here I sit once again looking at the many rows of cells inside Jackson State Prison. Everything has changed and I must readjust my thinking pattern from the free world. No more money, cars and clothes, women or drugs for a long time.

Over the next few years I would experience being alone and being a father at the same time. I can't complain and must admit that I lived a wonderful life. I'll use the memories from the past to help me through the present which will allow me to envision the future. To sum up the next few years of my life won't take long but must be mentioned.

In my first few years in lockdown a lot took place. My boy Tashaun had got locked up the same year as I did and had to serve four years on a gun charge. My cousin Ray had also gotten locked up the same year for six years after running to Kentucky after robbing me of my jewels. Even little Damien had been caught up and had to do five years out of state for his snatch and grab schemes. CB had stayed loyal and remained a friend along with Lyve, Leon and SkirBi.

A lot had changed with the family as well. My support group was really small and unsteady. Several people came in and out of my life or wrote ever so often to check on me. My famous roster of women all faded away with time. Rochelle had hung in there for a few months then got married to some dude she knew. I learned that from CB when I called to check in with him. I was hurt that she could be bold enough to kick me when I was down, but after a few days of crying inside, it was what it was.

Carlin stayed around at a distance for months. She would write or let me call until she finished school. I wanted her to be there for me on many levels but I guess a long distance relationship wasn't her thing. I tried everything to make her stay in my corner and she never went too far but was distracted enough to let me know I wasn't her number one anymore.

Sharice had wrote once but failed to stay in touch when her baby daddy came back home from doing a short bid. I found out later she had gotten married to someone else. Nikki had stayed around for about a year then turned away to live her own life. Once word got back that she had another baby, I just pushed her out of my mind like all the rest.

Candy played a major role and continued to send money, pictures and letters for the first few years then she got caught up in the fast life. She had become a Muslim and vowed to be by my side, then she disappeared only to come back with a baby boy. It hurt of course, but this was life. Alaya had found me in the system and showed me she still had love for me. She wrote and sent me pictures. I knew that I wasn't her only one, but played my role as a trustworthy companion. She remained ranked but her lack of dedication showed me that she wasn't worthy of a number one position.

Seta had stayed a true friend and sent her support over the years through mail, phone calls and pictures. I respected our relationship and never tried to pursue anything further. Nisha had come on strong in the beginning and played her role to the max. Once she started getting serious about me committing only to her, it threw me for a loop. I knew she had a man and the thought of her fucking every night and claiming to love me just didn't sit well with me. Then one day she sent me a letter saying she was getting married. I just smiled and moved on with my time.

Several other women fell off during my stay, Beana, Nat and Adriana all had babies and Angie fell off once she sent me the results that her baby wasn't mine. She wrote, sent money but couldn't commit to being loyal to just me. It's cool, but I knew what my future held – prosperity and in order for me to share my life with any woman I would have to see sacrifices and loyalty.

Other females like Nicole, Erica, Parish, Pooh, and Trice all came in and out, writing for a couple of months then going back to their lives. As for family my mom and siblings had helped to a degree by playing a part of my support group. Uncle Cody had decided not to stay in contact at all along with Dris, Sho, Dean, Tina, Jay, Will and Joey. I figured that they had a life of their own and this is how they treated the people that they had love for. T.B. and Teri had stayed close during my bit by playing their roles as family. They always wrote, always sent money or made sure that Tee and Jay were ok. A lot of times they would allow me to call or came to visit to show their support. It felt really good to see them get married and become a unit under my watchful eye.

My brother Rook stayed by my side off and on too. I understood that he had a lot on his plate, so I never became a burden to him and his family. I give him much respect and credit because he never gave up on me or left me behind. He probably didn't do all he could or all I wanted but he did enough. He helped me through a lot of tough times. My nieces were growing up and Rook had a lot of responsibilities to uphold.

I still would call Lyve and Uncle Slybone to kick it, along with CB and a couple of others sometimes to get the latest gossip or the hood death toll. They would keep me up to date on who was hot and who was not. Doing time is a hard process and if you're not being kept relevant then you'll wither away like an old clothes fashion.

After a few years, I had come across Tashaun in the system and helped him walk out of the door as a free man and a husband. Yes, he had gotten married to a wonderful woman, after all that playa shit we had done. I also came across many real dudes in prison that helped me maintain my sanity. See, one thing about prison is your reputation follows you from the streets. If you were a paid or made nigga on the outside then you'll be respected as that on the inside. To lose sight of who you are or where you can be is very easy so that's why a support group is a blessing.

So if you have someone special in your life that is incarcerated, don't let them die! Help keep them and their fashion alive. Now as for me and the rest of my stay, I was ok and in good company with the likes of Doc, Doughboy, Jabar, Wood, Mike, Brandon, R-dub, Jay-x, Will and Wise. They helped me a lot and I owe them a lifetime of thanks for walking with me through this crazy journey.

"Life has options and then you make a decision. Which one will you choose? Choose carefully!"

P.S. I know a lot of people were mentioned during my sixty month struggle except for Tee and Little Jay. Well over the years I watched Jay grow into a bright young man and wonderful son. Even though Tee had a man prior to me being locked up she still stayed by my side the whole entire time. My first few years she came and saw me with my son and we grew as parents. Our bond started to expand through letters and visits and she became the only true person to accept my conditions without limit. She sent money, wrote me and kept the same number the entire time.

Once her man became dead weight in her life we agreed to give our love a chance by rebuilding from the start and learning from our past. Once she showed me that she was willing to sacrifice her life to give me life while staying loyal, our process began. For a couple more years we stayed on the right path and through time we fell in love on a higher level.

One thing I can say about Tee is that she was the one true person who always had my back and even now she didn't give up on me. Many people counted me out but she counted me in and gave up so much to do it. She had become a wonderful parent on her own along with the potential to become a loyal wifey.

Several years passed by and she stayed loyal and dedicated to us so we started talking about being a unit before God. After carefully reviewing my life and weighing my options

OPTIONS

I decided it was time to mature and plan for my future along with my son's. Everyone had seemed to move ahead in life except me, so the decision was made to marry Tee and become a family. My son deserved not to come from a broken home and this would lower the risk of him falling fragile to the underworld.

The love that Tee gave me allowed me to let my guard down and become a real man. So eventually in 2010 we were married on the prison grounds and continued to build an unbreakable bond.

Crazy, huh? Rome is married to little Tee-Tee after all that we had been through. In life we must realize that everyone loves you when you are on top of the world, only a real person loves you when you are down and then tries everything in their power to help you get back up.

Who knows what the future holds? Who knows what options will be displayed in one's life? The best thing you can do is be true to yourself and follow the path that Allah (God) had set for us. Aim for the clouds in life and if you fall at least you'll land amongst the stars. MAKE EACH OPTION COUNT!

DISCUSSION QUESTIONS

1. If you were Rome, what would you have done different?

2. If Rome had a father figure, do you think that would have changed anything?

3. Did you ever think that Rome would have picked who he picked to be his mate?

4. Who else was deserving of Rome's love?

5. At what point did you think that Rome's life had changed?

6. Do you agree with Rome's philosophy of the game and the morals and principles in it?

7. Who do you think was a best friend to Rome throughout his life?

8. If you were Rochelle at what point would you have called it quits? Or would you have?

9. Did Rome's relationship with his mom have an effect on his life?

10. Do you think that Rome will be able to be loyal and successful, once he is released from prison?